SWAN RIVER SETTLEMENT
One Man's Journey

SWAN RIVER SETTLEMENT
One Man's Journey

A fascinating historical journey from Ireland through Victorian England to the remote colony of Western Australia

MICHAEL LE PAGE

Publishing Details
Editing: Eddie Albrecht Pickawoowoo Publishing Group
Interior and cover layout Pickawoowoo Publishing Group - www.pickawoowoo.com

ISBN 978-0-6455350-0-6 (paperback)
ISBN978-0-6455350-1-3 (ebook)

First Printing, 2022

A catalogue record for this book is available from the National Library of Australia

CONTENTS

CONTENTS

BASED ON AN INCREDIBLE TRUE STORY

To Maria, my wife, my best friend, my research companion, my travelling companion, my accountant, and my advisor.

To Dr Bill Edgar, social historian, and author.

To Jewel, our friend, literary advisor, and educator.

To Shirley Scotter, Irwin Districts Historical Society.

To Martin Gibbs, Professor - University of New England.

To Eddie Albrecht - Pickawoowoo Publishing Group editor,

To Julie – Ann Harper Pickawoowoo Publishing Group

To the memory of John and Mary Arnold

Thank you for leaving your footprints on this earth for me to follow and document your story.

This is a work of historical fiction based on the real-life story of John Arnold who was convicted of burglary during the Victorian era in England and sentenced to death which was commuted to life imprisonment and transportation to the West Australian penal colony.

This is not an authoritative account of the events of Western Australia's convict period. A few historians have documented this including Dr Bill Edgar in his book 'Lags' – A History of the Western Australian Convict Phenomenon. I would encourage readers to read Dr Edgar's book as it is a fascinating and impeccably researched record of this period in history.

John and Mary Arnold's story comes from exhaustive research. In some instances, I have created characters and filled in details to provide a richer story around John's life. It documents the extraordinary challenges he lived through – an Irish childhood, the potato famine, the harsh life in Victorian England, draconian English penal conditions, a long sea voyage shackled in the freezing hold of a sailing ship – before arriving in a dry, harsh, challenging, and remote environment on the other side of the world from his wife and children. It was a life, that while cruel, offered glimmers of hope, for a new and better life not just for him but also for his wife, family, and descendants.

This is also a love story spanning many decades, countries, and hardships that beggar belief.

John looked out over the freezing, cold, bleak landscape. He pulled his old, dark, woollen overcoat tighter to keep out the damp and cold. He knew it would start to rain soon but it was not cold enough to snow. Winter was fast approaching. "You should make a decision," his companion said. "There is no future for you here. The potato famine is destroying the farmland and there are too may in your family to be supported by this farm. Of all the family members you are smart, know farming, milling and weaving, plus you could easily find work over in Liverpool or Bradford. I can help find work there."

Yes, there was death in the air. People in Ireland were dying of starvation or fleeing the country to survive and seek another life. John lived on the family farm near Dromore in the north of Ireland, and over to his left he could see the family cottage. It was small, made of stone with a thick thatched roof. Smoke was drifting out the chimney as the family needed the fire on to keep the cottage warm and cook their meals. He knew he needed to decide as the family was too large for the farm. His father had passed away a few months ago and his siblings would survive without him.

His companion was Mr James Jones who was the agent for the English owner of the farmland. Mr Jones was an educated man who knew enough about farming and the realities of current famine to realise that this family could survive and pay the rent as they were all hard-working people, but something had to give as there were simply too many in the family. John looked down and kicked the ground with his boot. The soil was dark and soft underfoot from the recent rain. He didn't want to decide. He had never made a serious decision.

John knew little of the world and England seemed so foreign to him. If he stayed the famine would hurt the family through starvation, eviction from the farm or both. If he went what would the future look like for him? He turned to Mr Jones, thanked him for his advice and started to walk slowly back to the cottage. Would John become a lonely stranger in a foreign land or stay and risk starving with the family?

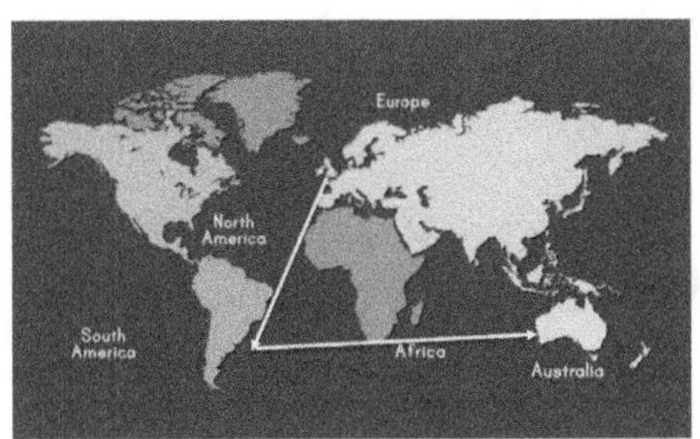

Ship route

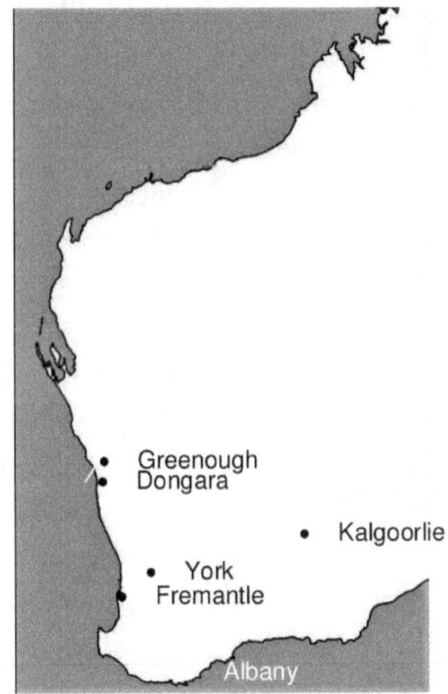

Western Australia

(For my Irish mother, Philomena Le Page – nee Condron)

May the road rise to meet you,
May the wind be always at your back.
May the sunshine warm upon your face,
The rains fall soft upon your fields.
And until we meet again,
May God hold you in the palm of his hand.
May God be with you and bless you;
May you see your children's children.
May you be poor in misfortune,
Rich in blessings,
May you know nothing but happiness
From this day forward.
May the road rise to meet you
May the wind be always at your back
May the warm rays of sun fall upon your home
And may the hand of a friend always be near.
May green be the grass you walk on,
May blue be the skies above you,
May pure be the joys that surround you,
May true be the hearts that love you.
Anon

The decision

It was a bitterly cold, bleak day when John was born in Dromore Parish, Down, Ireland to John and Elizabeth Arnold in the winter of 1815. It was a birth at home with Elizabeth's friend Catherine who lived in the adjacent farm. The local experienced midwife was also in attendance. It was Elizabeth's third child, so the experience was not new to her, and having a midwife and friend helping resulted in a complication free birth. Young John was healthy with his head already covered with fine auburn hair, the colour of his mother's. His father was working in the fields of the family farm just on the outskirts of the small market town they called home. Men did not get involved in the birth of a child, so John stayed away as did the six and four-year-old sons Henry and Thomas, but they all meandered around close to the farmhouse until they received a shout from Catherine. They rushed over and stood at the doorway. John held his old cap in heavily calloused hands and in his soiled working clothes he looked at his third child. He had secretly hoped it would be another son so he could teach him the ways of the world with the two older boys and in time provide help in the fields as it was demanding, challenging work.

The farm was small, and John raised a few cows, pigs, some chickens and kept several large vegetable plots where he grew crops including potatoes for the family and for sale at the town's market square on

Saturdays. He also sold eggs, milk and meat into the surrounding areas. It was a small but honest subsistent livelihood.

Dromore was an old, small town in the north of Ireland southwest of Belfast. The name is from Gaelic, *Droim Mort* meaning "large ridge" The original village of Dromore started around the site of a sixth century monastery founded by St Colman. In the nineth and tenth centuries the Vikings plundered the town and in the 1170s the Norman invaders, who were essentially from the Normandy region in northern France, built the fort. However, by the 1550s there were no significant buildings in Dromore except some old, thatched homes, a ruined church and the crumbling remains of the Dromore Castle. By the time John Arnold was born there were 360 inhabited houses and 1860 inhabitants living on both sides of the river Lagan. The roads throughout the town were narrow, and about half the houses had thatched roofs, the remainder used slate. The houses in Market Square and in the street between the square and the church were mostly neat and built of stone or stone and brick. The markets were held every Saturday. The only significant industry in the town was linen manufacturing. There was also a mill located next to the river for milling grains after the annual harvest. It was powered by an old wooden water wheel that turned all year around. Life was simple – pleasant, slow paced and driven by the day-to-day needs of food, clothing, and shelter.

There is a long history of the production of linen in Ireland. In 1685, some Huguenots who fled France settled in the north of Ireland. In France, troops ravaged their villages on an order from the king and up to 12,000 people were rounded up into camps, where many starved to death. The departure of the Huguenots was a disaster for France. Huguenots were particularly successful in the textile industry and were reliable skilled workers. They were also generally well educated and had the ability to read and write, and they brought with them the advanced skills for linen production. Many settled in the town of Lisburn near Dromore which resulted in Lisburn becoming perhaps the most famous linen producing centre in all of Ireland. When John was born most of the world's linen was produced in Lisburn and its surroundings like Dromore where at least three hundred people worked from home making handloom linens. It was also an enormous benefit to the education of the townsfolk in Dromore as literacy skills became more encouraged in the schools.

Mary and John's family farm was just outside the village. Their house was a small one-room cottage made of local timber and stones with a packed earth floor and thick thatch roof to keep the house warm in winter and the rain out. It had some windows for light. At the back wall was a fireplace over which an iron pot was suspended. They also owned a small wooden table, some chairs plus some rudimentary stools, cupboards and bedding. Mary was a short, thin but imposing five-foot tall lady with striking green eyes which complemented her long auburn hair. Her husband John was five and a half feet tall with blue eyes and ginger red hair which was prematurely receding at the front and thinning at the back. Like most men he wore a beard which was starting to show signs of grey. He was a strong man from all the manual labour he did on the farm and his heavily calloused hands showed he worked hard to survive. His one pastime was playing the Celtic fiddle which is like a violin. He could not read music, but his father had taught him to play the fiddle by ear from an early age and John planned to teach his young boys as well. In fact, he had already started with the older boys Henry and Thomas. As young John grew up his mother liked to sing to him and the other children. She had a beautiful voice that gave her much joy, and she particularly enjoyed singing hymns to her sons before they went to sleep in the evenings. Her favourite was an old cradle song:

Sleep, my babe, lie still and slumber,
All through the night
Guardian angels God will lend thee,
All through the night
Soft and drowsy hours are creeping,
Hill and vale in slumber sleeping,

> Mother dear her watch is keeping,
> All through the night
> God is here, you'll not be lonely,
> All through the night
> 'Tis not I who guards thee only,
> All through the night
> Night's dark shades will soon be over,
> Still my watchful care shall hover,
> God with me His watch is keeping,
> All through the night

John would smile at his mother and even his first words came out like a little song. The church was a big part of the Arnold family and each Sunday throughout the year, regardless of the weather, they would walk together into town to go to the church service at Dromore Cathedral on Church Street. It was Church of Ireland. The Catholics also had a church nearby at the corner of Banbridge Road with a small cemetery next to the river. It was a roughcast stone building only one hundred feet long and was built originally in 1661. Mary loved going to church as it was an opportunity to catch up with her friends and sing in the choir. While the choir was dominated by men, she had an exceptional voice, so she could participate. They did not have an organ, but the parish was discussing the potential to buy one and had started to collect money for it. John was not that religious and while he was raised and married in the church, he kept his distance and rarely went in. Occasionally when it was raining, he would sit quietly at the back of the church during the service to avoid the rain. The tall, lean reverend would see him there, nod and hope that someday John might re-join the fold.

When young John was five years old, Mary would take him with his brothers to the church school. It was a one-room, old, rundown stone building with a thatched roof but the teachers, whilst strict, taught the young children the things Mary thought were vitally important and did so with compassion, patience and a touch of discipline if any of the children were disobedient. The education was based on the Bible as it was one of the few books they possessed, and they instructed the children about what was right, what was wrong and the Ten Commandments. Every session started with prayers and a reading from the Bible. This was followed with the singing of a hymn. Sometimes they would tell the children stories about people like Abraham, Moses, Jesus, and Mary. John loved the story about the Good Samaritan and the singing.

Mary also wanted John to be able to read, write and learn numbers like his brothers. Simple things like how to add up and take away could sometimes be complicated to her. Mary believed if her children could read and write and be good with numbers it would make her so proud and help them in life. Mary was illiterate and understood literacy and numeracy were vital to do well in life. After school in the morning, they would walk home along the river talking and singing along the way. That walk was one of John's fondest memories of his childhood and one of the daily experiences that Mary treasured, her son's little hand in hers as they walked alongside the river. After the walk and a simple meal, the boys would help their dad in the fields to the best of their ability. They loved being with their dad working beside him, looking up to him. Their dad was a quiet, strong man. He did not drink as his father was a big drinker and it left him with some sad memories of his upbringing. While drinking was a thing that many men did, he never drank. Mary loved him for that as well. Times were tough as it was, but a non-drinking household was a blessing. Sometimes in the evenings and on Sundays John would bring out his fiddle and play some favourite Irish ballads to which they would all sing. Over time young John and his brothers would play the fiddle as well.

When John reached the age of eleven, he was the oldest in the school and had mastered reading and writing so much so that he would be asked to read the prayers each morning to the younger children and helped the teachers explain simple words and pronunciation to the younger children. Numbers had come to him easily, so Mary would get him each Saturday to count the money they earned from the markets and subtract it from what it cost to buy things for the farm. The older brothers had now left school and were helping their dad on the farm.

One Sunday a lady noticed young John at church and heard from her friends that he was respectful, diligent, obedient and clever at school so she asked Mary if he could work for her husband in making high-quality linen. He was looking for a youth to learn the trade – help, clean, fix things when they broke and package up the product for sale. Unfortunately, they did not have any children and many people in Lisburn wanted his linen as they regarded it as high quality.

Mary was perplexed. She rushed home to see her husband and they discussed this at length into the evening. John needed the help on the farm because he was getting older, but the older boys were already helping, and they also could do with an income in cash from working outside the farm. It was also a promise of a good life for their son as the work could lead to John buying his own loom and house and make linen for himself. Finally, they decided it was the best thing to do provided John still had some time to help with the farm.

John's father's advice to him on his first day was, "John, wherever you work arrive a bit early, leave a bit later than required, work hard, do real quality work and learn to get better at what you do. Implement this advice and you will always be successful."

As time progressed John became very skilled at operating and maintaining the loom, packaging up the precious linen and dispatching it to customers. He was quick and skilful with his hands, and his master, whilst a disciplinarian, taught him well. The work room was always spotlessly clean and organised. The linen they produced was of excellent quality and in much demand. Despite his skill, John's pay was low, and the hours were long but he was comfortable with his lot in life and still found time to work on the farm with his father.

In Ireland, at this time, a "middleman system" existed for managing landed property. In John's family's case the owner of the farm – and many around the district – lived in England. John's father did not own the farm, so he paid rent to the owner's agent or middlemen as they were known. From this, the owner received a regular income as did the agent. Their agent was James Jones who whilst he was fair and helpful, he still regularly reminded John's father that the owner expected his payment without fail. The Irish, like John's family, effectively lived a subsistent livelihood near to poverty and it was a constant strain to pay James Jones and live. John's apprentice wage helped but the farm livelihood was weather dependent and any disruption to farm crop yields or an illness amongst the cattle or other farm animals could easily cause disaster. Consequently, while there was much love in the close-knit Arnold family, John's father was constantly concerned about any pending disaster.

One evening when John was returning home from his work in the village, he could see his father in the distance ploughing a field and his brothers working farther afield. He noticed for the first time in his life that there was no smoke drifting from the chimney of the house which was situated just off the narrow laneway ahead. Everything was eerily quiet. Even the birds seemed to have stopped singing. Normally he would hear his mother quietly singing to herself as she got the household ready for the evening meal when John and the family would return. The closer he came to the house the more he sensed something was amiss. He could understand that the younger children may be over in the adjacent farm playing so there would be no noise from them. But it was eerie. There was no sound, no activity and no smells of a meal cooking on the stove. He opened the front door and peered inside. Nothing but silence.

As he investigated the semi-darkness towards the unlit fireplace where the old cast iron pot hung, he saw his mother lying motionless on the floor. Her lovely auburn hair, which was now streaked in grey, spread out around her head. She was still, silent and pale. He rushed over and touched her hand and face. She was cold, icy cold. His hand pulled back in fear as he did not know what to do. Here was the person he loved the most in the world lifeless on the floor. A loud cry came from his mouth and tears started streaming down his face. He dropped his old leather bag onto the floor scrambled out of the house, and ran over to where his father was working. When he reached his father, the words could not come out and he started crying more in anguish and pain. Finally, he said the words, "Mamaí is dead on the floor in the house!"

The pain for the family in the aftermath was enormous. The person who loved, cherished, and encouraged them all through their lives was gone. They did not get to say goodbye or tell her one more time they loved her. His father had gone quiet in his sorrow, and he went through the motions of talking with the priest and preparing the funeral. Catherine, the neighbour, was an immense help and assisted them through those dark days. At the funeral, many people said how wonderful she was, how beautiful a singer she was, and most importantly, that she was a loving wife and mother. The words whilst appreciated washed over all the family and their father in their sorrow. As they stood next to her grave adjacent to the church it started to rain and slowly the large crowd of dark-clad mourners drifted away. As they stood there silent with their heads bowed, more tears ran down their cheeks. Catherine came over to young John and pressed a piece of paper in his hand. She repeated how sorry she was, put her arm around his shoulders and then slowly walked away.

After a while John looked at the piece of paper and saw that she had written the words of a well-known poem.

Do not stand at my grave and weep
Do not stand at my grave and weep,
I am not there...I do not sleep.
I am the thousand winds that blow...
I am the diamond glints on snow...
I am the sunlight on ripened grain...
I am the gentle autumn rain.
When you waken in the morning's hush,
I am the swift uplifting rush,
Of gentle birds in circling flight...

I am the soft star that shines at night.
Do not stand at my grave and cry,
I am not there...I did not die...

(Source – public domain)

After the loss of their mother, life was never the same on the farm. All the beauty in the household diminished with her passing. John's father continued to work hard to keep the farm going. John's older brothers helped enormously, and John continued to work at his job. All the wonderful things that Mary did – the cooking, cleaning, washing, mending the clothes, tending to the chickens and other animals – were taken up by John's younger sisters Marianne, Mary, and Charlotte. John and his brothers had now grown into men and their faces were darkened with beards. John and his older brothers were medium height and built like their father. John was strong from the farm work but nimble, organised, and detail-oriented from his linen-making training. His auburn hair was now fair, his white face which was now covered with his beard was covered in freckles from too much time working outdoors. He was a trusting young man. Some would say he was not worldly wise or street smart. He told the truth and if he did lie even about something small, a day or so later he could not help himself or live with himself so he would confess and apologise. He and his brothers had learned to play their father's fiddle and their singing provided some entertainment on Sundays in an otherwise sombre house.

As the three brothers wanted to earn some extra money, they all managed to find some work at the grist mill as well as doing their normal work on the farm – or for John at the linen factory. They applied their father's advice to, "Arrive a bit early, leave a bit later than required, work hard, do real quality work and learn to get better at what you do." This brought extra money into the family as well as some small money for themselves. The grist mill was on the edge of town near the river. It was used to process corn and other grains during the harvest season. Farmers brought their grain to the mill where it was ground into meal or flour for a fee. The mill was built a few miles from the village and supported by the farmers as the local community depended on the mill for flour which was a staple part of the diet.

The mill in Dromore was water-powered, where a sluice gate opened to allow water from the River Lagan to flow past a water wheel and make it turn. The water wheel was mounted vertically with the bottom edge in the water. It drove a large gearwheel which drove the mill-stones which were laid one on top of the other. The bottom stone was called the bed and was fixed. The top stone was called the runner and it rotated to grind the grains between the two stones. The distance between the stones varied to produce the required grade of flour, so if the stones were moved closer together, a finer flour was produced. The driving mechanism from the water wheel could be disconnected from the stones and connected to a sieve to refine the flour, or for turning a drum to wind up a chain used to hoist sacks of grain to the top of the mill. All three brothers learned the milling trade and after a while they could run the mill themselves – receive the grain, hoist it to the top floor and feed it into the mill, run it through a series of sieves and finally pack it up in woven bags. Given their farm upbringing they were also adept in maintaining the water wheel and mill.

One day when John's father was working in the farm, he inspected a section of the potatoes and he noticed for the first-time brown freckles on the leaves, some with brown patches and a yellowish border spreading from the brown patch. He immediately knew what it was as the people in the neighbourhood had heard of this from some other regions. He immediately started to dig to see what the potatoes were like, and most were starting to rot and smell. This had not happened to him before, but he knew multiple potato crops, which were the staple crop of Ireland, had failed in 1832, 1833, 1834, and 1836 due to dry rot and curl. In 1835 the potato crop failed almost completely in Ulster. So, while John had been careful, this year the rot had infected his crop as well. The rumour in the town was that two main potato plant diseases had been identified. One was called dry rot or taint, and the other was a virus known as "curl" which was a parasitic organism like a form of algae. Frantically, he started to inspect all his potato patches across his farm only to find over 50 per cent of his crop was infected.

Potato with the rot
(Source – Public domain)

The impact on the farm and the community was immense and immediate. A failed potato crop quickly reduced a farmer's income and consequently the farmers who were already poor now were destitute. That year the yield loss due to the disease across the country was estimated to be between one-third to potentially one-half of the farm area cultivated. This resulted in the infamous and devastating potato famine. Property owners still demanded their rent. In John's case, James Jones the agent was more lenient as he knew John would always make up the rent. He could not get another tenant to take over the farm anyway as everyone was penniless. John was still managing through the sale of his other vegetables and crops plus the sale of eggs, milk and chickens coupled with his sons' incomes from the linen business and the grist mill. However, food prices were low and barely covered their costs. James Jones knew this would keep the family viable. John paid James Jones what he owed. He was an honest man and true to his word. What he could afford he paid and most times he paid more than he could afford just to keep the family on the farm.

However, the strain was showing on John's father and with it his health was deteriorating. He was becoming thin, and his once muscular frame was showing the strain. He never really recovered from Mary's death and the loss of his crop made him sad and more depressed. This crop loss was something he was dreading for years and now it was a reality. He started losing more weight but continued to toil away on the farm and no amount of extra work from his sons would result in their father working less. Work was his distraction from dealing with the loss of Mary and his crop.

One cold windy day his health failed, and John's older brother found him unconscious in a field. He called his brothers who helped get their father back to the house where they lay him in his bed. The cost of a doctor was prohibitive to them, but they asked the local nurse to visit. She advised that he was very frail, probably had a heart condition and had a fever. She cared for him on and off over the next few days but sadly he died, a broken man, on a cold Saturday afternoon. During the famine in Ireland, around one million people like John died and a million more emigrated, causing Ireland's population to fall by more than 20 per cent. Three-quarters of Irish labourers were unemployed, housing conditions appalling and the standard of living exceptionally low.

Once again John and his siblings found themselves tragically saddened by the loss of a parent. All the things that were precious to them had been lost. The love, humour, care and tenderness that was so much a part of their lives to date was gone and the cruel world of the famine era was upon them. Fortunately, John's job in the linen business was stable as their product was valued and in demand still. Much of it was exported. The work in the grist mill was still essential to the community.

A week after their father's funeral when he was laid to rest next to Mary, John and his brothers met with Mr James Jones the land agent. Mr Jones, although an agent, was still a reasonable and educated man. He talked with the brothers and worked out a plan to keep them on the farm. As Mr Jones walked out to his horse John walked with him and they talked. They had talked like this the previous week. Mr Jones asked him about his plans and ambitions again and repeated that there was no future here on the farm for all members of the large family. Something had to give with the famine and extreme poverty. He said to John that he was a smart man with his ability to read and write plus his skills in the linen business and grist mill. He suggested that he could leave and go to England and work in one of the big mills in Liverpool or Bradford. Mr Jones said he had connections that would help and suggested John could get a letter from his employer at the linen business and one from the boss at the grist mill. John did not know where Bradford was, but Mr Jones explained it was just across the sea and inland from Liverpool near a city called Manchester. He could simply travel by boat across to Liverpool and walk on to Bradford. No one ever had a discussion like this with John before. Even though he was in his late 20s he just expected to continue to work and live here all the days of his life. These places seemed so far away and foreign, yet they represented in his mind an opportunity that he had never considered before, to escape the poverty and helplessness in Ireland.

(Source – Unsplash)

In the mid-19th century, Ireland experienced a social and economic disaster from the potato famine. In 1847 alone it has been estimated that one million people died and more than a million fled the country. Between 1845 and 1855 more than two million people left Ireland on overcrowded coffin ships in one of the greatest mass exoduses from a single island in history. The main cause of the famine was a potato blight which also infected potato crops throughout Europe during the 1840s causing over 100,000 deaths outside of Ireland.

2

Into the unknown

John stood on the old wooden deck of the overcrowded vessel in the cold and wind. He was chilled to his bones but refused to try to find a place to stand in the hold of the ship as it was even colder, more crowded and filthier. People were sick and coughing inside. He could not afford to get sick. There was no one to care for him if he fell ill and no place to find shelter. Occasionally the ship would rock back and forth, and the bitter vomit would gag in his throat. He tried not to throw up on the people nearby. He edged towards the ship's rail in case he really did need to vomit. He was not used to the sea or a ship's rocking motion. The vessel was on its way from Belfast to Liverpool. Some people called the vessels coffin ships due to the chronic overcrowding, disease and hunger. Nobody would be missed if they fell overboard or died on board as many were alone and left their families behind. John had paid two shillings and sixpence for the passage and was told it would only take fourteen hours so he would stay on the deck until they landed. He tried to distance himself from the other passengers but that was impossible. He had never seen the sea before, and the wide ocean terrified him. He could not swim nor had ever tried. Before leaving his village he collected his meagre belongings and took two keepsakes to remind him of his parents. He had his mother's much loved, well used, rosary beads and a fiddle that his father had given to him. On the back of the fiddle were the simple words in small writing, To my loving son John – Dadai.

John also packed a tin plate, a fork, knife and spoon and a tin cup. He had on the clothes he owned including a well-worn but warm coat and solid boots. He carried two woollen blankets and nothing else. He was warned to be constantly aware of pickpockets and to trust no one. So, he wrapped the money he had in a long strip of linen and knotted it tightly around his now thin waist. Whilst he was naïve to the ways of the world, he realised quickly not to show any outward signs of money and he only carried a few small coins in his pocket on the inside of his coat. Being from a farm he was not a social person, so he kept to himself. He was not comfortable with nor trusted strangers.

Back at the farm a few weeks earlier, John had agreed with Mr Jones that his older brothers and his younger brother William could stay and work the farm and mill to survive. John wanted to stay and be a farmer but felt life in the English linen and milling businesses might hold opportunities. Mr Jones planted the seed of thought in young John's mind that he could migrate to England to restart his life away from the famine, death and destitution in Ireland. John left the conversation aware that someone needed to leave the farm, nervous about the unknown but determined the family must survive.

For the first time in his life John was making a life-changing decision. He discussed this with his siblings, and they sadly agreed that it may be best if he left in search for a new life. They had some savings which he could take to help him survive in the short term. His sisters wept as John discussed quietly his decision. Not only had they lost their parents but now they were losing one of the big brothers who had supported and loved them all their lives. John was nervous as he knew it was a big but necessary decision. He also knew he might never see his family, Ireland, or the farm again.

Mr James Jones walked away from the discussion with John feeling relieved. His landowner, the earl, would appreciate that he had managed to continue to see the farm operating. All the improvements the tenant had instituted over the past 20 years would be maintained and the rent would be paid. He also had earnt himself a small commission plus he felt he had done the best thing for John. James liked him because he felt of all the family members, John was the most likely to take on the challenge, grim and dangerous as it was. There was no future for the young man in this famine ravaged country. He had also given the young man a letter of introduction to some contacts in Bradford which would provide him with a basic accommodation initially if he needed it and some work in a woollen mill. He knew that even though John was literate, a highly skilled linen craftsman and a trained miller, the English employers would not value him or his skills highly. He felt however that John would survive in that tough environment plus with fewer mouths to feed on the farm the better the chance of all of them surviving – and the rent being paid.

On the trip to Belfast, John witnessed first-hand the devastation from the famine. Many people were on the road walking slowly to Belfast carrying their few meagre possessions to escape the country. All were pale, thin, hungry and desperate like John. Some walked like John and others crowded onto carts. Food was scarce. Occasionally they would see sparsely populated villages and newly dug graves on the outskirts indicating the impact of the disease. In some cases, the houses were abandoned as the former occupants could not pay the rent to the property owners so leaving was their only option. John even saw a few cases where the thatching on the roof was burnt to stop people from occupying the abandoned homes. According to rumours, the agents sometimes burned the thatching to stop the families from living in the cottage if they could not pay the rent. Most of the people on the road did not know where to go and like many others headed towards the port to leave the country and head for Liverpool and for many onwards overseas. There was no future for them in Ireland.

The City of Liverpool is located on the river Mersey on the west coast of England. It had long been a destination for Irish migrants but in the late 1840s there was a huge influx of Irish people desperate to flee the famine and poverty. For many, the Port of Liverpool was a staging post on their way to North America, Australia or settling in England.

For John it was a steppingstone on his way to Bradford where he hoped to find work and a place to live. Considering the teeming humanity around the port in Belfast and the multitude of overcrowded vessels heading to Liverpool, his optimism to find a job and a place to live was waning. Had he passed up one hard life for one which was even tougher, more uncertain and possibly dangerous? It was too late for him to turn back now.

In 1846, 280,000 Irish people, who were refugees, entered Liverpool and approximately 100,000 moved abroad. However, during the first half of 1847, about 300,000 Irish refugees arrived in the city and of those an estimated 130,000 emigrated. One of those who arrived was John Arnold. Within a few short years at least one quarter of Liverpool's population was Irish born. John quickly realised that Liverpool was no place to stay and started walking east towards Bradford spending a few coins for some bread and stew along the way. He slept in the wooded areas by the roadside. He wanted to leave behind, as quickly as possible, the overcrowded cellars and houses in the Vauxhall and Scotland Road areas near to the port where many Irish were congregating in abject poverty.

The walk was lonely at times and one day John passed another Irish traveller on the road. "Where are you from?" he was asked. John looked at him and was undecided whether to reply or ignore him and keep moving. So far it was a long, lonely journey and he decided to stop. He responded, "Dromore, just southwest of Lisburn." The other man looked at him in a quizzical way and John quickly realised he had no idea where Dromore or Lisburn were. John thought for a few seconds and added "Just near Belfast," to which his new companion responded "Oh, I'm from Sligo. It's terrible there. The famine is the worst in all of Ireland. People are starving and along the road I met lots of people leaving Sligo and the areas around it like rural Mayo." John had heard of Sligo but not Mayo. Sligo was in the northwest somewhere. So, he introduced himself as John Arnold to which his new friend replied, "I'm Sean...Sean Walsh." Sean was a dark-haired, short youth around 20 years old. Like John he was very thin, pale and gaunt but despite this he was jovial in his ways and like John a simple youth not used to the wide world outside their village. John said, "Sean have you eaten anything?" Sean replied, "Well John, food is a bit scarce but I did have some bread last evening." John replied, "Well, have some of this," and broke off a piece of stale bread he was carrying and gave it to Sean.

So, Sean and John started walking together on the road to Bradford. It was nice for John to have someone to talk with and he recounted the death of his parents, the work at the farm, mill and in the linen business. Sean's story was similar. His parents were still alive, but they were living in poverty as their potato crop failed and his father encouraged Sean to move away and find a new life as there was no future in Sligo for him. His family was large, and he was struggling to feed them all. With that his father gave Sean some of the little money he had, his blessing, and Sean hugged his mother, shook hands with his father and set out on the road to Belfast carrying his few possessions. Sean had been working the farm with his father and did not have any other skills but was determined to find work in Bradford too as he had also heard it was the centre of the wool business. He was illiterate and spoke some English with a heavy Irish accent. Gaelic was his first language. If life was going to be hard for John then it was going to be even more difficult for Sean.

Sean recounted the tales he had heard of the prosperity of life in Britain. He had heard wonderful stories of large towns and cities with bright street lights, music, shops and public houses. What both men did not realise was the truth was completely different. The influx of the Irish refugees into the industrial towns resulted in appalling mortality rates, isolation, frustration and despair. On top of this was the reality of bigotry, prejudice and extensive poverty especially with the Irish.

John asked Sean of his plans for when he arrived in Bradford. Sean replied that there were many Irish people in Bradford from the Mayo and Sligo areas, and they were congregated in an area around Nelson Court and Bedford Street. He was going to head there as it would provide some companionship and security. He had a contact, and he was sure someone would help him get a room to live in and help him find work. He said St Mary's Catholic Church was also near there and Father John Motler was the head priest of the local Catholic community. He also would try to see Father John to seek his help and guidance. John thought it would be good to join Sean. He also had some contacts from Mr James Jones.

The deep-rooted prejudice against the Irish in Bradford was significant and Sean's advice that the Irish areas on Nelson Court and Bedford Street were a secure place to stay was good. Forty years before, Bradford was a Protestant town, and this industrial urban community was over time seeing an increasing Irish peasant culture who were mainly Catholic. This Irish culture was maintained through kinship ties and social clubs. Assimilation was not normal and actively discouraged by the Protestant community. The Irish were also considered to be a burden on the community and earned much less than the English for the same work. The Irish proved useful to employers by keeping down the level of wages even for the English. John had gone to the Church of Ireland but for some reason he also aligned with the Roman Catholics, especially now that he was unsure if the Church of Ireland existed in Bradford.

Finally, Sean and John entered the outskirts of Bradford. They were tired, hungry and had not washed for days. The city was crowded and grimy. Smoke from the chimneys of the factories coated the walls of the houses with soot making them dark. When they commented on it to the people they met, some people said, "If you think this is bad you should go to the industrial areas around Wolverhampton to the south. It is so covered in grime that it has been called Black Country."

Based on Sean's advice they located Nelson Court and asked around for his contacts. The area was a filthy slum and the people on the street were friendly enough, especially the ones who spoke with an Irish accent. They were referred from person to person as renting a room was more difficult than what they had expected. John did not mention that he had some money tucked away. Finally, they found a room they could share with the help of one of Sean's contacts. It was in a cellar which was cold and had poor ventilation, but the door locked, and it was something they could afford together. In the room were two small wooden cots with old, well used straw mattresses and a wooden chair plus a stool. A few nails were driven into the sturdy wooden door so they could hang their coats. That was all. There was a metal tub outside in the small dirt courtyard with a hand pump for water. The water looked clean as it came from a well. At last, they were able to wash and clean themselves after their journey.

Forty years before Sean and John arrived in Bradford, it was a small rural market town of approximately 16,000 people. Wool spinning and cloth weaving were industries performed in people's cottages and farms. Now Sean and John found Bradford had at least 38 worsted wool mills in the town and 70 in the surrounding areas where approximately two-thirds of England's wool production was processed. John had been expecting cotton or linen mills as well. Instead, he found just woollen mills. Worsted yarns and fabrics and woollens were both made from sheep's wool, but worsted yarns are stronger, finer, smoother and harder than the latter. Worsted wool fabric was normally used in the manufacture of tailored garments such as suits and coats. Woollen wool is used for knitted items such as sweaters.

The next day John and Sean went separate ways and agreed to meet back at their room in the evening. Sean was going to track down some contacts who might have some labouring work for him. John was going to visit Mr James Jones's contact who he believed could provide him with an entry into a skilled job in the mill. John finally tracked down the address he had and knocked on the large solid door to an imposing home. It was in a tidy, impressive, cobbled street and each house was two-storey and expensive. John felt very intimidated, but he needed to be courageous to survive. A well-dressed servant appeared at the door promptly and peered at John with distaste. He was about to shut the door. John was prepared and said quickly in his best English, "Excuse me sir, my name is John Arnold and I have a reference from Mr James Jones who is the agent for the Earl in Dromore, Ireland. He asked me to present myself and this document to his lordship, the owner of this house." The servant was taken aback with John's confidence and the quality of his language. He took the sealed envelope looked at the front and back and stated briskly, "Wait here," and shut the door. John waited.

Over an hour later, the servant opened the door and handed back the envelope that John had presented together with a second white envelope. He said it contained a letter and added, "Please present yourself to the Old Mill on Victoria Road at 8 am tomorrow morning and ask for Mr Brian Smith Chadwick, the senior clerk. Present him with your references and this letter."

The next morning, John arrived 30 minutes early and waited by the mill gate. It was cold and rain was sprinkling down. The guard looked at him and told him to go away. At promptly 8 a.m. he showed the guard the envelope and said it was for a Mr Brian Smith Chadwick. The guard looked at the letter blankly. John was unaware that the guard could not read, and the guard handed the letter back to him and grunted. John persisted and said the letter advised him to be here at 8am and ask for the senior clerk. At this point the guard knew he needed to do something or potentially get a rebuke from the senior clerk, so he locked the wrought iron factory gate and walked across the factory laneway to a tall, imposing dark coloured brick building. He entered a side door and disappeared inside. Shortly afterwards John was standing in front of a neat desk in a small front office at the mill. Mr Chadwick was a tall lean man with dark hair and a long sharp nose. He was good at his work, but this interruption caused him some concern. He examined the paperwork thoroughly. It all looked genuine. A skilled weaving craftsman with fifteen years' experience in linen manufacture who could read, write and calculate numbers. Yet he was Irish. Chadwick was in a quandary. The two letters were written by an earl's agent and the mill manager's uncle and major shareholder of the mill. Finally, after reading the paperwork a third time, he stood up, sighed, and walked out of the office door to see the factory supervisor.

John was left standing there in front of Mr Chadwick's desk wondering what to do so he simply stayed standing. He had his cap in his hands. He looked at the desk and it was very neat and well organised. A pile of papers was stacked neatly to one side and what looked like a fancy pen with a cap sat next to the papers. In the corner behind the desk was a coat stand and Chadwick's nice dark woollen coat hung alone on the stand. John had never seen such a nice coat before nor such a nice desk and pen.

Eventually Chadwick came back, produced a form, and said, "Sign here and you can start tomorrow morning at 7 a.m. Ask for Mr Black, the foreman, at the front gate." Brian Chadwick had seen this type of case many times. A poor but educated well-presented Irish craftsman looking for any work to put a roof over his head and some food on the table. An enormous amount of high-quality wool and cotton materials poured out of the local English mills enabling the community to clothe itself more inexpensively than ever before and, in the process, making money for the mill owners. Industrialisation was sharpening the division between the rich and the poor. The benefits were apparent, but it ignored the fact that craftsman like John with once prized skills earned from working in cottage industries with hand looms were now essentially redundant and their skills worthless. This was one of the significant downsides of the industrial revolution.

John found life as a woollen mill worker challenging, loud and extremely dangerous. The gigantic machinery thundered relentlessly all day long and was unprotected so it could sever fingers, limbs or even kill people in a split second if a worker was not concentrating. The air was constantly filled with wool fibres and dust, so much so, that dust covered the workers and got in their throats. John covered his mouth and nose with a rag tied at the back of his head. Young children, sometimes as young as six years old, carried out hazardous tasks, like clearing blockages in the mills. It was nothing like the small linen mill back home in Dromore. The hours were long, sometimes 12-hour days, however he kept up his work ethic, arrived early, left later, worked hard, did real quality work and learned to get better at his jobs. In 1847 The Factory Act, also known as the Ten Hours Act, was made law so women and young people 13 to 18 years old were only permitted to work 10 hours per day in the textile mills. Younger children were also banned from working at the mill. These conditions were now followed in the mill where John worked. Due to some poor drafting of the Bill these changes did not include men, but all the men knew at this time a new law was planned to be implemented sometime in 1850 limiting their daily hours to 10 hours as well. There was some relief in their work conditions in the future. There was also some sense among the mill workers that through the organisation of workers better working conditions were possible.

John's initial role was a junior maintenance person on the weaving equipment where his hard-earned skills were useful but not fully utilised. However, he had a job and while the income was low, it enabled him to live and pay the rent of the room he shared with Sean. Initially he was suspicious of Sean, and he was careful to sleep lightly and be cautious with the little money he had but he quickly realised Sean was an honest, trustworthy Irish country youth.

He found that the pay at the factory was dependent on the role performed. So, if he worked hard, was productive and developed new skills he could gradually move onto better paid roles. That was his plan. The reality was that the Irish, unless they were exceptional, would stay in the low paid operational, cleaning or maintenance roles. He had also never had much to do with girls before. For the first time he was working with them and watched them with fascination as they did 'piecer' work which consisted of re-joining thread that had broken on the Spinning-jennies. The girls were quick as this work had to be done whilst the machine was in operation. Many a finger was lost this way. When he was home in Ireland, he never had time to socialise with the girls in the village. His only time was on a Sunday and even then, he merely walked to church and returned directly back to the farm. Now he was fascinated by the girls, their shape and the way they flitted about. Occasionally he would see one working and glimpse a bare ankle or calf.

They also giggled a lot especially if they caught him looking at them. He was now working six days per week with Sunday off. Sunday was his day for church in the morning which left time to catch up with his newfound friends and even talk with a few of the Irish Catholic 'piecer' girls from the mill.

Coffin ship
(Source – public domain)
I'm bidding you a long farewell, my Mary, kind and true
But I'll not forget you, darling, in the land I'm going to.
They say there's bread and work for all, and the sun shines always there
But I'll ne'er forget old Ireland, were it fifty times as fair.
Source -Lament of the Irish Emigrant (a ballad published in 1840.)

3

Romance at the mill

On a Saturday evening after work John and Sean would go to the public house to meet up with their newfound friends. Sean and his friends did not like British ale as they preferred Irish dark ale and reminisced about the great times they had at Thomas Connolly's pub on Holburn Street in their hometown Sligo.

When the friends heard that John had a fiddle and could play, they suggested he bring along his old fiddle so they could hear some Irish music on a Saturday evening. So, John became a Saturday night fixture playing the fiddle and singing. His music was good and lively, but he felt his singing was poor. However, after the crowd had a few ales they were happy with any music and singing. Most of his songs were from the north of Ireland which suited Sean and his friends from the Sligo area, but a new friend, also called John Arnold who came from Tipperary, could sing a few Irish songs from his area in the south of Ireland. As John had a reasonable ear for music, he picked up the tunes and started playing the fiddle to the other songs as well. Soon between the two men they had a good selection of songs to provide traditional Irish music and a few rowdy Irish tunes as well. One of the new songs John learned was a folk song called "Black Velvet Band". He was not aware at the time of the eerie implications this had for him in the future.

In a neat little town, they call Manchester,
apprenticed to trade I was bound.
And manys the hour of sweet happiness
I spent in that neat little town.
Till bad misfortune came o're me
which sent me away from the land
far away from my friends and companions
betrayed by the black velvet band.
Her eyes they shined like a diamond
you'd think she was queen of the land.
And her hair hung over her shoulder.
Tied up with a black velvet band.

(Source – Swindells of Manchester circ -1796 and 1853)

One Saturday evening in summer when John and Sean went to their favourite public house it was crowded. As the night wore on the friends got drunker, the conversation slurred into gibberish that John failed to understand as the local Sligo Gaelic slang crept more into the conversation. Finally, John left to go outside and pondered waiting for Sean or walking back to their room. It was still early but he decided to go home alone as he did have church in the morning. The streets were getting dark but just one street away from the public house, he passed a group of lasses and one said, "Hello Mr Maintenance Man". It was one of the 'piecer' lasses from the mill. He was embarrassed and did not know what to say but managed to reply shyly, "Oh hello". The lasses who were confident in numbers laughed and then chatted with him. He liked them all but fancied the one who called herself Mary. Finally, they said they needed to go before it got dark and left. As they walked away John watched them go still fascinated by their shape and giggles. Mary turned around shyly and waved.

At the mill on Monday John noticed that Mary also worked at the mill, and she appeared occasionally throughout the day. He did not understand why he had not seen her before. Eventually she passed him by and said hello. She was English not Irish, short and thin like his mother with dark long brown hair and brown eyes. He guessed she was about 18 years old. John pondered how he could get to know her better and asked Sean. Sean was of no use as he preferred drinking at the public house compared to talking with the lasses. Talking at the mill was difficult as it was noisy, and nobody wanted to let the supervisor see them being idle. As Mary passed one day John asked if she went to St Mary's Catholic Church, to which she nodded and kept moving. So, the next Sunday John looked around the congregation inside the church looking for a sign of Mary. He though perhaps she would be with her family. Eventually he sighted her away on the right-hand side near the front. John always stayed at the back of the church. After the mass was finished he approached the priest Father John and politely asked if he would introduce him to Mary and her family.

The priest looked over at Mary and was not aware of who she was but knew she arrived on her own every Sunday over the past year. Nonetheless he walked over leading John and said politely to her, "I am Father John, and I am sorry I have not spoken to you before. Is your family here?" Mary was surprised and taken aback to be speaking with the priest but managed to reply, "My name is Miss Casey, and I am boarding with the O'Brian family. I moved here to work. My family lives in Manchester." The priest nodded and said, "Well God bless you and I wish you well. This gentleman here is Mr John Arnold."

With that the priest was suddenly interrupted by an old lady with short grey hair who was talking about how the priest wanted the flowers arranged on the altar at the front of the church. He then left leaving both John and Mary standing together. They stifled a small laugh as the old lady led the priest away continuously talking in a high-pitched voice and obviously overly concerned about some flowers. She did not want to upset the priest or in her mind God with an inadequate arrangement of flowers.

John asked if he could walk her back to her home and she agreed. Mary chatted about her childhood and the fun times playing with the children in the street. Her parents were poor, and her mother supplemented the family income by making clothes. She was a dressmaker before getting married and continued making clothes to sell while she was at home with the children. In many ways this extra income was vital for the family to pay the rent and buy food. Each week she would buy material, cotton thread, buttons and some small pieces of wax for the thread. Then she would spend the week making clothes and selling them at the weekend market. From an early age Mary learned to sew from her dressmaker mother. Together with her sisters they made clothes at home during the week. Mary proved to be the nimblest with the needle and could sew perfectly within a year. Her mother also taught her how to cross-stitch and embroider so on each of her garments she made she would embroider or cross-stitch a colourful design, a flower, or an animal. Her speciality, she told John, was her small intricate colourful birds. The people they sold the clothes to liked these special touches on the women's and girls' clothes and paid a penny more.

Initially, John and Mary met on Sunday mornings at church and then spent the afternoons together. John learned that Mary was alone in Bradford having travelled here to gain work after growing up in Manchester. She was adventurous and wanted to move, travel and explore areas outside Manchester where she grew up. As she told the priest, she was boarding with a family called O'Brian in Bradford on Mill Street and her rent helped pay their rent. The O'Brians were an Irish family and when they met John liked him immediately. Often, they would have a simple Sunday midday meal together. On some Saturday evenings John would still go to the public house to play the fiddle and sing but he would always see Mary beforehand and walk her home from the mill if he finished on time. Mary did not go to the public house and the O'Brians were protective of her and her safety.

One Saturday evening John did not go to the public house, and as he walked with Mary back to the O'Brians' house he suddenly stopped, looked at her and said, "Mary, I have been thinking. We should get married as you are a wonderful person and I think we will have a great life here together." Mary looked at John and even though he was much older than she was, she felt it was the right time and he was the right person for marriage so she said, "Yes I would love that." Mary's father had passed away from an accident in a mill a few years ago in Manchester so John was not able to ask him for permission, and he did not have enough money or time to travel to Manchester to see Mary's mother.

The courtship had lasted 12 months, but after some thought John and Mary were certain that it was time to get married. Mary's mother agreed with their decision after John wrote to her. Their marriage was a simple affair with their few friends in attendance at St Mary's and then they went back to the public house for a celebration. Like John, Mary did not drink but many of their friends did, so it was nice to celebrate the event. Sean agreed to get one of his friends to move in with him, and John moved into sharing a single small room with Mary at the O'Brian's place. It was the first time, in either of their lives, they had any real privacy even if it was just one small room. Gradually, Mary started to make the room more comfortable, but they lived within their means and they both continued to work at the mill. Mary continued with her dressmaking in her limited spare time and the sale of the clothes helped cover the rent.

During that first year they were married Mary became pregnant and their son James Charles was born. It was 1851. Shortly afterwards Mary's mother became extremely ill in Manchester. Mary asked if she could move there for a short while as her mother was dying and needed some help. Mary knew a family called McManus with whom she could stay at 42-5 Ludgate Hill, Manchester. Mrs Margaret McManus' husband was absent, and she worked as a vegetable hawker. She needed the money so gladly accepted Mary as a lodger. Mary got work at a local mill and James Charles would be looked after by Margaret's four children. She also continued with the dressmaking in Manchester. Margaret had particularly good connections at the market and helped sell the clothes

Mary made. Mary and John had no idea the extreme difficulties they would face in the future with that simple decision to separate briefly.

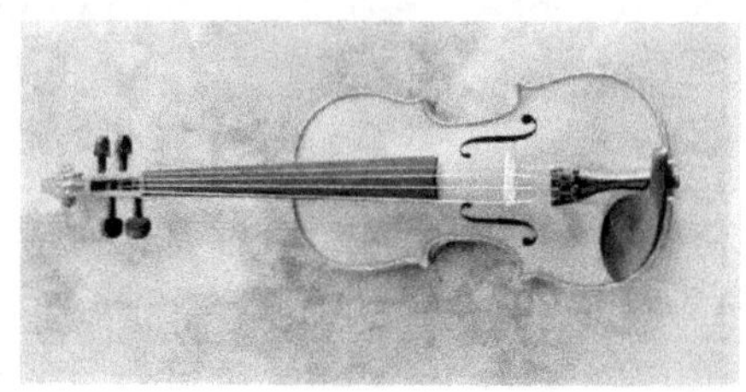

(Source – unsplash)
'till bad misfortune came o're me
which sent me away from the land
far away from my friends and companions
betrayed by the black velvet band.

4

Richardson

In Mary's absence John caught up increasingly with Sean again and one Saturday evening Sean let John know he had lost his job and was now doing some work at night and on the weekends for a man called Richardson. He asked if John would like to meet Mr Richardson as he was looking for some nice Irish lads to help him with some simple work at night. "He is an important Englishman, and he pays very well," Sean said. John thought about it and decided he should be respectful and meet him.

John and Sean met Mr Richardson down by the canal that night. It was dark, quiet and cool with a slight mist of rain. Nobody else was about. Mr Richardson was tall and gaunt with a long-pointed nose. His dark hat covered his head and cast a shadow over his face. His long greasy hair fell out the back of the hat and covered the top of his collar. His teeth were cracked, blackened and yellow in some places. His dark long coat fell to his black scuffed boots and the collar of his coat was turned up, so it was difficult to see any of his features well. He spoke slowly and deliberately with a deep voice. He said to John, "Well Mr Arnold, where are you from and where do you work?" "I am from Dromore in Northern Ireland, and I work at one of the woollen mills doing maintenance work," John replied.

Richardson thought for some time while staring at John. After a while he said, "I have some work for you John. I will pay you well and all you need to do is wait outside while Sean and the others go in to visit an old friend to collect some of my things I left there. Remember if you see someone nearby just whistle so Sean and the others would know about it." John thought was this odd, but Mr Richardson was an important Englishman. John was still naïve in the ways of the world, and he simply replied, "Ok."

Richardson was not his real name. He was a criminal with a long history of petty crime who had avoided capture. He had come perilously close to being caught by the police a few years ago so he was extremely careful. He only worked in the dark of night and never where anyone could see him clearly or follow him. He always stopped every few minutes and checked to see if anyone was following him. His long dark old coat was worn to completely cover his normal clothes and help him blend into the shadows at night. He was aware of the English law covering the punishment of rogues, vagabonds and sturdy beggars. It meant that convicted vagabonds would be whipped and returned to their parishes of birth or last residence. It was an old law enacted in 1597-98 and it led to transportation where courts could banish convicted criminals to overseas colonies. In addition, if any convicted criminal returned without permission, they could be hanged. The laws became progressively harsher to try to discourage the accelerating rate of crime in England due to the breakdown of the feudal system and movement of many dislocated people into the cities and large towns. The industrial revolution accelerated the change. By the mid-1700s, 160 offences carried the death penalty. This included minor offences like burglary, stealing 40 shillings from a house, cutting down trees in an avenue, sending threatening letters, stealing linen and sacrilege. It even got to the point where stealing objects of no more than five shillings could be punishable with death, but the death penalty was often commuted to life in prison and transportation to an overseas colony.

Approximately 60,000 convicts were transported from England to the colonies in North America in the 1700s and 1800s under the Transportation Act 1717. After the loss of the war in October 1781 with

America, England lost the ability to send convicts to America, so they began looking elsewhere to send the convicted criminals.

In mid-1786 the English government decided the newly discovered area of New South Wales in the southern hemisphere would be an acceptable place to set up a new penal colony. Over time Port Arthur in Van Diemen's Land was added as a penal colony.

Much later when New South Wales and Tasmania started to cease being penal colonies the inhabitants of the struggling settlement in the southwest of Western Australia asked the English government to send convicts because the settlement was desperately short of labour. So, the very isolated Colony of Western Australia was added as a penal colony where convicts could be sent.

Consequently, Richardson now got other people, who were not fully aware of the risks, to do his dirty work which included breaking into a property he selected and stealing valuables like cash, silverware and watches. Sometimes they stole guns as well. He collected the stolen goods in the dark of night down by a secluded part of town, paid the petty burglars well and then sold the stolen items. He found the poor Irish migrants were extremely keen to do his bidding for some extra cash as they did not understand the magnitude of the risk they were taking and generally were very poor and saw this as a way to alleviate the desperate situations they were in.

The next Saturday night John joined Sean with four other people. John thought he heard Sean say the owner of the house was Hutchinson, or Richardson, and it was near Lord Derby's estate. John did his job. Nobody came by. Sean and his friends met Mr Richardson again down by the canal and handed over £56, a watch, a gun and some expensive silverware. Sean explained to John that the friend in the house was away, so they collected the items that Mr Richardson said were owed to him. Mr Richardson carefully inspected each piece of silverware, weighted it in his hand and gently put it into his sack. He looked at the watch for a long time. John never owned a watch, but he was fascinated at the care Mr Richardson took with the timepiece. The watch was carefully wrapped in some woollen material and placed in one of Mr Richardson's deep coat pockets. With the gun he checked to see if it was loaded and dropped it into another one of his deep pockets. In the end he calculated what the goods and cash were worth and paid them all handsomely. John went home with more than a week's wages. John still did not get a look at Mr Richardson's face, nor did he speak very much other that summarising what the goods were worth to them. Although John was not worldly, he realised that it was a burglary, but he was just standing outside not participating. He was just watching. He was not stealing so he was not breaking any commandments, he reasoned, and the money was good.

John went home in the early hours of the morning and was incredibly careful to stop every so often and check no one was following him. Mr Richardson mentioned this to him. Once he thought he saw a small boy lurking in an alley fifty yards behind him, so he waited for over ten minutes in the shadows. Eventually a small dark-haired boy walked out of the alley and went back down the street. It was not until the boy was out of sight that John recommenced his journey home. He was sweating and anxious even in the cool night air.

Over the next few Saturdays, they did not get a contact from Mr Richardson who normally sent a small boy along to the public house to pass on a meeting time and place to Sean. One evening after John played the fiddle and sang a few songs at the public house, Sean introduced a man called John Cosgrave who looked a few years older than John and Sean. He too was Irish, and like John came to England due to the famine in Ireland but settled in Liverpool. John Cosgrave was vague about what happened to his wife Bridget Stoney, but he said they were married in Liverpool in 1841 and he had two daughters – Ann who was around eight years old and Catherine who was six maybe seven years old at that time. He was working as a dock labourer in Liverpool and was having trouble with money like everyone else. He was poor but not destitute and wanted to do better for his daughters. He said he was renting a room with his two young girls in Darwen Street, Liverpool down near the docks. It was close to his work he said. John Cosgrave went back to Liverpool the next day but said he needed more work if they had any.

Soon Mr Richardson was back in contact, and the same group of men met and broke into another house which Mr Richardson advised contained, £100 in a secret drawer. The house was about three or four miles away from the previous house. Once they broke in, they only found £8 and missed finding the secret drawer. Once again John acted as the lookout outside the house. No one came past.

The burglaries started a trend for them, and the police were on the lookout for a group of men who had started regular break-ins in the Bradford and Liverpool areas. When Mary came back from Manchester, she was unaware of the extra money in the hiding place they had in their room and believed John had simply found another job on a Saturday night from time to time to earn extra money.

The next house was about five miles from Bradford and was near the junction of the Bradford and Leeds railway, close to the canal. Mr Richardson said it was a magistrate's clerk's house. This time John went inside and helped to look for the things to steal. They ended up with some cash. John was getting increasingly anxious. He was now helping with a break-in and stealing goods. His guilt was overcome by the adventure and the cash rewards. One evening he said to Sean, "I am not sure about this Sean. We are stealing and getting paid to do it." Sean replied, "Don't worry John. Mr Richardson would not send us into a place where it was dangerous or possible that we would be discovered." John was saving all the money he received and hid it back in the room he shared with Mary. They made a secret hideaway in the flooring where he stored his cash from Ireland, any savings from his weekly wage plus the cash he was getting from Mr Richardson. He hoped to surprise Mary with an idea to rent a place where they would have more space for their children, and they could take in lodgers themselves.

John Cosgrave got in contact again and he joined John Arnold, Sean and four other men to burgle the next house. It was about one mile from Bradford. Mr Richardson provided them with pistols to scare the inhabitants if they were home, so they took the pistols and covered their faces with black woollen masks. They found a substantial amount of money and fourteen pounds weight of high-quality silver plate. Once again, they met Mr Richardson down by the canal where he paid them £17 for the money and the plate. So, John Cosgrave became a regular part of the group. As the robberies became riskier in the Bradford and Liverpool areas Mr Richardson sent the men down to Abergavenny, where they robbed a house but only found six half pennies, an unloaded pistol, and a larger pistol. John was given £5, 10s.

It was now 1852, when on the 9th of August Mr Richardson gave them another address. The house was owned by John Owen in West Derby east of Liverpool. It was about three or four miles from Liverpool near Lord Derby's estate. Here they broke in. Mr Owen was at home, came out of his bedroom and challenged the burglars demanding they get out of his house. One of the men who was new to the group – young, tall and strongly built – stepped right up to Mr Owen, grabbed him by his nightshirt and bashed him across his face with his fist. Owen fell and blood tricked out from his now broken nose. He staggered trying to get to his feet shouting at the men when he was hit viciously again. John and the others cowered silently. This is not what they had planned nor what they had done before. "What is going on?" said John. "Let's get out of here," replied Sean. It was supposed to be a simple break in, steal what they could and flee with the goods. The young man grabbed Owen by his night shirt again and dragged him off the floor and demanded he tell them where the money was hidden. When he did not get an instant reply, he hit him again. Owen now fearing for his life cowered bleeding on the floor and pointed to the bottom drawer of a bureau in the room. Here they stole £70 in money and collected on the way out six tablespoons, six teaspoons, twelve forks, three watches, and other property. Once again, they met Mr Richardson down by the canal side. It was the last time John would meet Mr Richardson. He paid £9 plus £5 for the three watches, and £50 for £65 of the paper money. This was an enormous haul and John wanted to rush home and put the cash away as quickly as possible.

On the way home back to the O'Brian's house he again noticed a small child who appeared to be following him. Every time he stopped the child disappeared into the shadows. He veered away from his house and still the child seemed to tag along in the distance for an hour. Finally, it appeared to John that the child disappeared, and he quickly made his way back to his house and home to bed.

How wrong he was that the child had disappeared, and he was not being followed.

Richardson
(Source – public domain)

"To err is human but in Victorian times the punishment was often life itself."
Michael Le Page

5

Gores General Advertiser

The following morning, Sunday, John rose early, washed, and headed off to church with Mary and James. He needed also to go to confession as he was feeling very guilty about the robberies. He hoped the priest would hear his confession and forgive him. Instead, the priest was angry at John in the confessional and forcefully whispered to him that he needed to obey God's law and stop this stealing. He needed to be honest and respect God's commandments especially, 'You shalt not steal' and 'You shall not covet your neighbour's house; you shall not covet your neighbour's wife, nor his male servant, nor his female servant, nor his ox, nor his donkey, nor anything that is your neighbour's.' He was given a harsh penance of prayers and the priest wanted a commitment that this behaviour was to stop immediately. John was distraught and promised to the priest to stop. The priest then had a long sermon during mass extoling the virtues of being honest and respectful. "Blessed are the meek for they shall inherit the earth," he declared and looked directly at John.

When he finally left the church, John was feeling better and was determined to stop meeting Sean and never rob again. As they walked back to his home, he entered through the back gate which led to a small courtyard area where the pump and wash basin were located. Here he was confronted by two tall sturdy constables and beside them was a small boy. The boy looked at John and said in a loud voice, "That's him!" to one of the constables who then gave the boy a coin. The boy took the money and quickly ran out of the back gate. John thought the boy matched the lad who followed him back from the house he robbed last night. John's elated feeling vanished, and he was filled with dread. The constables grabbed him forced his hands behind his back and put on him some rough iron handcuffs. He was then walked down to the police station where he was questioned. He told them he was not guilty of any crime and his name was John O'Brian. Based on the child's eye-witness story that he had followed John and the other men from the house that was burgled, down to the canal where a meeting took place with a tall person in dark clothes and then back to this very house coupled with Mr Owen's statement, the police decided to formally charge John with burglary with violence. He was transferred to Kirkdale Goal and House of Correction awaiting trial.

As John was allowed a priest to visit, he asked if he could see the priest. John explained his confession to the priest and how he was sorry for what he had done. He also asked if the priest could pass a message onto Mary in Bradford through their local church. The priest agreed to make the contact and he asked if John felt he was guilty to which John replied that he was. The priest then asked John to pray in silence over the next few days and consider in his heart if pleading not guilty was consistent with his upbringing, his values, his religion and the confession he had recently with the other priest.

Later, on October 7, 1852 John Cosgrave handed himself in to police, explained the misadventure and pleaded guilty. The trial date for both men was set at the Liverpool Assizes for December 9, 1852.

Gores General Advertiser
Number 4548 – Volume LXXXIX – Liverpool December 23, 1852
'The Bradford and Mirfield burglaries
Confession by one of the gang.'

'At the Liverpool Assizes on Saturday last before Mr Justice Cress-well, John Cosgrave, 41, and John Arnold, 37, were indicted for having at West Derby, burglariously entered the dwelling of John Owen, and stolen therefrom £70 in money, six tablespoons, six teaspoons, twelve forks, three watches and other property.

'The prisoner, Cosgrave, pleaded guilty and Arnold not guilty.

'Mr Owen, his party and other parties having given their evidence in its bearing on the above daring burglary, Mr George Adams, Governor of the Herford Gaol, said that Arnold was in his custody on the 5th of November last, on a charge of house breaking in West Derby when Arnold sent for him (Mr Adams) and made the following extraordinary statement showing his connection with various burglaries in different parts of the country, among others those at Mr Clough's, solicitor, near Bradford, and at Mr Ledgard's, solicitor, Mirfield, in the following statement:

"It is no use my waiting here. I was in this. I want to tell you some-thing about it. That name I gave (O'Brian) is not the right one. My name is John Arnold. I have been middling well brought up, till I came here sometime back. About 6 or 7 years back, I fell in bad company. Earl Fitzwilliam's agent, Mr James Jones, knew me to bear a good character when I was in Ireland. The minister, Mr Archer, knows me also. I have been in several things of the sort. There is one man who led me into two of them; He has been apprehended, and turned evidence; and, through him doing so, I have been afraid of starting to work. There is £100 reward offered for my apprehension and others, for house robbery like this, at Bradford. I believe the person robbed had been sheriff for York, or something: It is about one mile from Bradford. Two or three months ago, there were seven of us: We had pistols and our faces covered. We stole money and fourteen pounds weight of plate. A man (I think his name is Richardson) in Birmingham was the receiver of the plate. He paid us £17 for it, by the canal side, near Liverpool. The other house was broken into by myself and four others. It was, I think, the magistrate's clerk's house. It is about five miles from Bradford. It was about harvest time. We stole some money there. There was three of the party taken. The house is about the junction of the Bradford and Leeds railway, close to the canal.

"The other house we broke into in June last, was Mr Owen's, about three or four miles from Liverpool near Lord Derby's estate. There was six besides myself there. We took £75 in paper, two sovereigns and about £3 in silver and eight pounds weight of plate. Richardson had this plate also. The money was paid by the canal side. He gave us £9 odd for it. There were three watches taken. He got them also. He allowed us £5 for the three watches and £50 for £65 of the paper money.

"A man, name's Green I think, has been convicted, and death recorded against him, who was not present, nor ever in his life knew anything about it. I never saw Green and knew he was not there. There was another house broken into by myself and five others. I think the name was Hutchinson, or Richardson, something of that name: It's near Lord Derby's estate. This was about two years ago. We stole £56, a watch and gun. I think there was three or four convicted; neither of them were concerned or knew anything about it. The same party who was with me at Hutchinson's house, broke into another house about the same time, about three or four miles off, and stole £8 and in a secret drawer was £100 which was missed. One of the inmates was shot in the jaw. Neither of the party were ever taken. There was some persons taken into custody and convicted, but they were innocent. A captain of a merchant ship's son was taken with another for it on suspicion. There was £200 reward. All the money, at Abergavenny, that I saw in the house was six ½ d. The pistol I took out of the house; it was not loaded; it was in a press cupboard. I saw a watch; silver it was; I did not meddle with it; an old one it was. There was five there besides myself. Those two others who are taken are two of them. The tallest, the one taken for passing the bad half crown, was not inside; he was outside watching; the other one was inside with us. The larger pistol, found on the one who was not inside, was stolen from the house.

"After the robbery we went, four of us, down as far as Cardiff, the same night. We all slept at the Poolmans. The next day the tallest, and the one who came to Herford with us, but escaped being taken, gave me £5, 10s., part of the money."

'His lordship then summed up and the jury found the prisoners guilty.

Cosgrave, on being asked what he had to say why a sentence of death should not be recorded against him said, "I am sorry for what I have done. But there was a man sentenced at the last August assizes for this offence, and he knows nothing about it; he is innocent. I am willing to suffer for what I have done; but he is as innocent of it as you are. His name is France, and I never saw him until I saw him at Kirkdale gaol. He lived in Scotland Road. That is all I have to say."

"His lordship then ordered sentence of death to be recorded against the prisoners.

'By the vigilance of the police, in different towns, this gang of desperados has been completely routed, and all, save one or two still at large, transported for different terms for one or other of those daring burglaries, which struck terror into the minds of the inhabitants of the rural districts of this riding, some three or four months ago.'

The Huddersfield and West Yorkshire Advertiser printed a similar article on Saturday December 18, 1852.

After the trial, John was registered as a convicted felon and his details were recorded as follows.

> Name: John Arnold
> Alias: John O'Brian
> Convict Number: 3521
> Birth: 1815
> Data: Married with one child, semi-literate.
> Occupation: Miller
> Conviction: Liverpool 6.12.1852, burglary of the house of John
>   Owen and stealing £70, six tablespoons, six teaspoons, twelve

forks, three watches and other articles, death sentence commuted to life.

Physical: 5ft 61/4 inches tall, brown hair, grey eyes, round visage,
middling stout, much freckled.

The interviewing prison officer asked John if he could read and write
to which John replied he could read very well and write also. He said
that he went to school in Dromore for six years. He was proud of that.
The prison officer looked at him, an Irish criminal, and he doubted he
could read so he asked John to read a passage of the Bible that he had in
his desk. John read it fluently. The prison officer grunted then pushed
a small piece of paper to him and told him to write his name, where
he lived and his occupation. He wrote in beautiful script writing. The
officer looked at the writing, crumpled the paper and tossed it into a
waste bin in the corner. He then grunted again and wrote out semi-
literate while thinking no Irishman like this could read and write like an
Englishman. He also had seen that John said he was a linen craftsman,
grist miller and woollen miller as his occupations so he simply recorded
miller as John's occupation. He thought that there was no need to
complicate things plus the only milling he would be doing was working
on the corn treadmill in Kirkdale prison.

After the check-in, John was physically exhausted and emotionally
depleted. He laboured along the narrow, dark corridor of Liverpool's
Kirkdale prison down to his prison cell with his head bowed. He had
been here before prior to his court case and knew the harsh reality of
solitary confinement. His legs were in irons which forced him to shuffle.
His hands were in cast iron handcuffs. Both irons and cuffs were tight,
rough and cut into his skin. The tall lean prison guard behind him was
silent as was his way. The only way John knew he was there was the
rustling of his uniform, the stench of his body and the regular rough jab
in his back from the wooden truncheon he carried. It had a well-worn,
turned wooden handle with a leather strap with which he used to twirl

the truncheon around his wrist then prod John again. The guard didn't care if he hurt John. He just wanted to make sure John knew who was in charge.

The corridor was cold, damp and silent, and John knew the solitary confinement cell ahead was grim. It was thirteen feet long by seven feet wide and nine feet high with a small, barred window which provided some light and air. The stone walls between the cells were eighteen inches thick with close joints so there was no transfer of sound. They stopped outside the cell door and the guard motioned John to step aside as he unlocked the thick, black, steel door and then grunted at him in his disinterested, deep voice, "Get inside". The cell door shut with a thud. The key turned in the lock and with it John realised this would be his reality for the next 12 months – a dreadful beginning.

A whitewashed cubical with a metal basin supplied with water, a hammock, two blankets, a stool, a desk and some eating utensils were all he had. There would be no contact with any other prisoners. There would be cell visits by the chaplain and the prison officers, but he would be alone with his thoughts. For 23 hours a day this would be his home. He would be allowed out only for silent exercise and to attend the chapel. The daily routine would never vary. At six o'clock in the morning John would get up and wait for breakfast. He had a tin plate and tin mug with him, and he would stand in front of the prison cell door. The door would open, and he would typically get a brown six-ounce loaf of bread on his plate and three-quarters of a pint of gruel which was watery fare of unknown character but mostly oats, wheat or rye. Sometimes the bread was fresh and sometimes it was very stale. He ate it anyway. The door was then closed and locked. After the meal, a bell would ring and the door would open, and all the prisoners would march away for chapel. Not a word was spoken by the convicts or the guards.

He sat on the hammock and let his thoughts wander over the last few days. He burgled a house with six others and someone, not him, bashed the occupant to get him to turn over the money. There was £70 plus some silver plate and watches. The conviction crushed him.

The death penalty commuted to life imprisonment and transportation. Never again would he see his village, his friends or walk along the beautiful River Lagan in Dromore, Ireland. Would he ever see his pregnant wife Mary and his son James again? What would become of them?

A few weeks later one of the prison guards pressed into John's hand some dirty folded paper as they were walking to the prison chapel for a church service. He tucked the paper into his prison jacket and continued walking with his head down as if nothing happened. Later, after the service, in this prison cell he looked at the paper. The folded paper was greasy and dirty like it had been left in with a pile of trash. It probably had been. It was stained but he was still able to read it. It consisted of a page from the Liverpool Mercury newspaper dated December 14, 1852. Part of the newspaper was the transcript of his court case and his confession. He quickly read it. It all was accurate. He winced at the mention of the death penalty. Another part was a transcript of the other court cases held around the same time. The following caught his attention.

Liverpool special assizes
Crown Court
(Before Mr Justice Cresswell)

Friday December 10

The Judge took his seat soon after 9 o'clock.

'Evan Huyton, aged nineteen, pleaded guilty to having committed, at Scarisbrick, an abominable crime. Sentence of death was ordered against the prisoner.

Gross and Criminal Assault.'

Saturday December 11

Robberies at Manchester

'John Walker, aged thirty-five, was found guilty of having, at Manchester, in company with two other persons, assaulted and robbed John Stelfox of a watch, value £5, on the night of 12th November. A previous conviction was also proved against him. He was sentenced to 15 years transportation.'

Manslaughter at Manchester

'Thomas Laidler, aged forty for having at Manchester, feloniously killed Carolyn Miller, was sentenced to four months imprisonment with hard labour. '

John mused to himself. *John Walker stole a £5 watch and got 15 years and transportation. He knew that included one year solitary confinement, but Thomas Laidler killed Carolyn Miller and got four months imprisonment.* He felt disgusted at the injustice here and wondered if John Walker was an Irishman and John Stelfox English, while Thomas Laidler and Carolyn were probably both poor, destitute and Irish. "You can kill someone and that was a minor offence but steal a watch and you get 15 years and transportation. Where was the justice in that?" he said aloud to no one in particular.

Street Robberies

'Richard Holt, aged twenty, was indicted for having, at Selford, stolen £1 from Robert Sharrock. It appeared that the prosecutor was intoxicated at the time, and Mr Sowler submitted to the jury that he (the prosecutor) was not in a state to say who robbed him. The jury acquitted the prisoner.'

Bigamy

James Arthur Skerriff, aged thirty, pleaded guilty to having, at Manchester, on the 24th of March last, married Elizabeth Cance, single woman, Mary Anne Skerriff, his former wife still being alive. His lordship then sentenced the prisoner to be transported for seven years.'

Stabbing at Eccleston

'John Fearix, aged twenty-one, was indicted for having, at Eccleston, feloniously stabbed, cut and wounded John Hewitt, with intent to do him some grievous bodily harm. The jury found the prisoner guilty of unlawfully wounding and convicted him of the felony. His lordship sentenced him to be imprisoned and put to hard labour for three calendar months.'

Sentences

'Henry Howe, aged twenty-three, for having, with other persons, assaulted Francis Richardson, at Manchester and robbed him of £195, was sentenced to 15 years transportation.

John Clifton, aged twenty-one, for robbing the house of Anne Spencer, at Manchester to be transported for 7 years.

'John Simm, aged forty-eight, and William Stead, aged thirty-six, who had severally pleaded guilty to bigamy, were sentenced – the former to three months and Stead to four months imprisonment.'

Again, John mused to himself. *James Skerriff, got seven years transportation for bigamy yet John Simm and William Stead, got three months and four months imprisonment respectively for the same crime. Why was the court so harsh on one man yet so lenient on the other two? Was one Irish and the other English? He committed a few burglaries and got life imprisonment commuted to transportation. He would never be allowed to return to England!*

Monday, December 13,

Burglary at Pendlebury

'James Fenton, aged seventeen, was indicted for having, at Pendlebury, burglariously broken and entered the house of James Gordon, and having stolen 5s, 9d, in copper, sugar, cheese, starch and a drawer. The prisoner was found guilty and sentenced to twelve months imprisonment with hard labour.'

Horse stealing

'James Brown, aged forty, was indicted for having, at Chadderton, near Oldham, stolen one horse, the property of Sarah Simpson. The prisoner was also found guilty on this indictment, and he was sentenced to seven years and transportation.'

John thought again. *Somebody can kill someone else and get four months prison time but someone else steals a horse, does not even kill the horse, and gets seven years and transportation. The owner got the horse back too. John realised he was guilty of his crimes but who made up these laws and what was more important, someone's life or a horse? Apparently some wealthy person's property was far more important than someone's life,* John thought.

Saturday December 11

Assault

'Six young men, whose ages vary from 17 to 20, were indicted for a gross and criminal assault upon Maria Wright, a female upwards of 40 years of age, a Manchester factory operative. Maria Wright is the wife of a transported felon. Mr Justice Cresswell, in passing sentence, dwelt upon the necessity laid upon him for punishing in a marked and severe manner the perpetrators of so abominable and disgusting an outrage, for the commission of which it was no apology that the prisoners were under the influence of strong drink. They were each sentenced to transportation beyond the sea for 20 years.'

His thoughts immediately turned to his wife Mary. *Was she safe or would she become a victim of assault like Maria Wright when he was not there to protect her? Was Maria Wright viscously raped? The newspaper did not say. There were so many questions. Where was Mary? Did she get his message? Did she leave Bradford? How was her pregnancy going? How was young James?* John bowed his head into has hands and started to weep. He had done this many times in the past few months. He felt cheated, worthless, useless and alone... So alone.

"I found solitary confinement the most forbidding aspect of prison life. There is no end and no beginning; there is only one's mind, which can begin to play tricks. Was that dream or did it really happen? One begins to question everything." – Nelson Mandela

(Source: Unsplash)

6

Mary

Mary rushed out of the O'Brian's house on Mill Street, Bradford. She had not eaten but she needed to get to the factory on time. She made time to feed young James but not herself. It was cold as she hurried down the side of the lane pulling her coat around her body and fixing the covering on her head. Her pregnancy was showing now but she was also gaunt and thin. Her face was grey from worry and lack of food. She was starting to look much older than her 22 years. The blossom of youth was starting to fade but she discovered an inner strength in herself that kept her going through these tough times. She had cried so much but realised that was of no help and she needed to be determined and resilient. She needed to increase her pace. The supervisor was very harsh on people who did not arrive before the starting whistle and she could not afford to lose her job no matter how loud, hot or dangerous the work was. There were plenty of people lining up to take any vacancies that arose.

A few months ago, after mass on a Sunday morning, her local priest called her aside and passed on more news of John. Mary was frantic beforehand as she had not heard any news for a while and the priest was the best source of information. She was there that morning when the two constables were waiting for them in the courtyard after church and took John away in handcuffs. She had not seen him since. She did not even have the time to say goodbye. She was hysterical when he was cuffed and taken away, screaming, "You have the wrong man! Let him go!" Fortunately, the O'Brien's were there, and Mrs O'Brien took Mary into her arms as Mary sobbed. She thought the robberies were so unlike him. She had no idea as John told her he was just doing extra work at night for some money. He lied. She knew about the linen strip of material in which John hid their savings and the hiding place, but she never looked inside. Since then, the O'Brien's had still been getting the rent money from her wage and the money she made from dressmaking. She also regularly thanked them for their friendship and support over this tough time.

The priest filled her in on the details of the charges and court case. He even had the page from the newspaper. As she could not read he read the whole confession to her. She was puzzled why John would make such a confession and plead guilty. This did not seem to be the kind, respectful, hard-working person she married. The priest also showed her the article in the *Gore's General Advertiser* which documented John's trial. She looked at it blankly. She nodded with her head down and wiped away the tears that streamed down her face with a strip of cloth. "Mary," the priest said kindly, "as John has confessed to the crimes willingly, he is guilty, so no matter what you think, he will be in prison for a long time, so please forgive him and pray for him." The priest looked at Mary and wondered what would become of her. She was young, pregnant, poor and has lost her husband. She was on her own. The slums in Bradford were no place for someone like her.

One day she made sure no one was at home and looked inside the secret hiding place John had fashioned inside their room. She took out the linen money belt which was now darkened with age. She counted the cash that was there and rewrapped it. She put it back into the hiding place in her room and realised that to her, it was a lot of money. She also knew she would need it to survive over the next few years until John was released, especially with the baby being due. Never did it occur to her to leave John, and the priest omitted to advise her that John's sentence was for death commuted to life imprisonment and transportation overseas.

The priest knew that John would never be able to return, and Mary would probably never see him again.

Shortly afterwards she received a letter from John. It was dated the 13th of January 1853. She asked the priest to read it to her.

'Dear Mary,

It is with great sorrow that I must inform you that I got a hard sentence of life imprisonment and transportation over the seas from my home. My heart tis broken that I must leave you and our young James behind. What am I to do? I don't think a man has loved a woman as much as I love you.

They have locked me up in a cell all day and all night. I be here for a year at Kirkdale. It is retched. You must let James know that I am very well. Please speak kindly of me to him. I expect I will not see you before I depart but if God is willing, I will send for you and James after I get to the new land in the south. I will see you both agane. May God have mersy on me.

Your husband who loves you.

John Arnold'

She noticed she felt less secure with John in prison. The men at the factory looked at her differently now that they knew John was a convicted criminal and away in prison. Some openly leered at her which made her scared and she planned her trips to the factory and back with care to never be alone, especially near any alleys or in the dark. She pondered her plans carefully and considered to stay in Bradford with the O'Brian family as it was convenient for them both. It could be that simple. However, she started to feel uncomfortable even there.

One day she was harassed by a group of young men in the street on the way back home from the factory. She needed to work later than normal that day due to a breakdown in the factory, so it was getting dark. The young men appeared like they had been drinking and they crowded around her as she was alone and started pushing her back and forth. She felt terrified and screamed as they pushed her around and edged her towards an alley. She screamed again, then stumbled and fell. Suddenly they were laughing, and she felt their hands groping her body, feeling her legs, lifting her skirts and lifting her to carry her into the darkened alley. As quickly as it started it stopped as she heard a loud voice bellow at the men and a police whistle. They departed quickly as a police constable appeared and some of the neighbours came out of their homes responding to her screams. The constable gently picked her up asked if she as all right and then set off to chase the young men.

After this episode, she packed up and moved back to Manchester to live with Mrs McManus as she felt safer there with that family and she knew she could find work in a mill. She had enough money to support her if times became tough, plus she would get extra income from her dressmaking. She would wait for John. She was married, and as simple and hard as her life was, she was determined to honour her marriage commitment. She loved and adored him. Soon she would have two children to look after. She also wanted to avoid the dreaded workhouse for the poor which was just like a prison without the conviction. She also silently thanked her mother who taught her how to sew, so she could work and make clothes in her spare time to provide extra income so she could survive without John. Shortly after Mary Catherine was born in Manchester. It was 1853.

Source – unsplash

"

Irish blessing
May God never weaken you. Nár laga Dia thú

"

7

Kirkdale House of Correction

In England, during Victorian times, people were concerned with rising crime as offences increased fourfold between 1800 and 1840 to 20,000 per year. The consensus in Parliament and with the public was that very firm punishment was the answer. Most people did not question why crime was increasing but only considered how to punish the offenders. There were prisons but they were small, poorly run and lacked consistent punishments. Prisoners were mixed; sometimes hardened criminals, petty thieves, men, women, children and the insane were all crowded together in the same cell, in the same church pews and in the same exercise spaces. The person who ran the prison made up the rules. A criminal or their family could pay for extra benefits like better food, visitors and mail, and if you could not, the basic treatment was harsh.

The common punishment was to get rid of the convicts by sending them initially to America and subsequently to places like New South Wales or Van Diemen's Land (Tasmania), Australia. The name given to this new continent by the Dutch was New Holland. It was then changed by the British to Terra Australis, or the Great South Land, and then to Australia in 1824. In 1829 a further settlement was made, this time on the Swan River, and the name Colony of Western Australia was soon coined to refer to this isolated settlement on the southwest side of Australia. It was 2200 nautical miles from Sydney and 11400 nautical miles from London It was initially known as Swan River Colony and was established as a free colony on 2 May when Captain Fremantle formally took possession of the land of Western Australia in the name of the King of England. By the 1830s, New South Wales and Tasmania were complaining that they did not want to be the dumping ground for Britain's criminals.

The other alternative was execution – and hundreds of offences, just like John Arnold's, carried the death penalty,. However, twenty years before John was sent to prison people were concerned about these punishments, especially the level of executions. They found the answer was prisons, more of them, so the old prisons were extended, and a lot of new prisons were built from 1842. The prisons and the prison processes were made to be more consistent. They needed to be harsh places to deter new crimes and the repeat of previous ones. Convicts needed to be isolated with a lot of time to reflect on their crime; the food was to be basic but consistent – the same poor food all the time. People also insisted the inmates needed hard, reflective work like working on a treadmill as an additional means of punishment. The rules also changed with the new prisons. In the 1840s 'the Separate System' was introduced where prisoners were kept in their own cells for up to 23 hours per day and were only allowed out for chapel or for exercise. They sat in special isolated seats in chapel and wore special masks so that they couldn't even see, let alone talk to, another prisoner.

(Source – public domain – exercise hour in a Victorian era prison)

Not surprisingly, many convicts went insane under this system of isolation, and asylums were often built near to the prisons to house them.

John Arnold found himself at the Kirkdale House of Correction which opened in 1821 and had a capacity of around six hundred prisoners. It was the county gaol for the whole of the southern division of Lancashire. Some prisoners were made to work on the treadmill used for grinding corn and it used up to 130 prisoners per day to keep it running. Kirkdale had the highest death rate of any prison in England at the time. Coupled with the isolation, the heath of the prisoners was terrible. A report written a few years before John Arnold went there documented that 50 per cent were unable to name months of the year, 39 per cent were unable to name the reigning monarch and 15 per cent were unable to count to one hundred. Sixty-seven executions were also held at Kirkdale prison, the highest number was four at one time. Some were executed in public.

(Source – Public domain – Kirkdale House of Correction)

John's first year of incarceration from late 1852 was in total isolation. During that year there was some deliberation in the government to reduce it to nine months but for him he had to endure one year's total isolation. He had a Bible to read, and he was fed his meals at the same time each day. The food was designed to just keep the prisoners alive but not much else. Initially he started to mark each day with a scrape on the wall so he could track the passing of the days. He knew that there were seven days a week and 52 weeks in a year so all he needed to do was record the seven days fifty-two times and he would be out of solitary confinement.

After a month he started to question whether he had marked the wall that day or not. Did he mark the wall yesterday or not? He could not remember. So, after two months he stopped marking the wall. He looked forward to exercise time so he could at least get out of the cell and hear other people if not talk with them. Due to the design of the Kirkdale prison he did hear noise coming down the corridor, so he was not totally without use of his senses. Often, he would hear the screams from other convicts. He longed for the priest to visit so he could talk with someone. From time to time one of the nicer prison guards would stop and update him as would the priest. He found out that year that his death penalty had been commuted to life in prison and transportation. The laws changed that year and only the convicts who had 14 years or greater would be transported. John learned this included him.

John's knowledge of geography was extremely poor, like most convicts and most of the guards as well. For all his early life he was fixed to his parents' farm, and they never travelled. His world then was a radius of no more than ten miles. Though he could read, he rarely, if ever, read much. He had read the Bible as sometimes that was the only book he could get. News was spread by mouth around the town. When he travelled to Belfast, Liverpool and Bradford it was the first time he had travelled outside his neighbourhood but still he had little understanding of the world. So, when the priest told him of his potential transportation to a southern land, he said, "Father, I don't know where I will go or how far away it would be. Will I ever come back?" The priest looked at John, thought a little and replied, "John, transportation of convicts has been to a few places around the world. Previously it was to America when England had control there but after they lost the war and America became independent America would no longer take English convicts. Recently it was to the Australian colony New South Wales to a place called Sydney and then to Van Diemen's Land which is an island to the south of Sydney I believe. Some time ago these two colonies wanted the transportation of convicts to stop. However, another colony in the isolated west of the country applied to the English government to receive some convicts as there was a shortage of labour in the colony." He paused, thought again how to respond, and continued. "The new colony was initially called the Swan River Colony, but the name was changed a few years ago to the Colony of Western Australia. Transportation would be by ship, and it would take about three months or more depending on the weather." At this stage the priest was running out of information as he really knew little about transportation as did the guards and prison administration. After a while he added, "I heard that the port in the colony was called Freeman or Fremantle or Freemanson...something like that and the colony needed convicts to help with work on the farms and to build roads and bridges in the colony." The priest continued. "John, regarding your return to England, I understand as your sentence is long, it will be a long time before you can ever return." He then quietly said to John, "Let us pray together."

After a while, the priest stood to leave and loudly knocked on the cell door as he was instructed to do. After a few minutes, a guard opened it and the priest exited, then stopped at the cell door entrance and looked back at John. What he saw was John sitting silently on his stool leaning forward with his face in his hands. He was very thin. It was past the time for tears and the priest realised that John had reached the realisation that he would be sent somewhere on the other side of the world, never to return and never to see his family again. He then turned and left, thinking there must be a better path to justice.

As John considered his fate, the months slipped by. Many times he felt dazed and lethargic, and his mind would wander dreaming of the farm and his parents in springtime, or the good times on a Sunday with Mary, only to be brought back with a jolt to reality. He found the confinement without much light, contact with other people, and activities like playing the fiddle and singing, reading, or even a simple change of scenery made it a form of cruel torture. He slept a lot and sometimes would wake up anxious or dizzy or with a chronic headache.

He thought he was losing his mind and yet the silence and isolation continued day after day, week after week, month after month. After nine months he found he had trouble concentrating and when the priest or a prison guard would spend a few minutes in his cell to talk with him he would lose track of what they were saying even though he craved their presence. He lost the ability to recognise their faces and remember names. He even struggled with finding the right words to use when talking. Finally, his twelve months of solitary confinement finished but his punishment was far from over. It was December 1853.

Around that time the experienced English ship's surgeon Colin Arrott Browning wrote in his surgeon's journal an account of transportation voyages to Australia between 1836-1851. In it he described how the convicts' power of thinking, their common sense and their memory seemed to have been lost after their time in solitary confinement. He documented that imprisonment had sapped the convicts' physical and mental energies and predisposed them to disease, often manifested by convulsions the convicts experienced as they stepped on to the ship's deck.

At Kirkdale prison after the twelve-month solitary confinement, John was put to work on the treadmill. It was a punishment specifically designed for English prisons. It sometimes was called a treadwheel. John would be placed on a wheel adjacent to other prisoners and he would step down on a wheel comprising of twenty-four steps at a set rate. The wheels turned an axle attached to air vanes which controlled the speed. The guard could vary the speed of the treadmill by turning a large screw. To make the prisoners' work harder the prison officer would 'turn the screw'. One prison officer called Smith seemed to take pleasure turning the screw and make the prisoners work harder and sweat profusely in summer.

At other times, the screw was looser, John could not get a firm footing with each step as the step quickly moved away from him, so it kept him continuously stepping with no real footing. It was like a never-ending staircase and was exhausting. He had a bar to grasp with his hands so he could maintain his balance. Sometimes in summer it was hot and in winter the weather could be bitterly cold especially if the wind was blowing and there was snow.

Each shift lasted from the morning until five in the afternoon and in each session a prisoner would complete 864 steps which would be followed by the prisoner being replaced by another prisoner who would do 288 steps. Then the original prisoner would return to the treadmill. The treadmill turned a long axle, and at one end it was connected to a corn mill which ground the corn. It was designed to be a useful device but was also a torture. Initially, after the twelve months of solitary confinement, John struggled with the exhaustion of the sessions and on more than one occasion he stumbled from exhaustion then slipped off the treadmill only to be placed back on the mill. When he slipped too often, he would be taken off the treadmill secured to a flogging frame and whipped with a cat o' nine tails. It was his first but not his last meeting with the Cat.

It was at the treadmill that he saw John Cosgrave for the first time in over twelve months. He looked much older, and his hair was starting to go grey. His eyes had lost their lustre, he stooped slightly, and his face was gaunt and grey. As the two passed John said hello to him but Cosgrave looked blankly at him as if he was trying to work out who John was. Maybe the confinement had taken his mind away. Suddenly, there was a flicker of recognition in his eyes followed by a slight smile. The recognition brought him some happiness. Then they moved apart.

During that year John learnt his transportation would occur in the next winter in early 1855, and in the meantime he would be transferred to Portland Prison which is on the Isle of Portland in Dorset to the south of England. Portland was a departure point for the transportation ships, and it would be his last time on English soil. His one wish was to see Mary and his family again but with each day at Kirkdale and then the move to Portland that opportunity was diminishing. Would he see them again or could he escape?

"Crime and bad lives are the measure of a state's failure,
all crime in the end is the crime of the community."
H. G. Wells (1866-1946)

(Source – public domain Treadmill for men)

8

Portland Prison

John survived Kirkdale prison. Many prisoners did not. He overcame the mental torture of the solitary confinement and the physical torture of the treadmill. However, his mind was weakened, his body was thin, broken down from the lack of food and his back was heavily scarred from the lashings of the Cat. Yet as he was loaded onto a coastal vessel for Portland from Liverpool, he was hopeful the tough times were behind him. How wrong he would be. He was still in the British penal system.

Portland's prison opened in 1848. Its purpose was to provide convict labour for construction of the harbour breakwaters and other infrastructure which were considered of strategic importance to the military. The change of design and use of the prison was a result of the work of Mr Joshua Jebb. He was a major in the Royal Engineers and worked with Mr Crawford and Mr Russel to plan and design the Pentonville Prison. Crawford and Russel were the main force behind the prison system design. They opposed any plan to allow convicts to work together outside the prison. After Crawford and Russel passed away Jebb further voiced his suggestions for improvements. The first was to use convict labour for public works outside the prison and not keep convicts locked up in their cells. This allowed Jebb to reduce the cost of the prison construction by making the cells smaller, built with less expensive materials like wood and iron and with less amenities inside the cells. Convicts would work during the day, take their meals in a mess hall, and only stay in their cells at night.

John and the other convicts were herded into the prison, registered and assigned their cells on arrival. The cells were smaller than the cells in Birkdale. On the first evening John asked one convict, who had been there for a year, why the cells were smaller. "The aim here is to work and the cells are only for rest and sleep," the convict replied. "We all work in the stone quarries near the prison cells, where we move thousands of tons of stone each week for use on the breakwater construction. We quarry the stone, move it up to the top of the incline railway where contractors take over and deliver the stone to the port. At the port it is dumped into the sea to build the breakwater." The convict paused and looked down at his hands which John could see were heavily calloused and bruised. "The conditions in both the prison and the quarries are harsh," he continued. "Don't forget that or expect they are not. A lot of convicts have died here including two of my friends so take my word for it and be careful, especially over the first few weeks until you get used to the risks." Like John, this other convict was there for a holding period before being transported overseas to a penal colony. John learnt he would be held at Portland Prison until a ship had been selected and fitted for the trip to the West Australian penal colony. He was not told any more information. It was now 1854.

The next day the newly arrived convicts were marched over to the stone quarry where John was assigned a role to load the rocks onto wagons. On his first day it looked like around five hundred convicts were doing the work in the quarries lifting out and stacking stone, loading it onto wagons and moving the wagons to and from the top of the railway. He saw some convicts building a store yard, what looked like a blacksmith's shop and a foundry. John had no skills in that area, so he was kept with the loading operation. It was backbreaking work, cold and the dust choked his lungs. Like in the woollen mills he found a cloth rag and bound it around his face to keep the dust out of his nose and mouth. The discipline was strict, but the guard told all the newly arrived convicts that in return for good behaviour, convicts could be given a Ticket of Leave when they arrived at the penal colony in Australia. This meant they would get certain freedoms in the colony including the ability to be employed within their designated district, not stay in a prison, get paid a small wage and only need to report to the magistrate twice per year. John thought about this, looked at the guard and thought to himself that he needed to find a way to get out of here otherwise he would never see Mary and James again.

In the quarry John noted the blocks were roughly shaped by hand, loaded onto wagons, and taken away. Horses and locomotives were used to transport the wagons from the quarrying area to an area where a series of wagons were connected to a locomotive which would pull them up to the start of the incline railway. There were about eighteen derrick cranes being used at the time and John worked on one securing the rocks to the crane's chains for lifting onto the wagons. The days were long and it was dirty, dangerous work. The rocks were very heavy, difficult to secure and the ground was uneven, so the cranes were un-stable. Many times, the rocks would move, or the chains would slip, and it was easy for a convict to be crushed. One day there were four of them working a derrick to load blocks onto a wagon. The block this time was less shaped than before, and they were having trouble fitting the chains to secure the block. Finally, they got the block secure, and they started to lift it when a chain slipped, and the block dropped with a thud and rolled into one of the convicts who was standing near the derrick. He screamed and was killed instantly. Despite all the effort to try to quickly move the block away from him it was futile. Eventually the block was moved with the crane, and the crushed and bloody body was carefully loaded onto a wagon and taken over to the prison. John looked at the wagon leaving the quarry and was ordered by the guard to get back to work.

John worked through spring and summer doing the same work and was told that when someone did a certain job they stayed on that job until their ship was ready for departure. John had not heard any more information regarding his ship. There were several other convicts who he now had worked with for nine months. William Chambers and William Morley were two. William Chambers was convicted of being a pickpocket in Preston, north of Liverpool and near Blackburn. He was given 15 years imprisonment and transportation. William Morley was convicted of burglary in Nottingham which is much farther away from Liverpool to the southeast between Sheffield and Birmingham. John was still unsure of the location of any of these places. Morley was given transportation as well. All three would most probably be on the same ship to the Colony of Western Australia.

While they were working Morley, Chambers and John drifted into a friendship and grew to trust each other. It was dangerous work so they needed to trust the people they worked with. One day during a work break the three were talking when Morley said, "John are you happy here or would you rather be back in Bradford?" John looked at him and replied, "What do you mean?" Morley said, "Well if you could get out of here, would you, do it?" Chambers and I have been looking this place over. You know watching the guards' behaviours, asking innocent questions like what is over those ridges and what is the beach like? We are thinking about escaping and making a run for a railway over to the west and then get back home by hiding in a rail wagon. We would need to lie low for a while and change our names, but it can be done. We have people who would help us at home."

Morley continued that they had a plan, but they needed a third person to help and asked if John was interested. John was tired. He worked hard all the days in the quarry and the food was no better than in Kirkdale plus his hands were heavily calloused, continually bruised and cut. He was thin as well. Some days he struggled to connect the chains together to lift the rocks onto the wagons and the guard regularly would walk by and curse at them for being too slow. He would threaten the use of the lash which they all knew would and could be used vigorously.

Chambers added that the plan was to hide in the quarry when work finished for the day and wait until it was dark. They would then make their way over the back of the quarry past the fence and down over the rough beach foreshore to the water's edge. They would walk in the shallow water to avoid leaving footprints and quietly move along the water's edge towards the mainland. Morley heard from one of the guards that the sandy beach ran all the way from the island to the mainland but there were several guard stations. To get past these they would wade out to deeper water and walk slowly past them in the dark. Once they were on the mainland, they could sneak past some farmhouses and steal clothes that were hanging outside so they could take off their prison uniforms.

Morley had noticed that the guards always counted the numbers of prisoners at the end of the day before they started to go back to the prison. However, many times the counts would not add up to the correct number. When that happened one guard would look at the other and they would nod and not do a recount as it was the end of the shift, they were hungry and wanted to go home. Besides there had not been any escapes for a long time.

John pondered the plan for a long time and asked what they would do after they changed out of their prison clothes. Morley quickly answered that he had thought about this and reiterated they would need to travel quickly along the beach to the mainland on the first night. Provided they moved quickly and silently they could be in the forest on the mainland before daybreak. They could then hide in the forest during the day and move only at night and raid the farms for chickens, eggs and other food. He said it would work if they kept off the roads and away from villages and farmhouses especially during the day.

As summer ended and autumn started it began to get colder. John knew if they were going to escape they would need to do it now. Otherwise, they would be on a ship very soon to the other side of the world and he would never see Mary and his family again. John also checked what the guards did with the counting and Morley was correct as the guards often got the count wrong by two or three and they nodded to each other and did not do a recount. Besides, it was getting darker at the end of the day's work as summer had passed. They needed time to escape and if the alarm was raised early, they would easily be recaptured. John knew the consequences if they tried to escape and were captured. It would be one hundred lashes of the cat o' nine tails. He had felt the savagery of the cat o' nine tails in Birkdale prison and had the brutal scars on his back as a reminder of the punishment but he knew if he went on the ship to Western Australian he would never see his family again. This would be his last chance. John knew the odds were against them. The people who would track them would be trained, have dogs – probably trained blood hounds – and people in the surrounding areas would notify the police if they were sighted or noticed things were being stolen but John still thought he should try.

The 15th of October was a cool and cloudy day. The three men kept some of their meals and water in reserve and at the end of the day they all hid behind some large stone boulders and waited for all the other convicts to be marched up to the assembly point. They waited and waited. As darkness descended on the quarry they realised no alarm had been raised so they waited until it was very dark before they looked out from behind the boulders – it was all clear. John felt frightened as he took his initial step towards the boundary fence. He knew what capture meant. He knew he would be punished severely but he wanted to take the risk as it would be his last opportunity to sneak back into society to see his family. The thought of being banished to the other side of the world in an isolated, strange and foreboding place terrified him.

The trio made their way carefully over the fence and the island's natural landscape to the water's edge. At the water's edge Morley suggested they walk on the beach for one hundred yards away from the mainland and then into the water to confuse the trackers. They then did what they planned and walked carefully in the water leaving no footprints. If they were discovered missing in the evening or morning the guards would scour the prison and quarry areas first and finally the island.

Only once this was done would they raise an alarm with the nearby villages and farms and start looking on the mainland, so moving quickly without leaving traces of their presence was critical.

On the first night their plan worked well. Once they passed the check points, they kept moving along the beach. Speed was critical for them as was the need to keep quiet and walk in the water. About an hour before sunrise, they decided to cross over from the beach to the forest near the coast. They carefully chose a place where a small stream came out of the forest to the water's edge on the beach and they waded along the stream until they were well within the forest. Here they rested and ate some of their food reserves. They realised by now that the alarm would be raised so they needed to keep out of site and quiet in the forest.

For six days they followed their plan and headed towards Exeter to the northwest travelling at night on the forest paths and keeping deep in the forests during the day. They slept in shifts with one on alert. When the opportunity arose, they stole some clothes and food. It was late in the harvest season but there was still some fruit and vegetables available in the occasional market garden. They also buried the prison clothes in the forest to cover their tracks. The agreed plan was to make for Exeter as they believed the railway passed there and it offered a possibility to get onto a goods train headed to the north. They had no money but believed they could get onto a goods train in the night. On the sixth day they were resting in the forest when they heard some far-off barks from a hound dog. Initially they thought that it was a dog from a neighbouring farm but then it got closer, and they picked up their few belongings and headed for the nearest stream to hide their scent. Their progress was slow, and the barking sounds got closer and closer. All three men were now exhausted, starving, and terrified. They knew what capture meant.

At last, the evening came, and the barking stopped so they left the stream and quickly walked along the forest paths again. However, by dawn the barking restarted. Morley said, "I'm done. Let's wait until they arrive then at least this will be over," but John replied, "We need to keep going. Let's get down to the creek so we can at least hide our scent and try to last until evening when we know they will stop for the night." Despite the diversion to the creek, the pace was slow as they were all starving and fatigued. The guards overtook them by 10 o'clock in the morning and all three slumped in submission. They had no more energy or fight left in them. They felt like dogs as they cowered and were beaten with truncheons. The chains were fitted and locked to their legs and wrists, then they started the long painful walk back to the nearest police depot. It was October 22, 1854, seven days after their escape.

Back at the prison the punishment was formal but swift and brutal. The magistrate listened to the evidence and decided that each escapee was to receive one hundred lashes of the cat o' nine tails and serve three months in solitary confinement. The cat o' nine tails was a multi-tailed whip made up of nine knotted thongs of cotton cord about $2\frac{1}{2}$ feet long and weighted 13 ounces. It was designed to lacerate the skin and cause intense pain. Some simply called it 'the Cat'. The guards who undertook the flogging were trained to hit in the small area between the shoulders, but the tails of the Cat often lashed viscously down the back, up around the neck and at the sides leaving cruel red marks. Often the nine tails of the Cat would be covered in blood and flesh so that the tails would stick together, and it would become a vicious whip which would tear the skin and flesh off the convict's back. When it came time for John to meet the Cat again, he was escorted out to the prison court-yard. His arms and feet were secured in a tall triangular frame so that his feet were spread, and his arms were tied together above his head. He felt very exposed and vulnerable which he was.

He looked down at the ground and could see splashes of fresh red blood on the ground from the previous lashing. Small pieces of skin and flesh were scattered as well. Some black garden ants were assembling around the flesh to cart it off. The prison's superintendent and surgeon were well dressed, stood a few yards behind John with their arms folded and watched on passively. They had attended many of these before and it ceased to affect them. Also in attendance was a group of convicts who were selected so they could observe the severity of the flogging with the prison's aim to dissuade they from breaking any prison rules. A drummer was present also to make a drum beat for each lash.

John's shirt was stripped from his back and a wide leather belt was fitted around his waist to protect his lower vital organs. Another wide leather belt was fitted around his neck to protect the main arteries that travelled up the side of his neck. Both leather belts were cold and firm. The belt around his waist was still wet from the blood of the previous person who was flogged. The farrier had tried to wipe the excess blood off the belt. John looked down and noted a small divot in the ground behind him. He soon learned that it was for the farrier to place his left foot to get leverage when using the Cat. The farrier then selected a fresh clean Cat from the collection that was kept in a wooden box in the small storeroom near to the area. The Cat used previously needed to be cleaned and untangled.

With the first lash John winced and tried not to cry out. The drummer beat a solitary beat. After each lash, the farrier quickly ensured the nine tails were not sticking together and then lashed again methodically. After ten lashes John arched his back and screamed. Blood started to appear between John's shoulders. After 20 lashes John slumped and tried not to pass out but he sobbed with each stroke of the Cat. He now hung down from the binding around his wrists on the frame. The surgeon periodically came over and checked John to see if it was safe to continue. Each time he nodded to the farrier to continue. The surgeon was not checking to see if the flogging was humane but simply to make sure that it did not kill the convict. The surgeon was long past deciding what was humane. Privately, he felt that nobody would treat their dog like this.

The same farrier kept on flogging until after the fiftieth lash, and he then handed over to another farrier so that he could do the remaining fifty. The punishment lasted half an hour, or one lash every eighteen seconds after which John's back was splashed with salty water and he screamed for one last time. It was a soul wrenching scream that could be heard across the nearby prison. He was then dragged almost unconscious back to his cell and left on the cold stone floor.

When John regained consciousness, he was back in a cell measuring thirteen feet long by seven feet wide and nine feet high. His back was raw like a piece of meat and blood dripped down his sides, over his buttocks and legs. He knew somebody would come along soon to clean the bloody mess that was once his back. He hoped the wounds would not get infected.

After the solitary confinement he was put back on the same job in the quarry but with a different work gang. Morley and Chambers were also split up into different work gangs. All three were monitored more closely than before but each was submissive and quiet. John's back had almost healed but it was heavily scarred from the beatings at Kirkdale and now at Portland. He was now a broken, submissive man more resembling a starved beaten dog than a human being.

Three months after their severe beating, John, Chambers, Morley and 257 other male convicts, thirty pensioner guards and their families set sail on the *Adelaide* on the 16th of April 1855. As John boarded the vessel he thought once again of Mary and tears streaked down his face. He thought that at least he was alive and while he was beaten, he was not defeated. The question remained about whether he would survive the journey. Many did not due to disease resulting from poor health, confinement, lack of exercise and poor diet.

In the eighty years between 1788 and 1868, about 162,000 convicts from Britain and Ireland were transported to Australia. Britain selected Australia as a penal colony to reduce the overcrowding of the country's prisons and hulks. The overcrowding was the result of the increasing harshness of penalties legislated by Parliament to reduce the increasing rate of crime. In the First Fleet to Australia, under the command of Captain Arthur Phillip, there were eleven convict ships and they arrived at Botany Bay, south of Sydney, in 1788. In these first ships, about half of the convicts were from London and were convicted for relatively minor crimes like theft of money, food and clothing. In total there were 1480 people including 568 male and 192 female convicts.

Britain later established additional penal settlements, firstly in Van Diemen's Land (Tasmania) in 1803 and then in Brisbane, Queensland in 1824.The Swan River Colony was established in 1829 but it was not a penal colony and only a place for free settlers. Due to a critical labour shortage in the new colony, the local people petitioned the English government to allow for convicts to be sent there. In 1849 an Order-in-Council was passed nominating Western Australia as a place that convicts could be sent and in1850 the first seventy-five convicts arrived on board the Scindlan.

(Source – public domain – Frigate Ship)

"Never underestimate the determination and resilience of the human spirit."
Michael Le Page

9

At sea – the Adelaide

The *Adelaide* was built in 1832, a wooden, frigate-style ship weighing 640 tons. It had been sailing for 23 years so it was old and had been to Australia several times transporting convicts and crew. It sailed from Portland on April 16 and was expected to take three months to sail to Fremantle, so the expected arrival was around the middle of July.

The captain's name was Longman. He was a tall, dark haired, lean but stern man who had risen through the ranks and understood the sea, navigation, geography and how to sail and run a vessel. He also understood how to run a convict ship. As he sat in his cabin, he read the list of convicts. He mused to himself that he was given 260 convicts all with over ten years imprisonment for their crimes with an average sentence of 14 years and sixty-two life sentences. So, these were more serious offenders than the earlier shipments to the Colony of Western Australia and they all would have completed 12 months solitary confinement.

Some could be insane. Some could still go insane, and most would be beaten down by the prison system. Physically, they would be unhealthy, thin, beaten and mostly submissive. Some would be rebellious if given the opportunity. Mutiny was not unheard of. Eighteen per cent had robbery with violence, 11 per cent burglary, 14 per cent robbery, 3 per cent horse/cow/sheep theft, one per cent attempted theft and 3 per cent for robbery and wounding. So, half the convicts were convicted of crimes relating to robbery. Were they thieves or people who had resorted to theft just to survive? He understood the level of poverty and desperation in many of the English cities especially that of the Irish who were forced to flee penniless from the devastation of the potato famine. The remainder had a range of convictions from forgery to sodomy. Five per cent were for military offences including one with 14 years prison time and transportation for throwing a cap at an officer. Insubordination should never be tolerated in the military Captain Longman thought and nodded his head unknowingly.

Longman was not a cruel man and he treated people firmly but well. He wanted to get everyone to Fremantle safely but believed in taking significant precautions to not give the convicts any opportunity to cause trouble. The main and forward hatchways were secured with iron bars and a small passageway was inserted so only one person could squeeze through at one time. At night, guards were stationed on deck with loaded guns for security. In addition, cannons loaded with grapeshot were ready for use and aimed forward in case of trouble. Captain Longman believed from experience that this settled the ship and made the convicts much less restless.

He read the details of the convicts and noted three had recently tried to escape so he made a note to ensure the convicts were kept in the cells below the deck, locked up and in chains. He also noted to get their chains checked for security regularly. Exercise would be allowed. Anyway, the convicts' wellbeing would principally be with Samuel Donnelly, the ship's surgeon general.

Samuel Donnelly was Irish and attained a diploma from the Royal College of Surgeons of Edinburgh. He was medium height with a fair complexion, stocky, reserved in his manner and felt he needed to look after all the people on the vessel including the convicts. They were people too he thought. His first role in the navy was on the *Talbot* in 1838 as an assistant surgeon and then in 1842 he was appointed surgeon on the *Phoenix* in the Mediterranean. The *Adelaide* was his third time to serve on a convict vessel. The first was on the *St. Vincent* to Hobart,

Tasmania in 1850 and the second was on the *Lady Montagu* to Hobart in 1852, so he was very experienced at sea and in transporting convicts to Australia. He hoped he could get all the crew, the pensioner guards and their families plus the convicts to the Colony of Western Australia without incident. He did not like having a death on board nor did he support the use of unnecessary corporal punishment. He believed the Cat should only be used as a last resort. He felt there were better ways to manage the convicts' behaviour. He also made sure there was a good supply of water and rations.

Donnelly wrote in his journal the following general remarks, "On the 4, 9 and 14 April 1855, 260 male convicts were received on board the ship, 116 from the hulks at Woolwich, 43 from Portsmouth and 101 from Portland. They were apparently in healthy condition, except for John Mitchell (case no 1)." Signed Samuel Donnelly, Surgeon General.

Samuel sat with his assistant and laid out broadly the processes he wanted followed. He wanted regular meals for the convicts, daily checks on the irons to ensure they were secure, and those who kept themselves clean and well behaved may over time be relieved of their irons. He wanted the deck cleaned every day with sand and never wet so the convicts' cells below stayed dry where possible. He wanted airing stoves installed to ensure proper air circulation and would allow about a quarter of the convicts on the deck at once while doing light tasks or taking exercise. He wanted the convicts below to be given classes for learning how to read, write and do arithmetic with supervision by an officer. Samuel also knew some convicts would be well educated. He found that typically those with forgery convictions were more than capable of giving lessons. Samuel had some musical instruments in storage as he found some convicts could play and some could sing. It certainly kept their spirits up and gave them some events to look forward to.

Samuel documented the daily routine that he wanted for the convicts and explained this to his assistant. He had used this routine before and it worked well.

5.00 a.m.	Tuesdays and Fridays were washing days after breakfast, Cooks commence their duties. Prisoners roll up and stow their hammocks and bedding. The hammocks are either lashed up and stowed or brought on deck in fine weather for airing. The cleaners muster on deck and commence their duties washing water closets, decks etc. and finish by 6.30 a.m.
6.30 a.m.	Daily allowance of water to be issued.
7.00 a.m.	Daily allowance of biscuits to be issued.
7.30 a.m.	The Surgeon Superintendent visits the sick.
7.45 a.m.	The convicts on meal duty are to be on deck to receive the breakfast allowance and all the other prisoners go below and wait on their own berth.

8.00 a.m.	Breakfast. Immediately after each meal, the convicts who are on meal duty clean up after the meal and wash the cooking and eating utensils. After breakfast all the prisoners are admitted on deck and the convict areas are then cleaned by the cleaners.
10.00 a.m.	Divine Service.
10.30 a.m.	School.
11.40 a.m.	The allowance of lime juice is issued.
12.45 p.m.	The convicts on meal duty muster on deck and all the other prisoners go below as at breakfast time.
1.00 p.m.	Dinner. After dinner, the prisoners to be admitted on deck and the cleaners sweep the whole of the prison deck.
1.30 p.m.	The daily allowance of wine is issued.
2.00 p.m.	School. After school, all prisoners go on deck.
4.45 p.m.	The convicts on meal duty muster on deck and all other prisoners go below.

5.00 p.m.	Supper. After supper, all the convicts are admitted on deck and the areas below deck are swept by the cleaners. Before dusk, the allowance of salt meat is issued. At dusk, the hammocks are taken below, and the beds made.
8.00 p.m.	All in bed.
8.30 p.m.	No talking or noise of any kind is permitted during the night.

John and the other convicts settled into the journey. He found having to share the cells with the other convicts good as each had their own hammock. The air was good, and the food was better than in the prison plus he was not having to slave away in the quarry moving boulders on unstable ground, so he gained some weight. The various cuts and scrapes on his hands gradually recovered. John enjoyed the exercise sessions as it was good to get some fresh air and look over the sea. Generally, the weather was still warm and calm. He also enjoyed participating in the reading, writing and arithmetic sessions. It was so good to have things to read and explain these to some convicts who could neither read, write or add.

John was surprised that the convicts were generally healthy despite the rigours of Portland Prison and the heavy manual labour. In the early part of the voyage there were some cases of diarrhoea and a few skin ulcers from the poor food at the prison. Some were mentally impaired from the time they would have spent in solitary confinement or from the brutality of the treatment in the chain gangs or in the hulks.

They were told the ship was sailing west towards the empire of Brazil past Tristan da Cunha to catch the trade winds which blow steadily towards the Equator from the southeast in the Southern Hemisphere. They would pass the southern tip of Africa then head east all the way to the Colony of Western Australia. Some crew talked about the trade winds and how they would bring stormy weather. John did not understand that when the ship passed the Equator it would switch from summer to winter hence bringing colder weather as they went south.

One evening an officer brought out some old musical instruments and among them was a battered old Irish fiddle. John asked if he could play the fiddle and since no one else could play it was handed to him. It looked old and worn but the case and strings were intact, and the bow was repairable. He had not played the fiddle since his capture, but he still was able to tune the instrument by ear and start to play. At first, he played some older folk tunes that he remembered, and most of the convicts listened. A couple sang along quietly. Over time, Dr Donnelly noted the combination of tasks, meals, exercise and music was improving the spirits of the convicts, and any small trouble that had occurred had quietened down easily. Samuel was impressed with the music, and he asked one of the crew to show the convicts a couple of sea shanties which were working chants generally sung by the crew while loading the vessel in port. The sailor thought for a minute and started to sing.

Oh, South Australia is me home
Heave away! Heave away!
South Australia is me home
An' we're bound for South Australia.
Heave away, heave away
Oh, heave away, you are rolling king,
We're bound for South Australia.

I see my wife standing on the quay
The tears do start as she waves to me.
I'll tell you the truth and I'll tell you no lie;
If I don't love that girl, I hope I may die.

And now I'm bound for a foreign strand,
With a bottle of whisky in my hand.
I'll drink a glass to the foreign shore
And one to the girl that I adore.

Heave away, heave away
Oh, heave away, you are rolling king,
We're bound for South Australia.

(First published by L.A. Smith in the 1800s in her collection, The Music of the Waters)

The convicts liked the song and although John worked out how to play some music for it, it did not need music as they all just chanted along. Another of the favourites of one of the crew was the "Wellerman" shanty as he had spent time over the past few years whaling off the Colony of New Zealand which was about 1200 miles across the sea from the Colony of New South Wales.

The sailor sang it first for the crew.

There once was a ship that put to sea.
The name of the ship was the Billy of Tea.
The winds blew up, her bow dipped down.
O blow, my bully boys, blow

Soon may the Wellerman come.
To bring us sugar and tea and rum
One day, when the tonguin' is done.
We'll take our leave and go.

She'd not been two weeks from shore.
When down on her, a right whale bore.
The captain called all hands and swore.

He'd take that whale in tow.

Soon may the Wellerman come.
To bring us sugar and tea and rum
One day, when the tonguin' is done.
We'll take our leave and go.

Da-da-da-da, da-da-da-da-da
Da-da, da-da-da-da
Da-da-da-da-da-da

(Public domain – 1800s "Wellerman" sea shanty)

When they passed the southern tip of Africa, the weather became unfavourable and some of the passengers and convicts fell ill. Scurvy also appeared. For about a week the convicts were confined below deck due to the storms and wind. The waves were enormous and washed over onto the deck flooding freezing water onto the convicts below. However, it cleared up and the sicknesses improved when the convicts were allowed some more time on deck and in the sunshine. A few days later a sudden change took place again and the temperature dropped ten degrees to 55°F and stayed at that level. Rain was accompanied by a strong wind. Although the convicts had been given one worsted frock, one shirt, one pair of trousers, a pair of stockings, a handkerchief, a hat and one pair of shoes before they boarded the *Adelaide*, some noted the clothes were already starting to wear with constant use. When the wintry weather came they started to get cold, and some suffered from dysentery.

Around this time there was a death on board. One of the pensioner guards died of fever from a fracture of the tibia and fibula in his leg. It was a result of a box of salt fish falling on him. His corpse was dressed in his formal uniform, covered with a Union Jack, and then moved to the side of the vessel where the Union Jack was removed, and the body was slowly slid overboard. All the officers and pensioner guards were in their formal uniforms and gave him a naval farewell. The convicts were locked in their cells. When the body entered the water, it slid rapidly downward into the deep blue sea assisted by the weight of the chains attached to the feet. It was the only death so far and Samuel Donnelly was extremely disappointed, especially considering as many as thirty convicts were taken ill at one time and all had survived so far.

The cold wet weather continued for several weeks and then suddenly it warmed up when the wind ceased. There were also several more cases of scurvy with swelling of the gums, blue-grey spots on the legs, weakness, tiredness and sore arms and legs. With the warmer weather, soap was issued. Dr Donnelly decided that the convicts should bathe each day in the morning to improve hygiene. He had seen this before and was certain clean cells and clean bodies would reduce disease. Each convict had to strip and wash with the soap and water. A bucket of water was then thrown over them. One of the crew could cut hair so he was used as a barber to keep the convicts' hair short. Donnelly was convinced short hair was better for convicts' health and it certainly reduced the number of lice.

After three months they saw the Western Australian coastline for the first time. When John was on deck for exercise, he looked at the foreign coastline in the distance. The sea was blue and a couple of small, low islands stood off to the north. It was a beautiful calm day and the sky was an amazing clear blue colour he had not seen since he'd left Ireland – and where it was not a common sight. For winter, the weather was cool and pleasant. The land looked barren and he could see white sand at the edge near the sea. There was little evidence of a settlement or human life from where he stood out at sea. One of the crew said the settlement was up along the Swan River to their south. John was not sure what lay ahead but he was alive, and with life there is hope and a future. He said to Morley, who was with him on the deck, "What do you think about this?" Morley thought for a while as he rubbed the stubble on his cheeks and replied, "I am sure it is much better than being in prison in Portland slaving all winter in the freezing cold moving boulders and crushing my fingers and toes. The assistant surgeon said that some of us will get an immediate Ticket of Leave and be free to live, work and earn money outside the prison. It sounds good to me."

On the 18th of July 1855, the *Adelaide* arrived at Fremantle approximately three months after departing Portland. John Arnold's character was described by Samuel Donnelly as good.

Extract from the Colony of Western Australia newspaper.

The Adelaide from England

'This fine ship arrived on Tuesday last, after a rapid passage of 87 days from Portland, which place she left on the 16th April, bringing European intelligence. The papers received by the mail are but few and almost solely of March dates, consequent probably on the vessel having left London for Portland. We have however been favoured by the kindness of Captain Longman, with a copy of the *Weekly Times* of April 15th, from which extracts will be found in another column. The *Avalanche* was to sail from London on the 20th of April, but a private letter reports a belief that Governor Kennedy would not proceed by that ship.'

In the age of sail, transport across the seas was fraught with many difficult issues. When it was extremely hot in the tropics vermin came out of the ship's woodwork. This included rats, lice, cockroaches, bedbugs, and fleas. They impacted everyone from the convicts to the captain. The bilges were putrid in all the vessels as typically they contained a rotting mess of sea water, urine, faeces, rotting food, dead vermin and vomit. When rainstorms occurred, the convicts who were in the bowels of the ship, had no dry clothes and could not exercise on deck so they were continually swamped by waves of freezing seawater as it sloshed over the ship's deck.

On the *Adelaide* Samuel Donnelly did a first-class job in minimising the loss of life and reducing despondence among the crew, the pensioner guards, other passengers, and convicts.

> "Happiness is the quality of the soul…not a function of one's material circumstances." – Aristotle.

(Source: unsplash – A desolate shore)

10

Colony of Western Australia

After the vessel dropped anchor off the port of Fremantle, the crew got to work unloading the passengers and their belongings. These included the pensioner guards and their families who were on board. Some pensioner guards stayed behind to help with the transfer of the convicts. The pensioner guards were soldiers who came as guards on the convict ships. Typically, they had served in the military for Britain overseas and were awarded government pensions for their long or excellent service, good conduct or if wounded. After acting as guards on a ship they could remain with the military or stay on as settlers. After serving seven years as a pensioner guard, they were entitled to a free land grant. Many stayed on as free settlers.

Once this was completed the crew moved their attention to transporting the convicts to the shore. Some warders from The Convict Establishment came to assist in the transfer. The Convict Establishment was the name given to the convict prison in Fremantle. All the convicts were in irons as they marched slowly from the sandy shore at Fremantle to the newly constructed Establishment. The initial stage of the construction, which was primarily done by the convicts, was completed just a month before. As John walked the mile to the prison, he thought the town, while small, looked new, basic but cheerful. Some people gathered along the side of the road to look at them, but they were quiet and curious. John thought they all looked just like him. Occasionally he saw an Aboriginal, but the people were white and English looking. He also saw a few convict work gangs which seemed to be working on building or repairing roads. They looked up and called out a few encouraging words. The sky was blue and a very cool wind was coming from the south. The area around looked green from the recent winter rain.

Above all the low single-storey houses in Fremantle, the prison stood prominent on a small hill to the north. One of the colonial warders who came to assist said it was called The Establishment. It was built in a white stone that John had not seen before. The same warder said it was limestone, a softer rock which was quarried on site within the prison. He added that it was a common stone in the Fremantle area and was easy to cut and move compared to something like granite. John never had good days moving the boulders back in Portland as it was typically cold, hard and dangerous work. He could never forget the death of the fellow convict when he was crushed by the boulder that day.

To John the main prison block looked impressive, four storeys high and a 15-foot perimeter wall. When they approached the main steel gate there were buildings to the right-hand side outside the prison walls which he guessed were cottages to accommodate some of the prison officers. As John passed through the front gate, the walls looked to be over two feet thick and well-constructed. Inside the prison walls on the right-hand side there was an area which looked like a quarry where the convicts were sourcing the stone.

The new arrivals were herded onto an open area in front of the prison inside the perimeter walls. John looked around. The main building was big and impressive for such a small town. It was aligned north to south, and the entrance was on the western side pointing to where they had landed. In front of him stood a large central prominent section which someone said was the administration offices on the ground level and the chapel was perched on the second level above the offices overlooking the entrance gate. A large set of wooden doors stood in the centre of the building and three tall arched windows were built into the chapel exterior wall. To the right John could see the prison cells. By counting the small cell windows, he confirmed to himself that it was four stories high. On the left-hand side of the prominent church and offices section convicts had started building what looked like the next section of the prison. The foundations the convicts were laying seemed to indicate they were building a replica of the newly built cell blocks on the right-hand side.

On the back left-hand side stood what looked like the start of another building which someone said was to become a hospital. At the back right-hand side, he could see some glimpses of what looked like workshops as they were mostly hidden behind the main cell block building. Behind the administration section was a low single-storey stone building with small high windows. It looked eerily like the solitary confinement cells John was confined to in Portland. John guessed he would either be put to work inside the prison in the quarry, building the prison cells or outside the prison in one of the road gangs they saw as they marched to The Establishment.

The ground beneath their feet in the assembly area was barren and looked like crushed white limestone which covered all the grounds, so it crunched softly underfoot. Once all the convicts were standing in the assembly area, a warder dressed in a formal military uniform entered from the office main door and walked to a central area in front of the convicts. He looked like The Establishment superintendent and about ten armed warders stood either side of the superintendent. He spoke to them briefly in a loud firm voice with an English accent and said his name was Superintendent Dixon. Beside him was another person who was introduced as Prison Surgeon, Dr Gilbraith. Dixon stated that any insubordination would not be tolerated. He added it would be treated harshly with time in irons, floggings, long-term restrictions within The Establishment's walls, use of solitary confinement and food limited to bread and water. He told them a solitary confinement block stood just behind this main prison block. He added that good behaviour would be rewarded well with a Ticket of Leave which would allow the recipient to work in designated areas of the colony and need only to report to the local magistrate twice a year. The Ticket of Leavers, as they were called, would need to follow a simple set of rules and would be paid for their work by their employer. He read out a list of the convicts who had arrived with John who would get immediate Tickets of Leave and they were marched off to a separate part of the prison at the far end of the building to the right, somewhere called the Association Rooms. The convicts who got an immediate Ticket of Leave had a shorter sentence or had served more time in England than John. The superintendent said the remainder of the convicts would stay in the main cell block.

John did not get a Ticket of Leave and neither did William Chambers or William Morley. Their escape in Portland bought them some extra time and restrictions. They marched with the other convicts to the cell block entrance to the right and John got a closer look at the quarry area. He saw a small hill area rise to the right so that it looked like the quarry was taking the limestone from the small hill and levelling the ground. The perimeter wall in that area rose and sat on top of the original small hill. The stone was being quarried, cut into manageable smaller rectangular blocks, and then carted over to the construction area.

When they entered the prison there was a long central passageway from the southern end to the northern end and it had three floors above the ground floor. It looked like it could hold about 450 convicts. He counted 64 cells on one side of the ground floor. When he was locked in his cell on the ground floor he looked around. It was small at seven feet by four feet and had a fresh earthy smell. If he held out his arms, he could touch the cool, rough limestone walls on either side. The cell was small, but it was explained that they were not designed to accommodate convicts all day as they would be working inside The Establishment walls or outside The Establishment every day except Sunday. A hammock was attached by metal pins to the front and rear walls of the cell. The sturdy corrugated steel door occupied the small space in the front wall which was not taken up by the hammock. A small, barred window about six feet above the floor let in some natural light. He wondered how many hands had held those bars trying to get a better look outside. Opposite the hammock in the middle of the side wall was a small, basic wooden desk and stool which were made from a strange dark wood. It was a similar wood used in the ceiling of the building and the warder said it was a local timber called jarrah. The cell was very cramped. There was a basin with running water in one corner and a metal bucket for ablutions but nothing else. There was a hint of a foul smell coming from the basin and pipes.

When Superintendent Dixon went back to his office, he read the papers provided to him by the *Adelaide*'s Captain Longman and saw that three of the convicts on the *Adelaide* had tried to escape in Portland, so he opened his book for superintendent orders and wrote:

1855 July 25

Orders

3521 - John Arnold

3525 - William Morley

3531 - William Chambers

Probation prisoners having made an attempt at escape from Portland prison they will be kept at work inside and particularly watched.

The Deputy Superintendent will not fail to caution Warders & Officers as to the strictest vigilance being observed with respect to these men.

Thomas H Dixon "Super"

Dixon wanted to make sure few escapes occurred under his guard.

When the Colony of Western Australia was founded the aim was for it to be an English colony made up of free settlers. Initially, the Colony struggled, and some dissatisfied settlers moved over to the settlements on the eastern side of the country as those colonies were more established and provided more opportunity. By 1834 around 1300 free settlers left and the population was less than 1400 and declining. The reason for the dissatisfaction was lack of infrastructure, transport and most importantly a lack of workers. After 18 years a persuasive group of the remaining free settlers petitioned the Colony's Legislative Council for the introduction of convict labour as they wanted labour to help work the farms, expand the Colony and build infrastructure. Convicts could not leave the Colony until they received their conditional pardon, so they were locked in for a time. The British government was still looking for a place to transport their convicts, and the colonies in Sydney and Van Diemen's Land were pressing to stop convicts arriving in their colonies. In late 1849 a dispatch was sent to the governor of the Colony of Western Australia and shortly after the West Australian Government Gazette announced that the Colony had been constituted a penal settlement. The first convict ship landed in Fremantle in 1850 and the new prison was built by convicts from 1852. When John arrived, he could see that the second stage to the north of the administration section would take another three or four years to build.

John noted the warders were a combination of pensioner guards, some experienced men from British prisons and men from the Colony. The warders seemed to live in terrace houses near The Establishment on the outside. The colonial men were interesting as they were more relaxed and communicative whilst still being disciplined. Their language, while English, had a distinct accent. He found it easy to understand as they spoke clearly and deliberately, not fast. He noted they sometimes did not understand him easily because of his Irish accent so he decided to make an effort to speak more like them, clearly and deliberately, not fast.

In The Establishment, like all British prisons, there were strict rules and routines. They were woken early at 5:00 a.m., got dressed and took their ablution bucket to empty in a drain. They had a drink of water and a compulsory role call to make sure everyone was present. They then marched to their workplaces at 5:30 a.m. for two hours after which they came back for a meal in their cells. After breakfast there was a time for prayers and around 8:45 am they would return for work until midday.

If they were working inside the prison, they would have a meal in the exercise yard or if they were working outside, they would have a meal at their workplace. Just before 2 p.m. they would restart work until 5:30 and be back in their cell for a meal at 6pm when they were locked up for the night. There was also an allowance to smoke after the evening meal. Each convict was provided a quarter ounce of tobacco every two days and a pipe. A 30-minute period was allocated for smoking, and this was called 'smoko'. The prison officer collected and held the tobacco and pipes after smoko. There were also strict prison rules and the punishment for breaking the rules was very harsh. The officers would not hesitate to use the whip. On Saturday they worked from 1 p.m. until 5 p.m. and on Sundays there was no work. A bath was available for each convict every two weeks.

A warder explained to them the scale of rations. For hard labour work they received daily 24 oz of bread, 14 oz of meat, 16 oz of potatoes, tiny amounts of salt, pepper, tea, sugar and soap. To John this seemed much better than how he was fed back in Portland or Birkdale and even better than he could afford when he was working at the woollen mill in Bradford. In the mornings it was normally gruel. The prison uniform was also strictly controlled. Each convict was given a leather belt, two pairs of boots, four pairs of socks, four handkerchiefs, four cotton shirts, two flannel shirts, one grey wool jacket, one canvas jacket, a vest, one pair of trousers plus a felt hat. This was like the issue John received in Portland. The prison uniform was coloured one side in deep brown and one side yellow. All the fabric for the convicts' clothing was supplied from England and the uniforms were made in the tailor shops in the prisons. Fabric was supplied twice a year. The trousers had three upward pointing arrows on each leg and additional arrows on the sleeve and coat. In some cases, the light colour was yellow. This branding was common across all British government property.

The uniform was made up of a coarse woollen fabric and the winter coat had six buttons of dark metal and a stand-up collar.

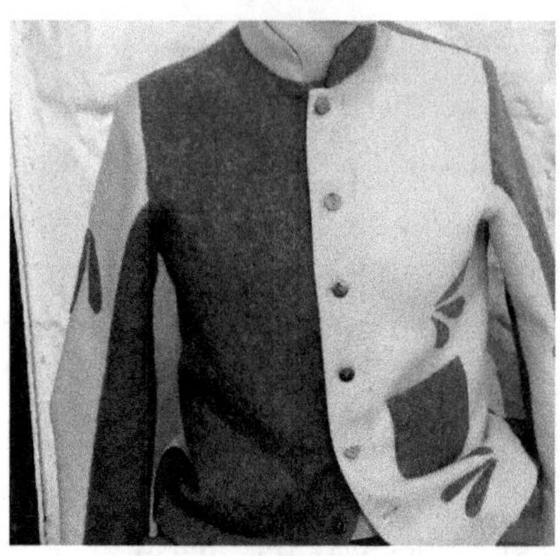

Colony of Western Australia – Convict uniform
(light colour is yellow)
Image – Michael Le Page

John's first role was within the prison working in the quarry moving finished stone blocks from the quarry to the construction site. The distance was not far from the quarry to the construction site. The blocks were loaded onto a wagon by derrick and the wagon was pulled by sturdy horses three hundred yards to the construction site where they were unloaded again by derrick. Compared to the work at Portland it was much safer and easier. The cream-coloured limestone blocks were more easily cut and formed into two-foot-long blocks which were easily lifted compared to the boulders at Portland. John noted the warders paid close attention to William Chambers, William Morley and himself. He assumed they were warned about the escape from Portland prison.

As July moved into August then September the weather warmed up, the rain seemed to ease later in September but the winds continued each day. Sometimes in the morning the air would be calm and cool but almost every day a strong breeze would start in the afternoon and clear the air. Storms with fierce winds would rage through the township regularly bringing squalls of rain. Communication within The Establishment was particularly good. The convicts seemed to know what was going on inside and outside The Establishment. Some warders would supervise the work and answer questions with ease while others would stay aloof. The colonial warders were the most communicative and from them John found out all the history and news around Fremantle. Further up the Swan River, about nine miles away, was the main town called Perth. It was said to be a nice place with a wide river in front. The town was small with a few nice new government buildings which were built by convicts, roads as well as businesses and a scattering of houses around the town.

The warder said Fremantle was a small town and there was bushland close by. There were more remote townships in York, 60 miles away, Toodyay, 55 miles from Fremantle and Albany, 240 miles to the south-east on the south coast. He added, "Albany was the first British settlement in the west of Australia as it had a big natural harbour. It has been said that the British government wanted to establish a settlement here in the west to secure the area for the King as the Dutch had been roaming the coastline for a long time. I heard that a captain called Dirk Hartog, on the ship *Eendracht*, landed up north as long ago as 1616."

John also learned of closer places such as Guildford which was seventeen miles away and just eight miles from Perth. With this information, some of the convicts, including John, whispered for days amongst themselves about the world outside The Establishment and the imagined opportunities. One convict, John Dawson, and John convinced themselves that they would remain in The Establishment for years. The warders did not know when any of the two would get a Ticket of Leave to work freely outside but they concluded it would be a long time. Dawson came out on the same vessel as John and they talked many times on the sea voyage. Dawson was an unmarried, literate grocer who had been convicted for robbery with violence. He, like John, was sentenced to life imprisonment. Suddenly, in early October 1855, John and Dawson were assigned to an outside work gang to help fix a road that was damaged from flash flooding after a strong storm lashed the town with forceful winds and days of torrential rain. It was a perimeter road at the eastern edge of town. As they had built up a small inventory of limestone blocks at the construction site, which was more than they needed for the construction, the warder at the quarry concluded they would not be needed for several weeks and could work outside The Establishment.

On the first day outside The Establishment, they were marched to the site of the damaged road by a single warder. There were ten convicts, and all were in long chains linked to a fellow convict to prevent their wandering off or escaping. They all wore The Establishment's distinctive clothing. Dawson and John started talking again about escaping. "John, have you noticed that the guard wanders off to relieve himself often and leaves us alone," Dawson commented. "He also gets bored and walks away to chat with one of the local people?" John nodded. He did not want anyone overhearing any of his comments in case they were related back to the guard. He just observed quietly while working.

"I think we could break these chains with the tools we are using and keep a broken link in place until the time was right to make a run for it," Dawson said. John looked at Dawson silently. Dawson had never felt the pain of the Cat or the horrible period of healing afterwards, but John had felt it twice now. The second time was for one hundred lashes and he was unsure of taking another risk after the beating he took in Portland and after the solitary confinement in Kirkdale. He also knew that Fremantle was surrounded by the river to the north and sea to the south. To the east and north was bushland he thought. The bush particularly disturbed him as he already had seen the black venomous snakes that were rumoured to have killed some of the townsfolk. It was a painful death with no cure he was told. There were no snakes in Ireland, and he had never seen a snake in England. Why would a snake live in a slum in Bradford he thought? He also did not know how to survive in this terrible sandy bushland. But still the two continued to whisper secretly among themselves.

John was terrified of another extended period in solitary confinement and the cut of the one hundred lashes. He had not seen any lashings since the journey on the *Adelaide* where the officers would use the lash for rule breaches to maintain discipline. However, he had heard of a birching occurring earlier that month on a prisoner called Corton, who was a 25-year-old unmarried locksmith. He had attempted to assault another prisoner. Birching was a flogging using a bundle of four-foot-long sticks bound together and it occurred out by the solitary confinement cells behind the main cell block. The other convicts said that the Comptroller of Convicts, First Captain Edmund Henderson, was a just man who was opposed to harsher forms of punishment like the cat o' nine tails. However, it was still used with birching in some cases around a dozen times a year. Typically, this was restricted to inmates absconding from The Establishment or public works, assault, robbery with violence, insubordination, threating language and other significant transgressions

Despite John Arnold's concerns, after a few days they developed a rough plan. They hoarded some food and watched their warder's routine. Every day around 9 a.m. he would wander off and relieve himself in the bush leaving the work gang alone. They were working on a road adjacent to some bushland and no houses were nearby. That day the two sprang into action as soon as the warder started to wander off and they used their tools to hammer through the chain which linked the convicts together. The eight other convicts did not want to participate in the escape, as most were close to getting a Ticket of Leave and did not want to take the risk. Most were also terrified on the snake infested sandy bushland off to the east. John and Dawson uncoupled themselves and fled quickly into the bushland. It was October 15, 1855, about three months since Arnold and Dawson had arrived in Fremantle.

When the guard came back, he counted the number of convicts and immediately noticed two were missing. He scanned the faces and quickly realised that Arnold and Dawson had run off. He was furious and screamed "Where did they go? The remaining convicts cowered and pointed that the two had run off to the south. Their fellow convicts wanted to give them a chance of escape and they knew they ran off to the east. While they feared corporal punishment, they still had a form of solidarity with the other convicts. The guard immediately lashed out at the nearest convict showing his rage and marched them back to The Establishment, alerted the officer in charge who marched into the office and saw Superintendent Thomas Dixon.

Dixon immediately took charge as he had recently had another escape from a convict named Henry Ade. He cursed under his breath about John Arnold as he had written a warning in his order book about him, yet it was not fully enforced. Dixon ordered his deputy superintendent to interrogate the remaining eight convicts from the work party to see if they could find out any extra details. He immediately put together a group of warders led by an officer and sent a message out for an Aboriginal tracker to join the search party. They then went to the point where the work party was located that morning. Carefully they looked around at the bushland adjacent to the road and saw plenty of footprints around the side of the road and saw footprints and broken branches that led further into the bush. The two escapees had not been careful and left traces of their escape in their haste. The search party led by the officer headed into the bushland to the east following the footprints and ignoring the advice of the convicts regarding the escape to the south.

The two escapees walked steadily through that morning trying to put as much distance between them and Fremantle. However, in their haste Dawson slipped into a small hole in the sandy soil and trapped his foot. His ankle quickly swelled, and he soon found he could not run or walk properly. After limping along for a while, he stopped and gave his food and water to John and said, "John you go ahead. At least you will have a chance. I will stay here. They will soon find me." John realised that it was his only hope and agreed. He then headed northeast. Later that day the search party with the aid of the Aboriginal tracker ran down Dawson and he was chained up and taken back to The Establishment. He knew his punishment would be formal, swift and brutal. It would be his first introduction to the Cat and would be an event that he would remember for the rest of his life. By the following day Arnold reached a river which he decided must be a south-eastern offshoot of the Swan River. Here he took a rest. Over the previous day and night, he had avoided any settlements and potential detection.

Back in The Establishment the deputy superintendent had some success with his interrogation of the remaining eight convicts from the work party. All eight were threatened with corporal punishment and each would not provide any further information except one. One convict was due to gain his Ticket of Leave, so he simply told the deputy what he knew. He confirmed that all of them knew nothing of the escape until just before the two ran off to the east. He said they had little water and supplies and seemed to just take the opportunity rather than carefully plan an escape. Their plan was to head east to a river and then go north. He added that they knew little of the areas off to the east or north.

This gave the search party more information. The next morning, the search party got better equipped and brought in another specialist Aboriginal tracker to help. The excellent tracking skills of this second Aboriginal had been a great advantage to The Establishment leaders in the past locating escaped prisoners. The tracker explained his methods simply saying he just walked around slowly, patiently sometimes in circles, to see more. By this time, Arnold had one day's head start.

He headed north after he reached the river to the east and stayed in the shallows near the water's edge. The water was clear, and the sand on the bank was white as was the bottom of the river. It was beautiful except John was in too much of a hurry to notice. It was still warm, and the sky was blue, so the walking was easy. He had not discarded his convict clothes as he could not find any settlements from which they could steal clothing. The river water was fresh and good to drink in the area as the salty sea water did not reach this far inland. However, food was scarce, and John did not have any skills or implements to catch fish or prawns. The land around the riverbank was dry sand with low bushes so he could not see anything he could eat. Hunger became a problem on the second day.

As he continued heading along the riverbank, John sensed the direction of the river was changing and bending towards the west where the sun was sitting low over the landscape. He did not understand the lay of the land around Fremantle and Perth, so he did not recognise that he was heading back toward the town of Perth but on the southern side of the river. As he detoured around a marshy area with stumpy trees and long grasses at the water's edge, John almost stood on a large snake that was black with gold and yellow stripes. It was long, over three feet, and thick in the body but quick. It was aggressive and flattened its body and reared its head at John before striking him at his boot level hitting him twice.

John screamed and jumped back five or six feet and fell to the ground digging his heels into the sandy soil scrambling away from the snake. The snake dropped its head to the ground and very quickly retreated into the marshy area and tall reeds leaving no sign it was there at all. John was terrified. His heart was racing as he examined his foot and boot only to discover the snake bites were on the outside of his boot and did not penetrate his flesh. He could see the venom dripping down on his boot. He sat exhausted and tried to calm down, but he was hungry and terrified in the strange unforgiving place. Still the sun beat down on his pale Irish skin.

The river was also getting much wider as he walked along, and it was impossible for him to get to the other side of the river. He could not swim. Still, he walked carefully avoiding open spaces and leaving footprints. After the fourth day his hunger became intense. He had not eaten since the first evening.

Trackers were often employed to work for The Establishment when an escape occurred. They enjoyed getting the money, and the work was easy for them. The main tracker was medium height, thin with dark wispy hair and a beard with some streaks of grey. He was wearing an old, cast-off military uniform without any badges and an old pair of scuffed boots. He wandered on foot through the bushland leading the search party. The search party had brought their supplies on horseback and all the party walked following the trackers through the thick scrubland. Often, they would stop look around, search the surrounding area quietly and then keep moving. Occasionally a tracker would point out the outline of a footprint or a broken twig to the officer in charge but most of the time they were quiet and walked slowly but steadily onwards. In the middle of the day the trackers would stop when the sun was high and hot and take a rest for an hour under a tree. They would then start again and walk slowly until the sun started to set when they would find a clearing in which to camp. The Establishment warders and the officer would set up camp with tents and a cooking fire while the trackers would watch almost in amusement. They only needed the blanket they carried, and both relied on the food provided by The Establishment guards. Otherwise, if no food was available, they could catch and cook something for themselves like a bush hen, goanna or snake or pick up some bush tucker. The following day they continued until they also reached the river and they turned northwards following the signs that the trackers found.

By the sixth day, John was exhausted, starving, sunburnt and dehydrated as he found that the water had turned brackish as if he was heading back down to the mouth of the river and Fremantle. He could not turn back as he assumed he was being followed. The day before he could see across the wide expanse of the river the small township of what he assumed was Perth. By that evening he was so fatigued and starving that he could not proceed any further, so he stopped and fell into a deep sleep under a small bush on the sandy ground. When he woke it was dawn and he remembered where he was. He had nothing to eat and was extremely thirsty but had no water to drink. He thought to himself, I can't go any further. I'm done, and he lay back exhausted.

Onwards the Aboriginal trackers proceeded relentlessly following the tracks John left behind. The main tracker pointed out that the footprints had become more obvious as if John stopped trying to hide his tracks. He also noted the escapee rested more often, and his footsteps were shorter. They sped up their pursuit. On the seventh day they located John lying under a nest of low bushes by the riverbank. He made no attempt to flee, and the officer was surprised as he was almost thankful that he was found. He had cracked lips from lack of water and was severely sunburned from the exposure to the bright sunshine each day. John lay down and made no resistance to being rechained but was unable to stand and walk so the officer ordered for a camp to be set up and they provided food and water. The officer wondered why the convicts bothered to escape as they had no idea how to survive here in this sandy dry landscape. Over the next few days with adequate food and water, the search party and John slowly walked back to Fremantle. He was recaptured on the 22nd of October 1855, seven days after the escape.

Once he was back in The Establishment the punishment decided by the magistrate was again formal, swift and brutal. It was documented in John Arnold's Fremantle prison character book that the magistrate ordered:

"Three years hard labour; first year in solitary confinement; 3 months bread and water; and 100 lashes."

Dawson and the other recent escapee from The Establishment, Ade, also received one hundred lashes from a Cat similar in weight and size to those used on board a man-of-war. The floggings were given by The Establishment's gatekeeper who was the designated flagellator. Most warders did not want to do the floggings so one warder was appointed as the flagellator and paid more for that service. John was escorted up to the flogging area which was just in front of the solitary confinement cells facing a tall limestone wall and at the back of the main cell block. Once again, his shirt was stripped off his back and the wide leather belt was fixed around his waist to protect his vital organs and a wide leather collar was fixed around his neck to protect his neck arteries from being slashed by the errant tails of the whip. Both belt and collar were darkened with the blood of the previous convicts who had been whipped.

John felt numb as his hands were fastened at the wrist to the high tie point on the whipping triangle and similarly his feet were each individually strapped to a separate leg of the triangle. There he was alone again, spread-eagled and vulnerable, waiting for the start of the rain of one hundred vicious lashes. He stared at the wall in front of him and saw where the white limestone stonework was darkened by the blood of the previous convicts who were whipped there. The white crushed limestone on the ground also held darkened spots where blood had sprayed during a flogging. Fortunately, there were not too many whippings in The Establishment which preferred to rehabilitate rather than severely punish the convicts. Work was considered the way to keep convicts busy and for those who followed the rules they were quickly released with a Ticket of Leave.

John heard the first lash whipping through the air, the deep grunt of the flagellator and then felt the pain as it lashed across his back. The solitary beat of the drum followed. Immediately he winced in pain, dropped his head forward and closed his eyes trying to take his mind off the present. The next lash brought him back to the present. A few officers were in attendance as was the medical officer. It was grim work for them to watch this.

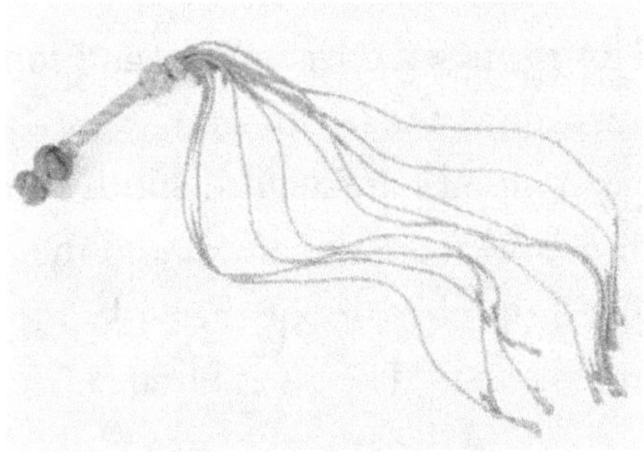

Cat o' nine tails
Source – public domain

While John was in solitary confinement he was allowed out for exercise each day and to go to the chapel. Fortunately, he was not given a solitary cell which was completely blacked out. In The Establishment there were eighteen solitary confinement cells – twelve were 'light' cells and six were 'dark 'cells where all sunlight was blacked out. He was thankful for that small mercy. The wounds on his back from the one hundred lashes were slowly healing and he vowed to himself that he would never run the risk of that punishment again. He figured that at his age of forty and having been whipped savagely three times – Kirkdale, Portland and now in Fremantle, the next time would kill him. He was struggling to recover, and the meals of bread and water were keeping him sick, very thin and weak. Thankfully, the wounds on his back did not become infected. He asked to speak to the priest after the chapel service one Sunday and the following day during his exercise time the Catholic chaplain called Father Donovan visited him.

They walked together around the exercise compound in the nice warm sunshine with their feet making soft crunching sounds on the crushed limestone underfoot. John walked slowly as he adjusted to the bright sunshine and the exercise. He could feel a nice cool breeze coming from the south. It was much nicer than being in the solitary confinement cell. After some time of slowly walking in silence and then saying a prayer quietly together, Donovan quietly updated John on some activities in the Colony, Fremantle and in The Establishment. John was thankful for the news, the company and conversation.

Donovan then explained the layout of The Establishment to John. "The Establishment buildings are aligned south to north," he began, "and at the front facing west are the offices and the chapel. What is in front of the offices and the chapel?" he then asked John. John thought for a few seconds and replied, "The assembly area."

"Yes, and what is beyond the assembly area?" the chaplain asked.

John thought and replied, "The front gate."

"And what happens at the front gate?" the chaplain asked quietly.

"That is where people come into and leave the prison," John replied.

The chaplain paused for a few seconds to let John ponder this. Slowly John said, "In front of the chapel is the gate and people leave the prison from the gate...so, the way out of the prison is through the chapel and through the gate." He thought again. He was struggling to keep his thoughts straight as the time in solitary confinement was robbing him of his ability to think, concentrate and talk coherently. The chaplain stayed silent and waited.

They had stopped walking by now and the chaplain looked down at the tired, thin, beaten man standing stooped in front of him who looked much older than his 40 years. He could still see where some blood was staining the back of his shirt from the whipping he had received. The chaplain did not believe in the severe punishment that was being inflicted at The Establishment and he made his views clear to the superintendent. He was politely ignored.

The chaplain continued. "In John's gospel (14:6) he wrote, 'I am the way, the truth, and the life. No one can come to the father except through me'." John thought and suddenly it came to him. He mumbled as the words could not come out. He started to cry. Tears dripped down his tired, bearded, ashen face.

Slowly John said, "The way out of the prison is through the chapel and through God. If I obey God's teachings, I will be saved and freed."

The chaplain nodded and said, "John, you were brought up a Christian from a loving Christian family in Ireland. You have a loving wife and children back in England and I am sure that when asked they will move here to be with you. But you have lost your faith and lost your way in life. Come back to God's family, renew your faith and you will be saved. Resist temptation. God will look after you and you will be freed. In prison you have your cross to bear for your sins, so bear your cross with dignity and in time you will be freed. The cross may at times be heavy but you need to bear your cross to find your peace."

"John, the Colony of Western Australia is a terrific opportunity for you. You should count your blessings. It is not like the cold cruel prisons back in England where you would be locked up for decades and tortured with the treadmill. Remember the Crank John? Where you would be forced to sit and turn the handles of the Crank for hours. This colony is not like the overcrowded slums in Bradford or the work in the mills where you were made to work long hours for a pay that hardly keeps scraps of food on the table and a roof over your head. Here there is opportunity. The aim is to provide rehabilitation through meaningful work for convicts, not the torture you experienced in Kirkdale Prison and the days locked in a solitary confinement cell. If you can be trusted, you will be given significant leeway to get on and work inside and outside The Establishment. You are only in your cell for approximately 10 hours a day to rest and sleep. The work gangs who perform work outside The Establishment give you time to be outside. So, engage with the system, follow the rules, work hard, renew your faith in the love of God and soon you and your family will be together once more."

John stood with his head down, listening. His eyes were focusing on the ground below as the priest's comments registered with him. After some time, John looked up at Donovan and saw a genuine man with understanding eyes looking at him with compassion. He knew then that Donovan was right.

Over the next few days John began to realise he had indeed lost his way. He had burgled a few houses, witnessed an assault and was being punished. It was a very severe punishment, but he needed to bear his cross and pay the price for his sins. He needed to resist temptation. With the time to think in solitary confinement he changed. He realised he was the master of his destiny, the captain of his own ship and the way forward was to be respectful, obey God's commandments and do the time for his sins.

Finally, he was released from solitary confinement. He was weak, emaciated and his hair was thinning and turning grey, but he felt alive for the first time in years. It was August 15, 1856.

Sometime after his release from solitary confinement, he asked to see the deputy superintendent one day and pleaded for an explanation of the arrangements for Tickets of Leave. The deputy looked at him, a downtrodden, thin, older convict in front of him and bluntly said in an aloof manner, "The scale of time for convicts like you with a life sentence was 12 months solitary confinement although this has now been reduced to nine months. You did the 12 months in Kirkdale. Once you are released from solitary confinement, you need to serve at least five years three months in public works then you would be given a Ticket of Leave. You have done some of this time in Portland and now here in Fremantle. You then work with a Ticket of Leave for at least four years and then you could get a conditional pardon. With a conditional pardon you have complete freedom except that you cannot return to England. After another 10 years you can get a full pardon."

John listened to the explanation and nodded.

The deputy superintendent continued. "Given you were convicted in December 1852 you could get a Ticket of Leave after six years and three months, or 1858 in March. Sometimes people can get their Ticket of Leave earlier based on good behaviour and the government's desire to provide labour for the Swan River community." He paused for a few seconds and continued. "Mr Arnold, however, you have tried to escape twice, once at Portland and once again here so your time here in The Establishment has been extended to June 1859. At this time if you do not incur any more infringements, you will be given a Ticket of Leave. Once you have your Ticket of Leave you can work freely in a designated region, for example York, Toodyay or the newly developing areas around Champion Bay and Greenough to the north and get paid. You can then apply to have your wife and children join you. According to the regulations for a Ticket of Leave, the wife and family of a well-behaved Ticket of Leave holder will be sent out to him free of expense upon the usual form of application to the Comptroller General through the Resident or Police Magistrate."

With this knowledge, the renewal of his faith and love he felt from his God, John bore his cross over the next years to June 1859. He remembered his father's words from years ago to start early, leave a bit later than required, work hard, do real quality work, and learn to get better at what you do. He did the hard labour. He loaded and carted limestone blocks without incident until his work on the northern cell block was completed in 1859. His behaviour was documented as excellent each month in The Establishment character book. During that time, he was moved to the probation party on March 13, 1857 and was appointed constable on December 16, 1858. These movements were a recognition that The Establishment officers regarded him as someone who they could trust completely. Sometimes during that time, he was given work outside The Establishment in work gangs building or repairing roads and bridges in Fremantle. Then on the 15th of May 1859 he was transferred to work on the construction of the nearby Fremantle Lunatic Asylum. Sadly, with the punitive treatment of the convicts in England, the use of extended solitary confinement, the treadmill in England and lashings – some of which were then extended in Fremantle – there was a significant need for an asylum as many convicts lost their minds during the inhumane processes and were unable to function normally ever again. John realised he had much to thank Father Donavan for.

Fremantle Prison – The Establishment

Fremantle prison cell – 7 feet by 4 feet
(Source – Michael Le Page)

"Power is of two kinds. One is obtained by the fear of
punishment and the other by acts of love. Power based on
love is a thousand times more effective and permanent
than the one derived from fear of punishment."
— Mahatma Gandhi

11

Ticket of Leave – The Miller

'I am free! I am free! My heart leaps in my breast,
And each feeling, each thought with grief late opprest,
Now thrills through my frame, as if a new life
Were given in mercy to meet the world's strife.
I am free, I am free! '
For the sins of my youth, I have suffered the pain.
I have felt the world's enmity, coldness, disdain,
The good have passed by me, 'twas torture, 'twas madness,
To see them avoid me in pitying sadness,
But now I am free!
I am free, I am free! What rapture is mine
How I bless, how adore that mercy Divine,
Which hath broken my bonds, which hath lightn'd my breast,
From my chains given liberty – peace for unrest.
Hurrah, I am free!

(Ticket of Leave song – source anonymous)

John was granted his Ticket of Leave. It was the 16th of June 1859. He was 44 years old. Mary was twenty-eight. John Cosgrave obtained his Ticket of Leave earlier on the 17th of November 1858 as he had not tried to escape and had a good record. As John Arnold was an experienced miller he wanted to work in a mill once again where he could use his skills and earn a living. He did not mind if it was a grist mill milling wheat. He liked that sort of work, and he knew how all the machinery worked. He also wanted to get away from Fremantle into the country like where he grew up in Ireland so he could have some space and freedom. John was told that people on a Ticket of Leave were permitted to work and be paid a wage. They could negotiate the amount they would be paid, and they were also given a district in which they could find work. He too moved into the Association Room at The Establishment and for the first time in years he was not confined to a small cell at night. He wrote to Mary. Over the past six and a half years he had written to Mary every three or four months and Mary had a friend answer the letters. The letters were short but for both John and Mary they provided a much-needed link to each other. These brief letters were often their little ray of sunshine in their otherwise dark and difficult lives.

'Dear Mary,

Tis with great joy that I write you. Today I got my Ticket of Leave. My hard life in prison is over and I can work for myself and be paid. God is shining a light on me. My heart tis no longer broken. Today I walked out of the prison freely in the bright sunshine and looked for work. People looked at me in my old clothes, but my heart sang "I am free, I am free"'. The Deputy Superintendent told me I can find work in York which is in the country and there is work in the wheat mills there as I am a miller. He also said I can apply for you, James and Mary to come here free of expense. I am so happy. I don't think a man has loved a woman as much as I love you.

I am no longer locked up in a prison cell at night and I sleep in the association room with many other men and not in a small cell. You must let James and Mary know that I am well and free now. Please write to me. I love you so much. I will see you all agane. May God have mersy on me.

Your husband who loves you.

John Arnold

John was given work in York in a grist mill. York was one hundred miles by road and track from Fremantle through vast bushland, hills and recently developed pasture for grazing and areas for agriculture. John also heard that John Cosgrave had found work out near York. He was not a miller but found labouring work. So, he set out on foot with a fellow Ticket of Leave convict. The trek was expected to take them three days and they were required to check in at the police station when they arrived. Each man had a sack containing some clothes, water and food on their backs. The officers at The Establishment issued them with a liberty suit, a blue cloth cap, a pair of boots, two shirts, two pairs of stockings, two neck handkerchiefs two waistcoats, a blue flannel, a leather belt, a pair of braces and a pair of blankets. They had their parchment Tickets of Leave in their pockets with letters confirming they had work. The Ticket of Leave was issued to John, and the government kept on file the Ticket of Leave butt which detailed John's name, the ship he arrived on, the date of arrival, place of birth, trade, date and place of trial and sentence, a physical description and the district to which he was confined. John and his companion talked as they walked. "I never want to return to The Establishment," John said. "If anyone asks me to do anything against the law, I will run one hundred miles away." His companion nodded. "Me too," he said as he kicked a stone along the dusty path. "I made one mistake and it nearly had me hanged, so never again for me."

The rules for the Ticket of Leave were documented over fifteen pages. John needed to always carry his Ticket of Leave, work in an assigned district, report to the local police magistrate every June and December, obtain and show a pass to leave the district, advise the police if he changed his employer or address, receive permission to leave an employer, not get drunk or loiter. There were many other restrictions about a curfew and working on seagoing vessels but both John and his companion believed the rules were reasonable and workable. It gave them freedom which neither had experienced for many years and they were very thankful for that.

Occasionally people passed John and his companion on the dirt road to York. All were friendly but they knew both men were Ticket of Leave men by their clothes. John did not mind as he was free and just being out in the open walking unfettered in this lovely country was an immense blessing to him, plus he had work arranged. Although it was the middle of winter, for John and his companion the weather was cool but not cold and fortunately it did not rain during the journey as it was apt to do from late autumn through to late spring in this region. From late spring through to late autumn it typically did not rain so it would be blue sky and sunshine.

When they exited The Establishment, they were given a pipe and some tobacco so each evening when they stopped to camp in the bush by the side of the road, they each took pleasure in smoking their pipes. Although they did not realise it, they were still following the rules of the prison and they smoked after their evening meal and only for 15 minutes.

York was the first inland town after Guildford in the Colony of Western Australia, and it was settled due to the fertile land around the Avon River. However, it was a small town with one short street with some buildings on either side and the Avon River off to the east. When they arrived at York, they immediately went to the police station to register and show their Tickets of Leave and letters offering employment. John's companion then went in search of his employer and John searched for Mr RG Meares who had recently built a new steam powered mill using a modern 12-horsepower steam engine, a pair of new French burrstones and a dressing machine. John knew the French burrstones were used for finer grinding of the wheat as he had seen some in Ireland years before. The millstones are made up from sections of quartz which were cemented together and bound with a shrink-fit iron band. Meares showed John around the mill on Lot 3 in York. He was proud of his achievements to build and operate the mill in this remote region. He was especially pleased with the steam engine and was pleasantly surprised with John's intelligence, knowledge of the milling process and the type of milling stones he had. However, he told John he already had a miller and John's role would be working in the mill loading wheat into the feed bins, bagging up the flour and preparing it for transport. Some cleaning and general maintenance would also be required.

It was John's first lesson – although he was now free with a Ticket of Leave he would only be considered for low level labouring roles until he could build trust or start his own business. He was after all still an ex-convict. He did not mind, and he reminded himself of the priest's advice back in 1855 to count his blessings. He also reminded himself of his father's words, John wherever you work arrive a bit early, leave a bit later than required, work hard, do real quality work and learn to get better at what you do. The other worker at the mill showed John where he could sleep and keep his few possessions. It was a reasonable hut at the back of the mill that acted as a small dormitory with a few wooden bunks and straw mattresses covered in a woollen material. Outside was a secluded area to wash and cook if he wanted. To John this was a luxury as the weather was warming up after a cool winter and the opportunity to not sleep in a cell with the solid steel door locking him in was wonderful. He would also be paid, and part of the arrangement was food and accommodation were included.

John started work early at 6 a.m. the next morning, had a meal break after two hours and then worked until midday when he took an hour off to have a meal back at the dormitory. He then went back at 1 p.m. for the rest of the afternoon. He enjoyed the work as he had been working in a quarry or moving limestone blocks for over five years and working in a mill was a great physical and mental relief for him. Meares quickly realised John really knew what he was doing. He trusted his work, so

John was not overly supervised and he was given sections of the mill to run reporting to the miller. On Saturday they worked a half-day and took a rest in the afternoon. Sunday was a day of rest and John found a local Catholic church to attend. The first Saturday afternoon and Sunday was the first free time outside of a prison he had experienced in seven years since November 1852.

After a few months John went to see the local magistrate at the police station to make enquiries about politely asking Comptroller General Edmund Henderson to give permission for his family to be sent out free of expense as per his advice when he was in The Establishment. He had thought about this a great deal and concluded life here in the Colony of Western Australia would not only provide a much better future for Mary and himself but for their children as well. Here there was opportunity, freedom from the slums, poverty, suppression, disease and class structure of England. He had observed the colonists and saw that many had worked hard to make a living together and depended on each other, so they developed less of a class structure. Sure, some people had come out from England with family money but the realities of life in the Colony was that everyone in the rural areas needed to work together. Labour was in short supply and people worked together including those who had money or property and those who did not.

John advised the magistrate he had written to his wife and received a response that she was willing to move out to the Colony of Western Australia. He showed the letter to the magistrate who then advised John that he would make some enquiries. The magistrate knew this was a sensitive issue as very many of the convicts' wives refused to move out to the colonies, simply remarried or had children with another man and never responded to any enquiries. He hoped John was correct in that she was willing to move. He was also aware that where the wives did not move out, the ex-convicts often had lonely, desperate lives and, in many cases, ended up physically and mentally broken down and in poverty. Severe alcoholism was also common.

The magistrate visited Mr Meares the following week to check up on John's work and non-work activities. Mr Meares advised the magistrate, who was a friend of his, that John was doing decent work. He added that John had a good working knowledge of a wheat mill, was diligent, worked hard, went to church on Sundays and never visited the public house or the "Dusty Miller" as it was called down the end of Avon Terrace in York. William Dunham owned the place, and while he was an open-minded businessman, he did not often see ex-convicts there. Later that week the magistrate wrote to the comptroller general forwarding John Arnold's request regarding his family. The magistrate also included comments that John was a hardworking, experienced miller who went to church and was supported by the mill owner, Mr RG Meares. When this letter arrived, the comptroller general looked at John's character book from The Establishment, noted his excellent record in recent years and decided to provide his support. He then wrote to the office in London to arrange transportation for Mrs Arnold and the two children to the colony. The comptroller general also knew the colony needed families as well as men to grow the colony, plus married men were generally much more settled and useful in the colony than the numerous unmarried ex-convicts.

As Mr Meares had a new operating wheat mill powered by a steam engine he occasionally had visitors who wanted to look at his mill and talk about business with him. One day a visitor arrived who John had not seen before. The miller sat down with John when they were having lunch and told him the visitor was Walter Padbury, a remarkably successful businessman not only in Perth but also further north in the colony. He had been in the colony for over 30 years, so he knew many people in the area. He originally worked as a shepherd in York from when he was 16, and then did many things like building fences, shearing and herding sheep. John was also told for the first time of a growing wheat and farming area over 300 miles to the north called Greenough, and Walter Padbury had been busy paying for the construction of a new wheat mill up there.

Later that afternoon Mr Meares and Mr Padbury came into the mill and walked around discussing mill stones, silk sieving screens, wheat and flour prices when Mr Padbury stopped and looked over at John who was filling bags with flour for sale. Mr Padbury was a wealthy man but based on his humble upbringing and tough working years he not only treated people very well but mixed with everyone as his equal. He recognised John as a Ticket of Leave man from his clothes but still he went over, shook John's hand, introduced himself and started talking with him. Mr Padbury was intrigued about John's knowledge of the mill, its workings as well as farming. He also asked John about the farming and milling he did in Ireland. It was clear to Mr Padbury that John was not only an experienced miller but an experienced farmer as well.

At the end of the conversation Mr Padbury stopped as he was walking away and came back to John and said, "Mr Arnold I can see you are a hard-working man who knows this milling business and farming. I have been in West Australia since I arrived as a young boy with my father, and for those who work hard it can be a land of opportunity. Learn from Mr Meares as he is a good businessperson. There are some things that are different here than in Ireland and England. The land can be difficult, the weather can be dry when you want rain or flooding when you want it dry. All this takes some time to understand so listen and learn. Next time I come back to York I will visit and say hello again. I will look out for opportunities for you." John nodded and said, "Thank you Mr Padbury." He had not had anyone take a genuine interest in him since Mr James Jones in Ireland, and Mary.

Afterwards, in Mr Meares' office, Mr Padbury asked if it would be acceptable if he talked with John sometime about the mill in Greenough and the opportunities for farming in that new area. Mr Padbury was convinced that Greenough would be the biggest wheat producing area in the whole colony. He also wanted to get more experience into the mill that he had financed in the area, and he thought John was a suitable candidate even though he was a Ticket of Leave man. Mr Padbury had a very tough upbringing and he wanted to help those who were willing to work hard and give them opportunities. He did not believe in the old English class structure and was extremely comfortable walking onto the work floor and talking with anyone. It was the Australian way he once told someone. Mr Meares agreed as he and Mr Padbury had some good plans of business together and he felt he could always replace John in York with another Ticket of Leave man from Fremantle. Mr Padbury left and made a note to contact John later. Mr Meares forgot about the conversation regarding John and continued as normal.

Early in the New Year John received a letter that Mary had been contacted in Manchester and she and the two children would arrive in Fremantle around the middle of that year. No vessel had been scheduled yet, but he would be informed of the ship's name and an expected arrival date when it was available. He would need to be in Fremantle to meet the vessel and take responsibility for his family. John was trembling when he finished reading the news. He realistically never expected when he left Portland to see Mary and his children again. He felt so alive again after the years of incarceration and brutal treatment. Shortly afterwards, in the New Year, Walter Padbury again visited York and met with Mr Meares. After they had finished discussing their planned business ventures together Mr Padbury walked into the mill to seek out John.

Mr Padbury once again discussed milling and farming with John and it seemed to Mr Padbury that since their last visit John had grown more confident, fitter and stronger. His once stooping frame was now erect, and he had built up strength and muscle in his body. Maybe it was the better food, physical work or simply a vision that he could be a free man again. This was a good sign to Mr Padbury, and he thought John was not just a survivor but someone who could do well. He said to John, "Mr Arnold, normally ex-convicts do not get more than unskilled menial work. When I was young, I could only get shepherd or fencing work, but I said to myself I could do much better than this, so I was determined to better myself. For you, the best way forward is to break free from this and be self-employed as a farmer or a merchant." With this vision for John, Padbury continued, "The Greenough area to the north has a lot of potential and is a good opportunity for you to become a farmer, miller or even a merchant. You could own your own farm !"

Mr Padbury explained to John that the Greenough flats are a long, narrow river floodplain in the north, which is approximately 1.5 to 2 miles wide and runs northwards next to the coast for about 18 to 19 miles ending about 15 miles south of the new area of Champion Bay, or as some people were now calling it, Geraldton. The Greenough River starts in the Murchison watershed, travels westward, and enters the flats in the south, then runs along the centre of the plain. High coastal sand dunes are to the west adjacent to the sea and a limestone ridge limits the flats to the east. The river veers westward at the north end of the flats and flows into the sea. In dry weather the river mouth does fill with sand and stops flowing resulting in pools of water near the river mouth. Over a prolonged period, inland rains along the river have caused flooding which deposited a rich layer of alluvial soils along the valley. Mr Padbury continued that half a dozen of the larger pastoralist families from the York region set up in this new area. He added that he decided a few years ago to invest in a new mill in Greenough as good farming land was available there.

Mr Padbury stopped and reflected for a while before saying "I can arrange a job for you in the mill in Greenough, transport up there, and a provide a cottage for your family to live in and in return you agree to move to Greenough." Mr Padbury continued, "You see, I have a substantial land holding there, had some land cleared and built some small cottages. My plan is to lease the land to small farmers like you at low rates. Eventually when you get better established you could buy land for yourself and farm there. You would be your own landholder and farmer and you could supplement your income by working in the mill. If you agree I will get my assistant to start making the arrangements." John looked at Mr Padbury. He never thought he could ever own any land let alone become a farmer on his own property but here it was coming from a person he felt he could trust. In Ireland and England it would be an impossible dream for him. Now it was a real possibility. He replied, "Thank you Mr Padbury. Yes, I agree to do that."

So, the plans were set. John would work in York until Mary and the children arrived and then they would travel by coastal vessel, organised by Mr Padbury, up the coast and set up home in Greenough. His aim was to take up some land and start his own small farm growing wheat and other crops. He would also work in the mill during the milling season. Walter Padbury and Mr Meares jointly arranged for John's Ticket of Leave arrangements to be transferred to Greenough with his first role to be working in Mr Padbury's mill.

It was late spring in Manchester when Mary, James and Mary Catherine started to pack. She had received a government letter stating the travel arrangements and timing. As she could not read, she asked the priest to explain it to her. The Catholic Church was also extremely helpful as it also wanted families to reunite. She was excited and terrified at the same time. Thoughts like where was she going, what would it be like, had John changed and would there be savages in the country crossed her mind. She also heard about the strange animals like kangaroos that were six feet tall and hopped around on two legs. She also heard about the multitude of dangerous snakes. James was quiet and supportive as always. Mary Catherine was excited. She loved the idea of going on a train and a big ship to sail across the sea. Maybe she would see some whales. The things that excited her terrified Mary. Soon the day came, and they set off with the small amount of luggage that carried their worldly possessions. Mary also made sure she had her sewing equipment and a ready supply of cotton, needles and buttons.

Mary arrived at Fremantle in Western Australia on the *Reubens* on the 3rd of July 1860 with children James and Mary Catherine who were aged nine and seven. It was almost eight years since John had seen Mary and James. It was the first time he had seen his daughter. John had now been in the Colony of Western Australia for five years.

(Source – pexels.com)

"In every person there is a sun. Just let them shine."
Socrates

Walter Padbury was born in England and arrived in Fremantle with his father, Thomas Padbury, in February 1830 on the vessel *Protector*. His father died shortly after in July that year leaving Walter in the care of some people who subsequently abandoned him. Padbury worked around Perth and then in York as a shepherd at 16 years of age. After that he did fencing, shearing, droving and sold stock he owned to butchers earning him profits. With the money he paid for his mother and the family to move to the colony. Over time, Padbury subsequently opened a butcher business, purchased property and built flour mills. From this he built significant property, flour milling and shipping businesses including in Greenough.

Due to his challenging upbringing he was reported to be helpful and respectful to his employees including ex-convicts.

12 |

Greenough

When Mary and the children arrived on the *Reubens* into the small bay off Fremantle they looked over the low-lying land in front of them. They had spent more than three months at sea, suffered badly from sea sickness but were comforted by their fellow passengers who were all travelling to this strange new land on the other side of the world. They saw themselves not so much as adventurers but people who were looking for opportunities, a new life, or in some cases to get away from the class structure, poverty and slums in England. Mary was also looking forward to a reconnection with John. They were glad to arrive and set foot on firm ground but anxious at the same time. What would this life be like, and would they ever go back to England and see their families again? Most of the passengers would never return to England.

The sea was calm now after the wild storms they had encountered on their voyage and given that neither Mary nor the two children had seen the ocean before it was a traumatic trip for them. From the crowded slums in Manchester with the smoke from the mills filling the air to the quiet of the ocean, the vast starlit skies at night and the never-ending sea. Mary Catherine loved going up onto the deck at night and staring at the millions of stars that dotted the sky. Some of the sailors loved her enthusiasm and taught her the constellations like the Southern Cross and Orion's Belt.

The land in front of them now looked dry and desolate compared to what they were used to in England. However, the sky was an amazing blue colour as was the colour of the water surrounding their vessel. When they looked overboard, they could see through the clear water to the sandy bottom below. White sand surrounded the shore at Fremantle and a scattering of low houses filled the landscape. A tall white building dominated the landscape at the back of the town. It was perched on a small hill. It was an impressive structure for such a small town and one of the crew told them it was called The Convict Establishment but was really the prison for the convicts who were still serving time. It was an ever-present reminder to everyone that this was still a penal colony. Mary wondered if John had stayed there.

Mary and the children were ferried to shore and a small crowd gathered to either welcome them or assist in unloading the vessel. The arrival of a vessel was always an exciting time in the colony as it brought goods and news of England including some old newspapers. As Mary looked around she saw a small, tall round stone building off to the left along the beach and a white stone building in front of her near the shore. It looked like a warehouse of sorts. There was a lot of activity with goods and people being ferried off the ship. Mary scanned the faces in the crowd and saw John at the back dressed in a suit with a hat clutched in his left hand. His hair was trimmed short as was his beard. His face was tanned, and he seemed older than she remembered. His hair was thinning and had turned partly grey. His beard was also grey in parts. However, he stood tall, and it looked like he was in good physical shape. There was strength in his stance and a smile on his face.

She walked up to him, took his hands in hers, looked into those green eyes and starting crying. She did not care if anyone else noticed. There was so much emotion to deal with; the sadness of when she lost him, the difficulty over the past eight years, the not knowing what the future held and the need to care and nurture her children. John held her for the first time in those eight years. He thought Mary looked beautiful and for the first time in such a long time he was held in a loving embrace. He did not care if anyone thought that showing affection was improper. It was such a lonely, harsh, painful eight years and now they were together again on the other side of the world. There was opportunity in front of them.

John then took the hand of his son James. He had grown tall with a head of dark hair. With his other hand he held Mary Catherine's hand for the very first time. Mary Catherine, like her mother, had long dark hair and at seven years of age she was blessed with a lovely smile. She did not know her father, but her mother had spoken about him so many times that she felt she knew him. Mary noted that while John still had his Irish accent he now spoke differently with a stranger choice of words and pronunciation with some words she did not understand. His speech was slightly slower as if he had subconsciously reduced the speed of his speech so people could understand him easier. However, she quickly saw again in John the wonderful man she married so long ago. He may have seriously erred in his judgement years ago but now she heard how he loved this new colony and the opportunity it provided. John knelt on the ground and spoke with both James and Mary Catherine. "This is a wonderful place. It is called Fremantle and it was named by Captain Stirling after Captain Fremantle who was the captain of the first ship which came here on the *HMS Challenger*. You will love it here. There is so much activity with people all about moving things to warehouses and working by the shore." He was so full of stories and excitement that they were all excited with him about this new adventure.

John had been saving money from his meagre wages. His accommodation and meals were paid for in York, so he had saved all his wages since he left The Establishment. He now had some funds to pay for accommodation and Walter Padbury's clerk had arranged and paid for their transport up to Greenough from Fremantle. He continued to be amazed at Mr Padbury's staunch support for him and his vision for John to be his own man and run his own farm. He also knew that Mr Padbury was a smart businessman and simply wanted skilled labour up in Greenough to support his mill investment and the growing community. John also knew that many pensioner guards had acquired land in the Greenough area for farming, but they were long-term professional military people who knew little about farming or milling. He knew then that his skills would be useful and valued unlike back in England where labour was plentiful, opportunities were scarce and the pay was poor.

They walked over to the Southern Cross Hotel where John had taken a room. The hotel, built in 1840, was on High Street, looked nice and was well run. Mary noted there was a scattering of stone and brick buildings on that side of Fremantle, and they looked like government offices to manage the port and the town. Also, there were a few commercial buildings and warehouses. It resembled what she had envisioned a small port town would be like, with small streets, some cobblestone paving and all sorts of carts carrying items back and forth. The children were fascinated with the activity, the new sounds, strange voices but most of all the warm weather and sunshine. It seemed so bright here even though it was winter. Their heavy English clothes made them sweat in the warm sunshine. Once back at the hotel John and Mary allowed the children to wander around just outside the hotel a little to just watch the activities in the area and at the port area just a few hundred yards away. Then for the first time in many years, they were able to hold each other in an embrace. John had endured the harsh reality of the whip, torture and confinement for years and now he felt a loving embrace so tender he wept. He missed Mary so much, and to be reunited again was indeed a wonderful blessing.

Mary had no misconceptions that life here would be different in the Colony of Western Australia, and like in Manchester, not easy, but she welcomed the change as she was swapping life with its uncertainty for another – but this time she was not alone on this life's journey.

Alone in their room Mary opened the old trunk which she brought with her from England. In it were her and the children's possessions and some simple family treasures to remind her of her family and England. She reached in and brought out a woollen bag which was tied with a string. She opened it and brought out John's father's fiddle and bow plus his mother's rosary beads. She had treasured these two items over the years and kept them safe as she knew how much John valued them. John took hold of them, held the rosary beads in one hand and the fiddle in the other. He looked at the fiddle, caressed it and turned it over to look at the inscription on the back. It brought back lovely memories of his family singing together back in Ireland. John looked at Mary and said, "Thank you for this. Having you all here means so much to me. It gives me hope and a future. Thanks also for looking after my fiddle and the rosary beads. They are incredibly special." His hope now was to establish a place where his family could call home, be together and sing together.

During the two days in Fremantle, John and Mary caught up with all the things that had happened over the time they were apart. Mary recounted how she stayed with Margaret McManus in Manchester for that time. It worked for them both as Mary worked the long mill hours five-and-a-half days per week – 10 hours per day during the week with an early morning start – and Margaret worked as a fruit hawker selling fruit in the market. It was manageable as the two women worked slightly different hours, and with the help of the older children, the smaller children were supervised. The money John had left behind helped keep Mary with a roof over her head and food on the table during those lonely dark times. Mary also continued with her dressmaking and with Margaret's help she sold the garments at the market. Mary Catherine had developed some skills at dressmaking, and this helped Mary enormously.

John told the story of the past eight years for him. He left out the brutal parts and the dark days in solitary confinement plus the torture in Kirkdale prison, but he could not avoid mentioning the whipping with the Cat. Mary saw his bare back and the cruel, long, red, raised scars that raked down from his neck to his waist. She thought it looked like a lion had clawed him from top to tail and she wondered how cruel and brutal one person could be to another. She was Christian after all and could not comprehend this brutality. She thought back to her own golden rule of 'treat others how you would like to be treated' and believed the world had a long way to go to begin starting to treat all people with respect and dignity.

After two days in Fremantle their vessel set sail for Champion Bay 240 miles to the north. Champion Bay was the port for a new area on the coast. A few years earlier in 1848 lead ore was discovered in the bed of the Murchison River to the north-east of the area. As the young colony was looking for sources of income a mine was started, and lead ore was shipped out of Champion Bay. A small town called Northampton was established near to the lead mine. Afterwards the land to the south was developed and proved to be fertile and suitable for farming. A small new village was established in the coastal plain thirteen miles to the south and called Greenough. The area was first explored by George Grey in 1839 and Grey named the area after his sponsor, Sir George Bellas Greenough, the then president of the Royal Geographical Society.

When John, Mary and the children arrived at Champion Bay, they felt like they had reached the very end of civilisation. If Fremantle was at the bottom of the world then Champion Bay was event more remote. There was little infrastructure, the roads were rudimentary and while there was some structure to the layout of the small town it was obvious that this was an outpost of the colony. Luckily for them Water Padbury's clerk had arranged for them to be met by a fellow mill worker and ex-convict who had a horse and wagon to transport them the thirteen miles to Greenough. It was warm and they were pleased not to have to walk. John did not mind walking for three days to York, but he did not want his family to walk the thirteen miles carrying their possessions.

Along the track to Greenough, they could see small farms scattered on either side of the road. Most of the work was being done by hand with farmers clearing land by axe and then ploughing by hand as well. Occasionally they would see some Aboriginals who did not seem to mind the farmers nor travellers like them, but John did hear stories on the ship of problems with the Aboriginals and the occasional skirmish.

They were also fascinated by the strange trees that bent away from the wind. In some cases, the trees were bent at 90 degrees ending up flat on the ground. John reasoned it must be very windy here from time to time or the trees were very flexible.

Finally, they arrived at the mill which was built by Mr Padbury and leased to Edward Whitfield and his partner Robert Sutherland. Mr Padbury had funded it with a £1600 mortgage on his land at Greenough and it was the first flour mill in the district. John Maley was the overseer for the mill construction. When John arrived, Walter Padbury had just installed a new experienced miller called William Forrest who was from Bunbury which is a small port town approximately one hundred miles to the south of Fremantle. He was experienced and welcomed John. Forrest needed experienced hard working people to work on the mill as it had been struggling to operate effectively, and he had been requested by Mr Padbury and the leaseholders to get the operating rates up and the costs down, as well as improve the quality of the flour.

Forrest explained to John that the mill was a well-built steam powered grinding mill made with the use of the local, cheap limestone. The limestone was easily burnt in pits and mixed with sand to provide a strong mortar plus it was used as a stone in the construction as well. The timber needed for construction was transported up from the south as the local timbers were inadequate for the structural beams. John remembered the trees bent over from the wind and understood that they would not be suitable as structural timbers of a mill. The roof of the mill was made of wooden shingles to keep the rain out.

Forrest welcomed Mary and the children and showed John and the family the small cottage near to the mill which was to be their home. It reminded John of his family home back in Ireland. It was simple, had a firm packed earth floor, walls made from the local limestone rocks and wooden slats called wattle daubed together with sticky clay, wet soil and sand. The roof was thatched. The thatching was very thick and was made from the leaves of the local grass trees which were a regular feature of the wooded areas to the east. Forrest also showed them a small plot behind their house which he said they could use as a garden if they wished. Mary looked around. She had grown up in Manchester and worked for a time in Bradford, so she had never lived in the country. Now she scanned the wilderness out the back of the cottage and saw nothing but tall grass, bushland and blue sky. She turned to John and said, "I think this will be simply fine. We can make a home here. If you show us how, James, Mary Catherine and I will build a vegetable garden here which will provide us with a good supply of vegetables and maybe some fruit in season."

They settled in quickly. Mary and the two children were not used to the isolated rural environment, but they enjoyed the open spaces, the fresh air, sunshine and freedom. In many ways for them it was extremely foreign to have so much space around them and freedom. Supplies came in regularly and there was free flour from the mill and water from the nearby creek which flowed into the river. John and Mary planted a small garden for vegetables. John had done this for many years when he was growing up in Ireland. Mary and the children were quick learners. James was responsible for bringing water from the creek to water the garden. Mary and the children grew vegetables and sold any excess at the weekend market where people would sell or barter goods. Mary also purchased some material to start making clothes to sell at the market. She had kept up and improved her sewing skills while John was away, and it helped to bring in some extra money each week.

Other families were in the area and the children met the other local children. Some parents did not want their children to mix with the children of an ex-convict but generally the children did not mind. There was even an ex-convict who was transported to the Colony of Western Australia for forgery back in London who was acting as a part-time schoolteacher in a rudimentary hut near the mill. For James it was good to continue his education and learn to read and write. For Mary Catherine it was the first schooling she had ever had as she did not go to school in England, and she learnt to sew to help her mother. There were a thousand people in the district when the Arnold family arrived and one of the original landholders, Frederick Waldeck, who arrived in 1857, donated some land for the local school.

John worked in the mill. He knew the work well and quickly established himself as someone Forrest could rely on. The milling business quickly improved with Forrest's and John's experience.

Throughput was improved, and with the high wheat yields that year combined with Forrest's passion to look for ways to improve the quality of his flour and mill throughput, profits were improving. Greenough was quickly becoming the biggest wheat producing area in the colony. Over the first six months John was curious and asked lots of questions about the working of the mill, the pastoral leases around the Greenough area and even the Irwin District at the southern end of the Greenough flats. He was trying to work out how he could progress into farming and stay in the milling business as well. He thought he could farm until the harvest was completed then work at the mill.

Walter Padbury was true to his word and John was able to sublet some land to farm in his spare time and during the times when there was no milling to be done. People in the region had started to grow a range of crops including wheat, barley, oats, rye, a small quantity of maize and hay. By then there was over 3000 acres cleared and under cultivation in the area. There were also thousands of horses and cattle with over 45,000 sheep in the area, so the opportunity was ripe for John to start farming.

He was also interested in the Aborigines. He wanted to know what they were like, if they worked the farms, their habits and culture. Some people cared about them, but many farmers saw them as a threat and were afraid of them because of the rumours of what they had done in the past. John heard the Gregory brothers first explored this area for pastoral land in 1848. Then they met with a large group of Indigenous Australians who were camped beside a swampy area adjacent to the Greenough River about two miles inland from the river mouth. The local farmers called the area Bootenal, from the Nyungar word Boolungal which meant pelican. John had seen pelicans around the mouth of the Greenough River, and they had passed by the Bootenal area which was to the west of the road on the way down from Champion Bay. These Aborigines were of the Yamatji people. They had lived in the area for an exceptionally long time and survived on fish and waterfowl from the river mouth, shellfish from the adjacent sea and kangaroos from the hills to the east of the Greenough flats. They also cultivated ajeca, a yam like plant on the river flats.

In 1852, according to talk in the settlement, farmer William Criddle used the Bootenal area to water his cattle and the Aborigines resented this intrusion in their traditional camping area. In 1854, large numbers of Aboriginal men including some from surrounding tribes, gathered in the relative safety of the swampy Bootenal area and made forays at night killing cattle and sheep and attacking homesteads. The farmers and graziers responded under the command of the resident magistrate on the night of the 4th July, and they rode to Bootenal area and drove the Indigenous Australians from the area. There was no official report of casualties or deaths but in some stories it was referred to as a massacre and with that the Aboriginal resistance in the area was finished. Maybe the stories were accurate. Maybe they were not. John and his family had little to do with the Aborigines initially but after being in Greenough for six months they had a chance encounter down at the beach.

Later that year Mary realised that she was expecting her third child. It was December 1860.

> "We are all visitors to this time, this place. We are just passing through. Our purpose here is to observe, to learn, to grow, to love and then we return home."
> – Aboriginal proverb

Grass tree
(Source – Michael Le Page)
The grass-like leaves at the bottom were used for thatching on a roof.

13

Down at the beach

John and Mary worked hard to settle in and create a new life in Greenough. The mill work was demanding, the gardens needed to be developed and tended, and the cottage always needed some repairs. The children helped. This left little time to do other things but after six months they decided on Sundays after attending a makeshift church in the school hut that they would take the afternoons off and explore the surrounding areas.

One of the first places they intended to explore was the beach. One cool day, they set off under a clear blue sky. Mary brought some food for them to eat, while John carried some water to drink and to make tea. He told James and Mary Catherine he would make a fire on the beach while they could explore the seashore, wade in the water, and see if they could find some shells to collect. It was the first time any of them had been to a beach.

They trekked across the river flats and climbed to the top of the sand dune, where they stopped and looked out to sea. They could see for miles and the ocean was calm, blue and beautiful. There was no wind which was uncommon as Greenough was a windy place. When they looked north or south the beach stretched as far as they could see. To the south all they could see was white sand for miles. To the north it was the same except on that day John thought he could see the mouth of the Greenough River where it entered the sea. At first, they thought that there was no one on the beach north or south but when John looked to the north, he could just make out a group of people walking slowly towards them. They were about two miles away. John could not work out who they were, but it did not matter, and they ran down the sand dune onto the beach.

James and Mary Catherine raced directly to the water's edge, took off their boots and splashed in the water. None of them could swim but they had enormous fun running along the water's edge, getting their feet wet, splashing each other, and squealing in excitement. The water was a beautiful blue colour, warm, enticing and a world away from the dark brown water of the River Irwell in Manchester. John and Mary walked down to the water as well and took off their boots – walking along the water's edge getting their feet wet was a treat for them as well. The sand was so beautiful, clean, and soft that they did not need to put their boots on all afternoon.

After a while John walked back up the beach and started to collect some driftwood to start a fire. There were some pieces of wood scattered along the beach that had washed up with the tides over many months. Much of this was dry and he easily started a fire so he could boil some water to make some tea. It was then that he explained to Mary how to make tea the Australian way. She was intrigued as she had always made a pot of tea. John had other ideas. "It is the Australian bush way," he kept saying, and he had learnt it from the men at the mill in York. He produced a one-gallon metal container with a simple wire-loop handle and filled it with water. John had previously put two holes in either side of the top edge of the metal container. The holes were opposite each other and John had threaded a loop of wire to create a simple handle

When the water was boiling John put some tea into the container. Mary looked at this oddly as she always poured the water on top of the tea in a tea pot. That was the traditional British way. John then stood up and held the container by the looping wire handle. He took five steps away and spun the container in a vertical loop with his arm around and around. After five or so spins he put the container down and said again, "That's the Australian bush way. The container is called a billy" before pouring the tea.

As Mary and John were drinking their tea, they noticed James and Mary Catherine had ventured further up the beach, and it was an Aboriginal family whom John had seen earlier in the day walking down the beach. The family also had two children with them. There also seemed to be three or four adults. The Aboriginal children had run further away from the adults and were now running to James and Mary Catherine. They were having fun running in and out of the water. Mary stood up. She was not certain what was happening. Should she be afraid or calm? John stood up as well and looked anxiously up the beach. They knew the children had seen and played with Aboriginal children occasionally back near the mill, but this was away from the local community. Mary said to John anxiously, "I need to get them back," and she started to call out when the four children met up and started playing together running in and out of the water splashing each other and having fun.

Mary stood anxiously for a few minutes. The urgent shout to the children died in her throat. She calmed down and then sat. "They look like they are having fun," John said. "The children all seem to know how to play together." With that the four children spent the next few hours playing along the beach. Occasionally they would run up the sand dunes and run back down again or tumble down rolling over and over. Later the Aboriginal children showed them how to dig for some molluscs and find some beautiful seashells. Language did not seem to be a problem.

The adults sat down further up the beach and like John and Mary built a fire. After an hour or so two of the men stood up and picked up what looked like long slender spears and walked down to the water's edge, stood for 15 minutes looking out to sea, and then waded into the water with their spears held at shoulder height. John and Mary looked at them and wondered what they were doing. Should they be afraid of these people with spears. Slowly the men waded through the water looking down as they went. Every now and then one would lift his spear and thrust it into the water only to produce nothing. "I think they are fishing," said John. After about 30 minutes one of the men produced a large fish on the end of his spear. "Looks about a pound," said John. From their distance it looked like a nice fish. It seemed they had located a small school of fish as they now speared several nice sized fish over the next few minutes putting the fish into a net bag made of string from the local reeds which hung off their waists.

When they had enough fish the two men slowly walked back out of the water and back to their companions who were seated around the fire on the sand. Still the children played. Mary and John started to eat some of the food they had bought with them when John looked up and noticed the two men were walking towards them with their long spears hanging idly in their hands below waist level. Both men were dark haired with beards and were slim but looked strong. Neither were tall but not short either. One was older than the other as he had some grey hair around the side of his head. Still, they walked up towards John and Mary carrying their spears. Mary looked over anxiously to John as she had no interaction with the local Indigenous Australians other than when some of the women and children walked past their house on their way to collect water from the river. They used to laugh and wave to each other. They seemed friendly enough.

John noticed that they were talking to each other. Were they scheming something? Would they attack and use their spears? John wondered. As they got closer, John and Mary stood up and Mary stepped back a little to be just behind John. She did not know what to do.

Suddenly one of the two men produced two lovely fish and handed them to John, smiled and said some kind sounding words. John took the fish, smiled, and said, "Thank you, that's very kind," and they were gone. John stood there with two fresh fish in his hands watching the men slowly walk away chatting.

John and Mary looked at each other and looked again at the men walking away and laughed. What a strange experience. They did not know whether they felt relieved or excited but as they chatted, they really appreciated the kindness of the Aborigines. Mary took the fish, cleaned, scaled and then filleted them. She had become skilled at cooking fish since she landed in Greenough. In England she never had fresh fish. John called the children over and the two Aboriginal children came over too. All six had a meal of cooked fish, some fresh bread Mary made the previous day and some boiled vegetables.

At the end of the day, they trekked back to their home. All were exhausted but Mary Catherine and James could not stop chatting how they enjoyed playing with the other children, found some molluscs in the sand near the water's edge and what pretty shells they collected. John and Mary realised that the Aboriginals were generous and nice people who simply needed to be treated well. John thought about the Irish and how the Irish felt that the English had taken their land and how in some ways it was the same here. They were farming on the Aboriginals' traditional land. After all, it was their land, originally.

"Once a jolly swagman camped by a billabong.
Under the shade of a coolabah tree,
And he sang as he watched and waited till his Billy boiled.
You'll come a-waltzing Matilda, with me."

(Accredited to Australian poet A.B. Patterson}

(Source – public domain)

14

Mary Catherine

Mary Catherine first saw the snake in the grass behind the mill. Initially she just saw the long slender brown body quickly weaving away from her further into the bushland. She had never seen a snake before in Manchester or on the journey out from England and the long slender brown body covered in glistening scales fascinated her. All the things here were new to her. The bright blue sky, the lovely sunshine, the big, tall kangaroos which lazed in the shade under the bush all day and the long lizard-like goannas with their muscular bodies and sharp claws all caught her attention. The kangaroos did not seem to mind Mary Catherine looking at them. Occasionally they would lift their heads, look at her and then go back to sleep. Once she saw two six-foot tall male kangaroos fighting each other. They were boxing like the young lads back in England with jabs and an upright stance. Neither seemed to win. Maybe it was just too hot at that time. She loved all the birds as well, and as she walked through the bush near her home she often saw the birds nesting high up in the trees. Her favourite was the black cockatoo with its distinctive white feathers underneath its wings. It was always around when rain was imminent. There were also plenty of white corellas which to Mary Catherine looked just like a cockatoo but pure white.

Goannas were plentiful too. The biggest she had seen was a monster about four foot long. It just meandered lazily swinging from side to side looking for food and occasionally scratching the ground digging small holes. All the goannas she had seen were deep brown in colour with a blotchy lighter colour pattern. She thought this was a wonderful pattern to camouflage them in bushland. The goannas did not mind Mary Catherine and many times if she kept still, they would just walk right on past her with their long-pointed pink tongues flicking out and their slanted eyes peering along the ground for food. Once she saw one running across the field and she was surprised how fast it could go, but normally they just wandered about slowly looking for insects, eggs and small reptiles to eat. The mice around the mill seemed to attract them and Mary Catherine guessed the mice attracted the snake as well.

Mary Catherine asked her father about the animals. Considering that John was lucky to escape alive from a snake bite back in Fremantle and the fact the colony was petrified of snakes, John forbade Mary Catherine from ever going near them. He said "Just leave them alone and keep your distance" and continued, "Be careful. The snakes are very poisonous, fast and some of the most dangerous in the world. They could easily kill a person and in fact one of the local farmers was bitten last year by a snake that he surprised in his shed. He tried to kill it with a stick but the farmer died within a day."

Still Mary Catherine liked to walk past the back of the mill looking for the big brown snake she saw that day. One day she saw it again and she stopped like she did with the goannas and kept still. This time she saw the whole snake and it was about five feet long and thick. It quickly slid in a weaving fashion through the grass once again from the mill. It seemed to flatten itself against the ground and moved with its head slightly raised. It had dark attentive eyes on either side of its small head. There was a gentle breeze blowing past Mary Catherine towards the snake and it stopped, lifted its head, and flicked its forked tongue out in the air. It seemed to sense Mary Catherine and immediately disappeared into the grass and beyond. Mary Catherine was surprised how fast it was and she followed trying to feel those lovely shiny scales, but it was gone. Mary Catherine was seven years old.

James did not share Mary Catherine's fascinations with the wildlife. He was really scared of snakes and stayed well clear of the goannas and even the kangaroos that lazed in the shade of the trees. He had to help build a high fence around the vegetable garden to keep the kangaroos away from eating the plants. To him the snakes looked evil with their dark shiny scales, dark eyes and reputation for venomous bites that could lead to instant death. Still Mary Catherine was fascinated.

Mary Catherine was loving her lessons in their makeshift classroom in the old hut near the wheat mill. The ex-convict teacher was knowledgeable, kind and patient with the children. He taught for a few hours in the morning then worked in the mill for the rest of the day. The mill owners and John Maley supported his time to instruct the children as they saw it a critical part of establishing a strong vibrant community in Greenough. They knew in time the government would build a proper school in Greenough but in the meantime they needed to support the activity. Many of the children had never had lessons before, and in some cases like Mary Catherine and James, their mothers had never had any education. From an early age they did chores and, in many cases, worked in the various industrial mills in Victorian England. Mary told Mary Catherine that she never went to school and at six years of age she was working in a mill. It was illegal now but then it was a normal activity. Consequently, Mary was illiterate.

After school Mary Catherine could play until lunch time and then she helped her mother with the chores and tending the vegetable garden. James worked helping his dad in the mill bagging flour and filling the mill feed bins with wheat.

One day after school Mary Catherine decided to skip past the back of the mill once again on her way home. She had forgotten about the snake now as she had not seen it for a long while. The grass had gotten longer as Greenough had experienced some rain from a recent cyclone up in the north, and with the summer warmth the area was greener and the grass taller. Quickly she skipped through the thick grass and suddenly she felt a lump under her foot. She looked down and screamed as the large brown snake she had stepped on viscously whipped around and bit her several times on her bare leg. It then dropped to the ground and rapidly disappeared into the tall grass. Mary Catherine staggered in shock as she went pale, fainted, then collapsed amongst the tall grass. The several red puncture marks on her white leg oozed with venom and mixed with blood as she lay stunned and motionless in the grass. Her dark long hair and pale limbs spread out among the green grass in the sunlight.

Several hours later Mary wondered where Mary Catherine was, so she walked over to the school to check on her. Sometimes she was late for the midday meal as she was playing with her friends or simply got lost in time looking at the birds or goannas. No one had seen her, and the teacher was in the mill working with John. She started to get worried and collected the other children and went searching for Mary Catherine. After an hour they found her on the ground, cold, silent and still, not far from the back of the mill. Mary slumped among the grass and sobbed in grief as she held her dead child's now cold little hand.

(Source – Unsplash)

"Words cannot cure a broken heart from the loss of a child...only time can."
Anonymous

15

Doherty's Inferno

The old proverb that time heals all wounds is true, however in the case of Mary and John the loss of their young daughter was heart-breaking. In the wilderness of the northern Colony of Western Australia families were close and worked together. In the short seven months that John knew Mary Catherine he quickly learned to love that beautiful adventurous child who loved nature and embraced her new country and friends with such enthusiasm that it was infectious. Now she and her laughter were gone forever. She would not grow up to be that lovely woman she deserved to be. It reminded John of the loss of his mother which, while many years ago, still felt like yesterday. Sometimes he could still feel her hand in his like when they walked together along the River Lagan in Dromore, Ireland.

By the middle of the year Mary was due to give birth. She and John were blessed with another daughter who they aptly called Catherine after her older sister Mary Catherine. She was a happy, healthy baby and the first child to be born in the region to the people who worked in the mill, so there was reason to celebrate and put behind the tragic sadness of the past six months. Forrest made his garden at his house available for the celebration and John once again brought his fiddle, played and sang a few traditional Irish tunes, a few new Australian songs plus the old ballad, "Bound for South Australia", which he learned on the voyage from Portland.

John had it in his mind to play one of his favourite Irish folk songs, "Black Velvet Band" but now the last two verses which he sang with gusto in Bradford no longer appealed to him.

> As I went strolling down Regent
> not intending to stray very far
> I met with a frolicsome damsel
> applying her trade in a bar
> a watch she stole from a customer
> and slipped it right into my hand
> the very first day that I met her,
> bad luck to the black velvet band
>
> Before judge and jury next morning,
> both of us were to appear
> a gentleman claimed his jewellery
> and the case against us was quite clear
> seven long years transportation
> right down to Van Diemen's Land
> far away from my friends and companions
> betrayed by the black velvet band.

*Source – Public Domain Swindells of Manchester circ
-1796 and 1853*

While John was sad, he realised they needed to move on from their loss. Mary too realised this and with her new daughter she gradually moved on from her sweet Mary Catherine. Later that year in September the family travelled up to Champion Bay and had Catherine baptised. It was the 8th of September, 1861. They lit a candle in the church and said prayers for Mary Catherine too, so she was not forgotten.

At that time Forrest had been helping John get a tillage sub-lease and in the following year, 1862, John and the family built a simple cottage of local limestone, wattle and daub with a thatched roof on their new property. It was like the cottage near the mill but slightly larger with a second small enclosure out the back for keeping tools and other equipment. John, Mary and James also established a vegetable garden next to the house to provide produce for themselves and for the local market on the weekend. The sub-lease made John, for the first time in his life, self-employed. Forrest had been a great support and he said he did so because John was hard working, trustworthy and reliable. He also wanted John to work in the mill in the milling season to maintain the mill properly and when John's harvest was complete John would work milling the wheat and other cereals from the surrounding farms. John's simple ambitions were coming true.

Over the next year John built a stable for the cow and horse he bought, and started growing hay, which was proving to be worthwhile, as well as wheat. He would harvest the hay before the seeds developed so that the hay was a nutritious feed stock for the graziers' cattle when extra feed was required. He stored the hay in his haystack next to the stable and would sell it to the graziers when the price was right.

Later that year Ellen was born giving James and Catherine a young sister. Once again, they visited Champion Bay to have Ellen baptised in the church, light a candle and say a prayer for Mary Catherine. It was December 8, 1862. The following year was fruitful for John and the mill in Greenough. The rain was adequate and the yields on the farm were good, as was the work in the mill. James was now thirteen and growing into a young man. He was getting taller and stronger so was an immense help to John on the farm and in the mill bagging and loading bags of flour. Forrest really appreciated this diligent hard working young lad, so he took the time to help teach him as well.

Later in the year a new Ticket of Leave man, John Doherty, arrived from Champion Bay to take up farming on a property south and adjacent to John. The land had already been farmed before and there was a hut that Doherty could live in. The land was already cleared but the wheat crop had failed the year before due to poor farming practices.

Doherty was new to farming. He told John his background was as a steam-loom weaver in Perth, Scotland, so he did not have the background to understand how to farm well – especially in these new lands. In fact, he had never farmed or lived on a farm before. He was used to the city. Perth is north of Edinburgh in Scotland, and it was cold and cool even in summer, so he was still struggling with the extremely hot weather in Greenough.

In the first few weeks he would seek out John and talk about farming techniques but still he struggled to even start working. He told John he arrived in February 1861 from Portland prison on the *Palmerston* and obtained his Ticket of Leave in December in 1863. Like John, he worked in the prison and then in the work gangs before he moved to Champion Bay later that month for work. Doherty was a bit shorter than John, had dark hair, was unmarried and about 20 years younger than John which placed him in his mid to late-20s. John would often see Doherty struggling to till the soil or clear new areas on his land.

Despite the good rains around the region Doherty continued to struggle. No matter what John and the other farmers told him, he seemed not to listen and be aimless. John and the other farmers knew it was difficult physically and mentally for anyone to go through what Doherty had experienced in prison. He would have been transported from his home region and family to Portland to work in the quarry, spent months at sea followed by a few years in Fremantle prison before ending up at the edge of civilisation on a farm on his own and with few skills suitable for farming. At some point in England, he also would have spent significant time in solitary confinement which John realised was very damaging to many convicts. Physically it was demanding but mentally it was very tough. It was the reason many prisons like The Establishment in Fremantle had an asylum nearby to house and treat the mentally disturbed prisoners who were crushed by the penal system. John really appreciated that Mary had come out to join him because it gave him the support and comfort of family around him. No matter how hard life was it was always better with Mary and the children there.

As the days went by, John kept a look out for Doherty. Some days he would not see him at all and he would walk over to check on him. Doherty was appreciative but to John he seemed to be sleeping. He was concerned about him and knew of the few cases he saw in Fremantle prison where prisoners would be taken to the hospital for observation as they had gone insane. John was not a doctor but knew Doherty was not well, physically or mentally.

Late in the year this all seemed to close in on Doherty and he snapped emotionally. One late December day he set fire to his house and stable. The thatch roof burst into flames which rose many tens of feet into the sky, billowing smoke which could be seen for miles around. All the neighbours came over from their work in the fields and out of their homes to try to put out the inferno. John and Mary came running to help as well. There was little water to use, and the inferno quickly tore through Doherty's hut destroying the few pieces of furniture he had and everything else in it. The strong southerly wind aided the fire. The inferno was so hot that none of the people coming to his aid could enter the house to retrieve any of his meagre possessions.

As John and Mary looked around from the help they were providing Doherty, they suddenly realised that their big concern was no longer Doherty's hut, which was now destroyed, but their own stables, haystacks and cottage. The sparks from the inferno flew with the prevailing southerly wind across the farm and started a grass fire, firstly on Doherty's property but then it rapidly spread to John's and Mary's property. With the hot summer wind, the dry grass caught fire and spread rapidly. Quickly they and the other farmers tried to stamp out the grass fire with their feet and shovels, but the fire kept moving with the wind and it was now fifty yards across. Swiftly it reached their stable which burst into flames along with the stacks of hay which were stored as cattle feed during the scorching summer months. Fortunately, their cow and horse were out grazing in the field.

John and Mary watched hopelessly as the flames reached high into the sky and black smoke could be seen for miles around. They then suddenly realised that their own home was in the line of the fire and rushed to drag out what possessions they could into the field away from the direction of the flames. The other neighbours abandoned trying to stop the grass fire and rushed to help the Arnolds rescue their possessions.

All the neighbours rushed in and carried all the Arnold's possessions away from the fire and tried to stamp out the grass fires that were now racing towards the house. Still the fire blazed in the stable and storage area sending embers high into the sky. John watched helplessly as the embers landed on the southern side of the thatched roof of their home and started spot fires. Within a few minutes the entire roof burst into flames and their home was engulfed.

Later that evening, around 6 p.m. as the sun was going down in the west, John and Mary looked hopelessly at the charred remains of their stable, haystack and home. All their toil had now gone up in flames. They and the neighbours were able to rescue all their possessions and tools, but their home was gutted. John gathered the three children and Mary and put his arms around them all. He thought to himself that he had been through the potato famine, lost his parents, been imprisoned, tortured, confined to solitary confinement and whipped so he had seen the worst many times over many years and survived. He would not let this misfortune define him or his family so he said, "We will not let this destroy us. It is a challenge given to us to prove how strong we really are. We have come a long way together and we will overcome this." Mary wept. The children looked at the charred remains of their home in disbelief.

With that John walked over to check on Doherty to make sure he was safe, but he had fled. Then John, Mary and James started the lengthy process of cleaning up the mess that was once their stable, haystack and home. Luckily, some of the home was made of stone so the base structure was recoverable, the crops in the field were intact and so were most of his tools. The vegetable garden was saved, as were Mary's sewing materials, buttons and threads. John and James still had work in the mill to earn extra money.

Forrest came over from the mill to help when he saw the smoke in the sky. When he saw the devastation to the Arnold's home, he and some neighbours went back to the storeroom at the mill and brought back some canvas to use as tents. With the neighbours' help they pitched two tents. One was for the Arnolds and the other was to provide shelter for the possessions. It was rudimentary but that was all they had.

A few days later in the New Year, the local constable, Police Constable Goodwin, visited John and Mary to inspect the now burnt-out farmhouses. He had in his hand two documents. One was a summons for John Doherty to answer for the fire he started but Doherty had fled and neither the Arnolds nor any of the neighbours knew where he went. Apparently, no one else in the wider community had seen him either. The second document was John's conditional pardon meaning he was now a free man and could travel freely anywhere except return to England. He could travel and work anywhere he wanted in this country. At the time this really meant little to John and Mary except that he did not need to report to the magistrate every six months and live by the Ticket of Leave conditions. However, he had always wanted to visit Adelaide and Melbourne as there was little history of convicts in those places and he felt he would be treated differently. So, these towns were now on his mind. He was free and could travel. Shortly afterwards Mary realised she was expecting again. This would be child number five after James, Mary Catherine, Catherine and Ellen. John privately hoped it was a boy to be a brother for James, but Mary would be happy if the birth was easy and the child was happy and healthy.

Later that month, on the 19th of January, John heard that Constable Goodwin had caught up with John Doherty and arrested him. John did not follow up on the issue and simply left it to the police and magistrate to decide what to do with Doherty. He did not want anything to do with the process of sending anyone into the prison system nor did he want to have anything to do with courts, magistrates or the police. He just wanted to be left alone in peace and out of that system.

Over the first half of 1864, John, with the help of James and Mary, painstakingly rebuilt the farmhouse in their spare time while living in the tent. It was a rough way to live but they had little choice. They had some money in reserve and used this to buy the building materials they needed and paid three Ticket of Leave men to assist with the heavy lifting and new stonework. They offset the cost of the labour by providing meals and a tent for them to sleep in. The Ticket of Leave men recently had just left The Establishment in Fremantle, so they were happy to be relatively free living away from the confines of a cell, the daily chains of the work gangs and the constant supervision. One man was a skilled stonemason from his work back in England so the stonework on the new house looked much better than the previous home. John felt pleased that he could assist the Ticket of Leave men just as Forrest and Padbury had helped him. He also extended the house to make it bigger with a little more storage out the back. The stable took a little longer but by mid-year with the help he brought in plus the reused materials the home and stable were rebuilt. In August, their new child was born. It was a girl giving them one boy and three girls. Again, they visited Champion Bay to have Teresa Jessie baptised plus light a candle in the church and say prayers for Mary Catherine. She was never forgotten.

About this time a Father Patrick McCabe, who had arrived at Champion Bay as the first resident priest in 1860, started building the first Catholic church in the Victoria District at Greenough. John volunteered to help build the church, but Father McCabe left the district soon after and the work on the new church stopped. The next priest was Belgian, called Father Adolphus Lecaille. He, John and some fellow farmers and ex-convicts helped restart the construction of the Catholic church in the district. John and Mary were happy as this was the start of a church for them in the area and, perhaps in time, a Catholic school as well.

Over the next two years the harvest was good for John and his small farm prospered. Little by little he tried innovative ideas in farming – some worked out and some did not. One season he planted an area for oats but the yield was poor and the price was low. He would have been better off just growing wheat. Another time he grew more hay and stored it in his shed. As it turned into a dry summer the hay was in big demand and the price rose. Every season he and Mary saved money. He was concerned however about the rumours in the area regarding the Greenough River. These came from the local Indigenous Australians whose families had been in the region for an exceptionally long time. Their concern was that approximately every ten years in late summer a very large and dangerous storm system would come down the coast from the tropical northern areas. Many times, the storm would rage and move inland where it would dump a large amount of rain in a brief period. This happened further up north regularly. The Greenough River was over two hundred miles long and the catchment area was over 5000 square miles or 3.2 million acres so if it did rain significantly in the catchment area, the flooding could be devastating as all the rainfall would then drain into the Greenough River and flow through the coastal Greenough flats where the farms were located before emptying into the sea.

John did take this seriously and felt he was lucky as his land was up the slope from the river to the east which gave him more protection. He also felt they had stayed long enough. About 18 months after the repairs to their home and stable, John and Mary decided after a particularly good harvest season that they would sell their farm, house and stable and move up to the Champion Bay area to live. The funds from the sale of their sub-lease and the money they had saved gave them enough money to take the chance and move. John also thought that Greenough was overdue for serious flooding.

Champion Bay was part of the small town of Geraldton. It was growing steadily, and John saw an opportunity to work as a builder constructing homes for the slowly growing population. He had stayed connected with the three Ticket of Leave men who helped him rebuild his house and he was keen to employ them in his business. It was 1866.

Padbury's Mill – Greenough
(Source – Michael Le Page)

"Our greatest glory is not falling but
rising every time we fall."
Confucius

16

Champion Bay

In January 1840 George Moore, the Colony of Western Australia's attorney-general, sailed into Champion Bay and named the bay after the vessel in which he was sailing. Ten years later Augustus Gregory explored the area and named the site of the town after the governor of the region, Charles FitzGerald. Hence Geraldton got its name. The town site was surveyed in 1850. When John and his growing family moved to Champion Bay, Geraldton was a crescent shaped town located on the shores of Champion Bay. The population was small with just a few thousand people, and most were located around that small coastal area.

The Arnolds initially moved into some temporary and simple accommodation that John had arranged prior to leaving Greenough. Shortly afterwards, he walked down to the convict hiring depot on Chapman Road with his son James. James was now a tall, dark haired, strong youth of sixteen who had been labouring at the mill in Greenough and on the farm for several years. He was a willing worker skilled in milling and had some experience in construction from rebuilding the farmhouse. He was getting stronger and used to hard physical work. John would often remind young James of his grandfather's advice: "Wherever you work arrive a bit early, leave a bit later than required, work hard, do real quality work and learn to get better at what you do. Implement this advice and you will always be successful." James consequently also had a decent work ethic.

The convict depot building was a relatively new single story, limestone building built in 1856 just three years after the first depot north of Fremantle was established in Lynton to provide labour for the new Geraldine lead mine. The depot was designed to provide accommodation for Ticket of Leave convicts and a place from which they could seek work or potential employers could visit to seek labour for their businesses. The police station was part of the convict depot and a warden's house was built at the back. John was looking for the three Ticket of Leave men who helped him on his farm as he knew all three were now living in Champion Bay. At the depot he was provided with some information on where he could find them. They were working on public works for the government as they could not find any private employment.

The same day John went looking for a friend of Forrest's back in Greenough. His name was Barry Johnson. Forrest said Barry might help John get established in constructing some of the new buildings in the area. Forrest's friend was true to his word and offered John and James some work on a project that he was constructing down at the port opposite the harbour master's cottage. It was to be the first permanent school building in the town. John enquired if his three colleagues could also find work with him. Johnson agreed that all three could work for John as he was having a lot of difficulty getting hard-working experienced people to work in Champion Bay. He said he could get labourers, but many had little or no skills, and some just did not want to work hard. John also explained that all three were good workers and one was an experienced stonemason while the other two were willing labourers. The building planned was a single-story limestone and timber building so it would suit all their skills. With the arrangements in place John and James went looking for the three former labourers.

They found them working on a town bridge construction project on the edge of the settlement. They were glad to see John and James again and willingly agreed to work for him. They were on government work so could easily move as there were some Ticket of Leave men available, provided they advised the magistrate and filled out the required government paperwork. Thus began John's small building business in Champion Bay.

Mary and their daughters settled in well. They were used to living rough in the country so the move to the town was easy as there were a few more small benefits like small shops which were close by, easier access to water and the community with their church. The small, basic house they were living in was on the north-eastern edge of town. It was suitable for their needs and had room for a vegetable garden and space to do their dressmaking. Mary found a small group linked to the church who would take the two older girls and teach them some Bible stories plus some basic reading and writing. She did not have any lofty expectations. She was illiterate and John had some skills in reading and writing but she thought it would be good for her daughters to meet some other children plus learn about the Bible. She also continued with her dressmaking and growing vegetables for the local market. It helped with their savings.

She also noticed that some of the ex-convicts in the town seemed to struggle with working and alcohol as they drifted through life. In Greenough she seldom saw this as it was remote and the people on the farms needed to work hard just to survive. Here in the town the convict depot provided a base for some ex-convicts where they could sleep and be fed. She would often see them in town, these seemingly broken old men. While John and his three workers worked hard, some others could not keep a job and ended up back in the depot repeatedly. A few re-offended from simple mistakes like drunkenness and vagrancy and then they would spend more time in jail. They just did not get rehabilitated and had no aim in life. She wondered why this happened. Maybe it was the isolation of solitary confinement they had endured. However, most of the ex-convicts, like John, never re-offended and lived perfectly ordinary lives.

One thing Mary noticed in town was the way the townsfolk regarded the ex-convicts and their families. Even though John had committed a relatively small crime and paid an enormous price, some people in the town still treated them like they were all hardened criminals, and not only could they not be trusted but neither could their wives and children. In England there were social classes based on who your family was and their status. This existed much less here in the Colony of Western Australia but there persisted a divide between the free settlers and the ex-convicts and their families. It did not worry Mary so much as she lived with the rigid class structure in England and was aware where she fitted into that class structure. People had made it clear she was working class. However, she resented that her children were being treated unfairly simply because John was an ex-convict, and that they were all tarred with the same brush.

For John, it did not cause him any concern as he had lived through an extremely harsh and unfair penal system, so a minor concern among townsfolk that he was an ex-convict did not worry him in the least. He walked like a free man because he was. His strong belief was that if he worked hard here in the Colony of Western Australia, he and his family would be able to do well, have their own home and look after themselves. He never had those opportunities in Ireland or England, and the thought he could own his own farm and house was never a possibility there. Here in the Colony of Western Australia he could do both as these things were the reward for hard work, saving and determination. Back in England and Ireland years of hard work bought survival, nothing more. The other thing John was aware of was that he was now 52 years old and had he stayed in England the harshness of the vast industrial slums and rampant disease would have meant a much shorter life for him. In England, the probability was that he would have passed away before he was forty years old.

The construction work for John and his labourers continued through late 1866, 1867 and into 1868. In early 1868 he and Mary agreed they were missing life on a farm and the farming community. He regularly had visits from people he knew in Greenough, and he heard that good blocks of farmland were becoming available further south in the Irwin district near the small village of Dongara on the Irwin River. The land available was adjacent to the river and was fertile. He also knew John Smith and John Malley who had built a wheat mill on the southern bank of the Irwin River close to the farming area a few years earlier in 1865. It was also not far from the small port called Irwin Port which had only recently been renamed Port Denison. The mill was on the south side of the river and about a mile from the port and a mile from Dongara. After some more enquiries John and Mary decided to buy one hundred acres of land in the Irwin district and start a farm. It was location 4303. Mary was pregnant again when they sold up their business and moved taking a cart down past Greenough to the Irwin River and beyond. It was 1868.

(Wheat field – source – public domain)

"If you are born in the country, no matter what you do you will always miss the country."
Anonymous

17

Dongara

In 1859 before Mary arrived in Fremantle, John Smith started farming in Irwin district. To have his wheat milled he built the first mill in the area in 1865 with John Malley who also had a mill in Greenough. It was the first piece of industry in that area. To ship his milled wheat and other products away, coastal boats anchored at the mouth of the Irwin River and men carried bags of wheat or other product on their shoulders out to rowing boats. These were then pushed through the shoals and rowed carefully through a narrow passage between coral reefs to the waiting schooners.

Later the next year in 1867 a jetty was built at the foot of Herbert Street by ex-convict Ben Mason to bring in provisions and take out products like wheat, other cereals, wool and flour which was milled in the area. Occasionally over time copper ore from the Wheal Arrino mine and other small mines located to the southeast of Dongara was also shipped out of the jetty. In addition, near the jetty George Shenton built a limestone warehouse the same year to store wool, wheat, flour and a range of agricultural products for shipping.

The Irwin area was first explored by Lieutenant George Grey in 1839. It was the home of the Warrandee tribe. He named the area the Province of Victoria and the river after his friend Major Frederick Irwin. He and his crew were walking back to the Swan River Colony after they were shipwrecked up at Gantheaume Bay to the north of Geraldton.

When John and Mary passed through the village called Dongara on the north side of the river on the way to their farm, they passed a hotel, a few businesses and some houses. The Irwin Arms hotel was relatively new and was built by Joseph Walton who was also an ex-convict. The main road in the village was called Waldeck Street. The roads were rudimentary but passable and there was no bridge over the river just a rough stone causeway called Walton's Crossing. They sensed there was opportunity here with the port development and the slow but growing town development.

When they approached the Irwin River the road passed down into a small flood plain, so John had a good look about. What he saw was some nice fertile land close to the river where some people were growing some small crops and vegetables. He saw one house being built by a young man called Titus Russ on the south side of the river to the east of the road. He knew, based on the comments from the Aborigines in Greenough, that once in 10 years or so the area would receive a significant amount of rain in a brief time and this area would be under water. Occasionally it would be unbelievably bad, and it would be under 20 to 30 feet of floodwater. It was not a safe place to build but he also knew many of the farming areas were adjacent to the river for many miles to the east. Shortly after their arrival Annie Arnold was born in Dongara.

In the Dongara area there were a few ex-convicts like John, so he already had a network of people he knew from The Establishment in Fremantle. They were able to help each other with advice and support when necessary. George Brand was one. He arrived in Fremantle on board *Stag* in June 1855 and received his Ticket of Leave in 1856 so he knew John from his time in The Establishment. George's wife Isabella and children joined him in 1859 in Greenough. By 1867 George had enough finances to support buying 90 acres, so when John and Mary arrived George was already established in farming and provided some advice about the district and how to farm the land effectively.

Richard Sparkes was another ex-convict who arrived on the *Stag* in 1855 and knew John from The Establishment in Fremantle. He moved to Dongara and was working as a mason and builder when John arrived. Richard was a useful builder in the area and had been contracted to build the stone obelisk at Port Irwin now called Port Denison. It was used to guide ships through the reefs into the port. Richard was able to help John and gave him many contacts for Ticket of Leave men who could help him, for wages, to clear land and build his modest stone cottage.

Not long after John and Mary settled in Dongara an ex-convict, James Mountain, arrived in Dongara with his wife Bridget and four children who arrived on the *Hastings* in 1864. John knew him as they both sailed out to Western Australia on the *Adelaide*. James was a carpenter and they worked together in Champion Bay. James took to farming like John and held several tillage leases which were off to the east of Dongara along the bank of the Irwin River. The land was fertile but prone to seasonal flooding. His farm was close to Mountain Crossing and Mountain Gap which were named after James' farm due to its proximity.

James Hibbert was another ex-convict in the Dongara area John knew from his transport out from England on the *Adelaide* and from time in The Establishment. James however struggled and was regularly involved with the police from problems with alcohol and drunkenness. Occasionally, John would travel into the town centre and see James sitting in the shade under a tree. He would stop by and sit with him for a while and have a smoke. However, James continued to struggle. Life did not work out well for many ex-convicts, especially those without a family who could work together and support each other.

John, Mary and James set about developing their one hundred acres and building a cottage. In many ways it seemed like they were starting over again but they had done this before. They knew what to do plus they had some money they had saved. Once they got started, they hired some Ticket of Leave men to help build the limestone, wattle and daub home with a thatched roof and clear more of the land for farming. It was back-breaking work to clear the land as they only had axes and mattocks to use. Once the trees were felled, the trees and scrubs were dragged into a heap and burned. The cleared land was then ploughed using a single furrowed plough and then the soil was hand seeded. A sickle and scythe were used to harvest. All of this was done by hand. They also built a stable and an area for hay. Once they were settled and the available land was cleared John decided to expand, and he later purchased the adjacent 100-acre farm on lot 5171 giving him two hundred acres. His land was now much larger than he had in Greenough, and it gave him a significant opportunity to prosper. He also was far exceeding his and Mary's dreams by owning that much land on their own. John and James put in their first wheat crop. Mary and the girls started their vegetable garden, dressmaking and regular trips to the markets in Dongara to sell their products and purchase the regular basic items they needed.

One morning when James was inspecting this first crop in the northern field, he noticed small brown patches on the wheat leaves which were odd to him as he had never seen them before. He went over to where John was working and together they walked back to examine the discolouration that James had seen. John had seen this before and he called it wheat rust. It was fungus he said. As it was warm weather, they noticed over the next few weeks the 'rust' moved quickly across the crop in this northern field. John assumed the fungus was spreading with the southerly breeze which was normal in the area, and he was now concerned as this could devastate his entire wheat crop. To stop the growth of the rust he decided to burn the areas where the rust was located to kill off the fungus. This worked for him, but he lost about 50 per cent of his crop. Many of the farmers in the area were not so lucky and they lost almost their entire crop.

With the loss of most of the wheat crop in the area the government decided to provide rations to the farmers to help them survive. For the Arnolds this was extremely helpful. For many others it was a matter of survival. To help with the loss of income John and James went to visit Smith and Malley to ask if they could work in the mill or take on any construction work which might be needed. As Smith and Malley knew John and James, they offered them work immediately to bring in the extra experience and muscle they needed. This provided the extra income for John and James to help fund the farm in that bleak year. The mill was also not far from their farm on the south side of the river.

Over the next few years, the weather was good with reasonable rain, and John was much more knowledgeable about controlling the rust, so his wheat yields improved. His two hundred acres provided him the opportunity to grow hay as well so he could sell hay to the pastoralists over the summer. Both John and James kept working at the mill and in construction outside the harvest and seeding times to provide much needed income. Again, John and Mary kept saving where they could. Around this time in 1873 John and Mary decided that they would like to consider moving to the east to see what living in Adelaide or Melbourne would be like and to provide more opportunities for their growing family away from the isolation of the northern wheat areas of Irwin and Greenough. Both Mary and John wanted to give their daughters in particular the opportunities that existed in the bigger towns. James enjoyed farming and was good at it and mill work so he would thrive anywhere.

It was also rumoured there was no convict transportation to Adelaide or Melbourne in the past so the stigma of being an ex-convict did not exist there as it did in places like the Colony of Western Australia and reportedly in Tasmania and New South Wales. Mary and now John felt the free settlers still treated them differently even though John had his conditional pardon for over 10 years and had operated his own businesses for much longer than that. He had never since been in trouble with the police, so he had a clean record. He was however asked one time to report in front of a magistrate for being on crown land taking timber. At the time Mary asked, "John what is this about being on Crown land collecting timber?" John was silent for a while and replied, "I really don't know. I was over the back of our property, on the eastern side near the road and some people from Dongara were riding past. I was carrying some timber that I had cut down from our property over to a log pile I was building so I could burn it. My plan was to start ploughing that area next month so it would be ready in time for seeding. I think that the travellers thought I was on Crown land at that time and not on our own land. Why would I go onto Crown land to collect timber when I had plenty on my own property?" This was dismissed by the magistrate as there was no evidence, just a complaint without any information and John felt to himself it was probably someone who disliked ex-convicts who were doing well.

It was the same, around that time, for John Holt who also was an ex-convict. He arrived on the *Merchantman* in 1864 in Fremantle. He received his Ticket of Leave soon after in 1866 and worked as a carpenter before moving to Dongara. In the early 1870s he had acquired land for farming and was also charged with unlawful removal of timber from Crown lands and fined thirteen shillings and six pence. He, like John Arnold, was furious of his treatment and later in 1877 petitioned the government, with others, complaining about the active discrimination against ex-convicts.

The police also seemed to find a need, even in this remote area, to check on them despite John and others having conditional pardons that said they were free to travel anywhere across the country. Mary was in fact a free settler and never a convict. John dressed like any of the free settlers and now spoke more with an Australian accent than Irish but still some people, especially the police, saw him as an ex-convict and treated him and his family differently.

In 1870 the police presence increased. Construction started on the first Dongara police station after the police were stationed in a room at Smith's mill for a couple of years. Joseph Walton, an ex-convict who built the hotel, also built the station. He was a good member of the district, a publican and builder. Prior to 1870, John Smith's mill seemed to be the centre of activity as it also acted as a post office. The police station was completed in April 1871, and it contained a court room, a magistrate's room, police office, a day room for police to do interviews plus jail cells. There were three two-person cells and a larger cell which could hold more people. On the outside was a veranda and at the back a courtyard. It was a nice building made from limestone rocks held together with local lime coupled with Jarrah timber shipped in from the south. Jarrah shingles were also used on the roof. With this came some more police.

Every month all through 1871 and 1872 either PC Pridmore, PC Waldock or later PC Kennedy would turn up at the Arnolds' farm for no other reason than to just check on them. On one occasion the police constable asked John about his dog which was on his farm. It was a dog one of the neighbours had given him as a pup. He asked if the dog was registered. John responded he was unaware he needed to register a dog on a farm several miles from the town of Dongara. The police constable responded he would need to report John had an unregistered dog and apply to the magistrate to see if John would be fined. John was subsequently fined one pound or one week's wages for having an unregistered dog on his farm miles from town.

John was terribly upset, not just by the penalty but the severity of it. It was also probable that if he was a free settler the police would not visit the farm and if they did, they would simply ask the farmer to register the dog or most probably not even inquire about a dog. If John did not pay the fine, it would become an offence for him and he could be incarcerated. This simply reinforced in his mind that it would be best for him and the family to look at moving away from the Colony of Western Australia to someplace where ex-convicts were not treated so poorly for extended periods. John also formed the view that government employees like police constables did not like seeing people like John prospering to the point where they were successful landholders and farmers. In many ways John was in a dilemma He knew the government officials like the police were strict on him and people like him, but he also knew that they were simply doing their job and following the instructions given to them by their superiors. When they visited, they were mostly friendly and respectful but the fact that they even needed to check is what concerned John.

With this decision in mind to explore the opportunity to move to Adelaide or Melbourne, James took on the main work on the farm aided by his growing sisters. James and John worked in the Smith and Malley mill after their harvest season and John took on some construction work with Mr Leverman who was contracted to build a new church in Dongara plus some other buildings. This provided John with some extra funds to save. He was earning four pounds and ten shillings per month from Mr Leverman.

Slowly over time they accumulated more funds and after the harvest and milling season John left the family just after New Year 1873 to travel by coastal vessel to Albany. Once in Albany his plan was to travel over to Adelaide to explore the area and see if it had good opportunities for the family and for work. He also wanted to see what the farming areas were like as a consideration to sell up in Dongara and buy a farm in South Australia. James was left in charge of the farming work. The older girls, Catherine, and Ellen were over ten years old now and were a significant help around the farm, the house, the vegetable garden and in dressmaking. Unfortunately, because they lived out of town, access to schools for the girls to learn to read and write was not available to them. At their age John did some teaching but essentially they were illiterate. James took John's place working with Leverman as Leverman was extremely comfortable having James working with him. James was now a strong, hardworking, experienced young man of 22 years.

John had not been on a coastal vessel since Mary arrived in 1860 when they sailed from Fremantle up to live in Greenough, so it was a long time ago. Occasionally when they were in Dongara the family would walk down to the beach on a Sunday after church past all the farms and over the sand dunes. John would sit on the sand and look out to sea wondering what it would be like to be at sea again. None of the family could swim but it was nice to sit on the beach and watch the young children run in the shallows and pick up seashells. It was quiet on the beach and often there would be no other people anywhere to be seen. The local Indigenous Australians would be there sometimes like they were up in Greenough, and they would spend hours showing the children how to catch fish, find shellfish and cook them on the beach. When they were in Champion Bay the water was a five-minute walk away, so they all spent more time along the beach than they did in Greenough.

After a long time working on the farm and in construction John enjoyed being back on a ship. As he was a paying passenger he was treated well and had the opportunity to enjoy the calm weather, sunshine and fresh sea air. No one treated him with suspicion and disrespect like an ex-convict. The crew gladly showed him how they operated the sails and pointed out the marine life along the way like the playful dolphins and the giant whales. Some even asked him what it was like to live in Champion Bay, Greenough and Dongara as they were interested in getting off the transient life on board a sailing vessel. The vessel stopped in Fremantle to discharge some passengers and cargo plus load up provisions for the trip back up the coast.

John got off the vessel in Fremantle and had two days in the town before his vessel was due to depart for Albany. He booked into the same hotel Mary, James and he stayed at when Mary arrived in 1860. The town had changed a lot. It was bigger with more people and more industry. However, it was still a small port town as he walked around it in an hour and a half. John did enjoy the time to just walk. As no one knew him he was treated as a free settler, and he liked that. Compared to when he walked these same streets many years before in his Ticket of Leave, prison issued suit of clothes, people treated him well. He had on a new suit of clothes, new boots and hat. He also stopped in at the barber shop and had his hair cut and his beard trimmed. He felt good and enjoyed the experience and treatment.

He walked up to The Establishment on the hill at the top end of the town and observed it from the outside. He stood across the road near the entrance. He had no interest in talking with anyone or going inside but it was interesting to see it again. It held a lot of bad memories with the flogging, solitary confinement, and chain gangs. When his mind went back to the Cat he remembered clearly being tied up, spreadeagled and vulnerable, the blood stains on the white limestone wall in front of him. And the beat of the drum. Why these things stuck in his mind he did not know. His memories of solitary confinement were fading as time passed, though he did remember the pivotal talk with Father Donovan and his kind and provoking words: "John," he said, "the Colony of Western Australia is a fantastic opportunity for you. You should count your blessings." Donovan probably saved his life he thought. Otherwise, if he had continued in his troubled ways, the prison system would have broken him and he too would be living in the asylum with his mind shattered. With that thought he turned and walked down Ord Street and stopped outside the now complete asylum. It too was a large building and he thought of his time there starting the construction and of the many convicts who had lost their mind due to the treatment in the prisons. He quickly turned and walked on back into town.

When the time came for him to board the ship bound for Albany, John was ready to leave. Fremantle did not hold any fond memories for him other than reconnecting with Mary, James and Mary Catherine when they arrived from England. He was looking forward to the next leg onto Albany then Adelaide.

As it was summer the weather going south was warm and calm. The storms and fierce winds normally came in late autumn and winter so the trip to Albany was peaceful. Once again as he was a paying passenger he was treated very well, unlike the three-month journey chained in the hold when he came from Portland to Fremantle so many years before. They saw a lot of whales while at sea and the crew taught John how to catch fish from the ship. He enjoyed the experience but from time to time wondered how the family and farm were progressing. John had not been to Albany before but knew it was the first English settlement in the west of Australia as the early explorers found an amazing safe and enormous harbour there back in 1791. Then Captain George Vancouver named the area King George III Sound and Princess Royal Harbour. It was more commonly known simply as King George Sound.

The ship's captain told John that Albany was settled by the English in late December 1826 and the Union Jack was raised for the first time January 21, 1827. It was a convenient place for a settlement as it was on the sea route from England to Port Jackson on Australia's east coast plus it allowed England to lay claim to the west of the continent.

When John landed in Albany in January 1873, he found a small settlement struggling to prosper but the surrounding areas were magnificent, and King George Sound was an impressive natural harbour. John only had a day in Albany before his vessel, the *Armistice* departed on January 27 so he asked where he could stay and was advised to seek out R Nesbitt's Spencer Inn just two streets up the hill from the main street called Stirling Street. As Albany was a small settlement it did not take long for him to walk around the area and find the inn. The following day he departed for Adelaide. On his departure he was disappointed to note that a clerk asked for his name and papers and if he was an ex-convict. He was then obliged to show his conditional pardon papers and his departure was documented as a departing ex-convict and conditional pardon holder. The government in the Colony of Western Australia kept track of him and all other ex-convicts.

The trip to Adelaide was uneventful. The sea was calm which was fortunate, and the wind was sufficient to get the vessel into Adelaide on schedule. On arrival he collected his few possessions and walked into the town near the port. He booked into the Railway Hotel on Commercial Road and walked down to the library further down the road and politely asked if he could see maps of the region. He was taken into the reading room where he looked over the maps and decided he would catch the train into Adelaide and then travel up to Hahndorf in the hills to the east. He was told there was a village there, relatively new farms and a wheat mill. He also decided he would go out to the northern region to Nuriootpa which also was a wheat area. He was not asked if he was an ex-convict at the port which made him happy. Adelaide was founded in 1836, and like the original Swan River Colony, it was a freely settled British province in Australia. Unlike the Colony of Western Australia, it remained that way and no convicts were sent there.

John found the town was located just twelve miles inland next to a small river called the Torrens and someone had designed a grid pattern for the street design with wide streets and many open parks. The entire town centre was surrounded by parkland with a very wide strip of undeveloped area along the river Torrens. It was small but well organised and nice and he liked it. He thought of Mary and the children and thought they would like it too. However, over the next few months as he walked around the city and ventured into the countryside to Hahndorf and Nuriootpa to look at the farmland he felt very lonely and isolated. He knew no one and missed the family and life on the farm, so he decided to return to Dongara and get back to farming and work.

He did not see the trip to Adelaide and South Australia as a failure but an opportunity to see the country and explore. He felt if he wanted to explore again the best thing to do would be to save as much money as possible, make contacts ahead of time and try to have somewhere to go and work. So, John returned to Albany, Fremantle and then Dongara to reunite with the family and get back to work on the farm and in the mill. He put away the idea of moving to Adelaide but was still interested in seeing Melbourne and the booming opportunities due to the gold rush in that state. Thousands of people from overseas were pouring into the country to take advantage of the growing economy and opportunities. All these new people knew nothing of the convict past nor cared. They were looking for gold and their fortune.

John heard that the gold exported from Victoria to England in the 1850s paid off all of England's foreign debt. That was a lot of gold so maybe it was an opportunity for him too. He just needed to find out how.

R Nesbitt's Spencer Inn – Albany
(Source – Public Domain)

18

Melbourne

John arrived back in early 1873 and simply restarted where he had left off. James and the family had managed the farm well in his absence, and James continued working with Leverman who had plenty of construction work to complete. In some ways the break from work was good for John as he, Mary and the family had been toiling away for years, and as he approached his 58th year, he needed to rest from the demanding work and take time to think about what he should do. He had done nothing but hard manual labour for 20 years since he left Kirkdale House of Correction in 1853 and went to Portland Prison. He came back glad he had seen Adelaide. He explained to all the family the experiences he had, and they marvelled at the stories of Fremantle, the sea voyage, Albany, Adelaide and the countryside around Adelaide They had never seen a whale and the places John described seemed fascinating and a world away for them.

Mary was happy to have John back. She missed him and his company. While it was hard working in a remote area on a farm, it was harder when John was away, and she made him promise to take the family if he wanted to travel again. John, Mary and the family worked on the farm over the next four years. Mary and her daughters continued to cultivate and expand their vegetable garden and walk to the market to sell their produce each week. The climate was warm in winter and hot in summer, so it was possible to grow a variety of vegetables all year. They also continued to make dresses and work clothes which they also sold at the market or made specially for the townsfolk and farmers when asked. Two years later their last child Elizabeth Arnold was born in Dongara. It was 1875.

Four years after John returned from Adelaide, in 1877 John was approached by Joseph Chivers to see if he would sell his two hundred acres of farmland to him. Chivers liked the way John had cleared his land with some fenced in areas. He wanted to combine several farms and make one bigger farm for him and his family to operate. Together they discussed the family's options, and it was decided to sell as the price was good and move down to Perth so that James and the children had more opportunities in life. Mary knew she and her daughters could continue to make clothes and sell them at the markets in Perth. This would help bring in some extra cash. John knew he and James would find work as they had many useful skills including in masonry and construction. John was relieved at the decision, particularly at 62 years old, as he felt farming was getting too demanding for him physically.

Once in Perth, the family moved into a nice home just to the north of the centre of the town. It was the first time they had lived in a house with more than three rooms and a yard at the back. James was 26 years old, Catherine was 16, Ellen 15, Annie 13, Teresa nine and Elizabeth two. The eldest four were able to work and after a few weeks they found work in various areas. James moved into building construction and the girls all either found work with a dressmaker or worked with Mary making dresses and clothes at the house. Mary insisted Teresa go to the local Catholic school run by the Mercy nuns to continue her reading, writing and become knowledgeable in the Bible. She could help Mary make clothes in the afternoon after school. Elizabeth was the baby of the family and was looked after by them all. Mary now reminded them of their grandfather's work advice – "Wherever you work, arrive a bit early, leave a bit later than required, work hard, do real quality work and learn to get better at what you do." She added, "If you implement this advice you will always be successful at whatever you do." The young girls took this work ethic into their work lives just like the older brother James had.

John wanted to travel again, this time to see Melbourne as he had heard so much about the town. It was civilised, they said, with more established buildings and nice stone bridges over the river. He promised Mary he would be away for only a short while. They had discussed this earlier after his trip to Adelaide and Mary acquiesced to John's request, besides the family was too big and settled to move again. She added that she would look after everyone for John's trip to Melbourne. Once again, he travelled to Albany from Fremantle catching a coastal steamer to Bunbury and then Albany. He stayed a few days there before catching a ship across to Melbourne. He left on the SS *Tanjore* on the 5th of November 1877. The *Tanjore* was built by Thames Iron Works, London, in 1865. It had an iron screw steam engine using propellers, known as screws. This was fascinating for John as he had only sailed on sailing ships. As they left Albany, he stood on the front deck with the tall funnel behind him blowing out smoke as the ship powered along.

John's aim was to see Melbourne, work for a while and see if there was an opportunity with the gold rush, but he knew realistically that he would not stay as the family was still in Perth and they were too old and established now to move again as a whole family. If he did move, some of the family would stay in Perth. Consequently, after a few months in Melbourne and in the countryside doing whatever work that was available, he decided to travel back and settle in Perth. He had now seen Adelaide and Melbourne and decided Perth would be his final home. Both Melbourne and Adelaide were nice, and it did not matter at all that he was an ex-convict. No one checked or even asked and even in Perth in 1878, with the influx of migrants from overseas to the east due to the gold discoveries, people cared less and less about who was an ex-convict.

(Source – Unsplash)

"The grass always looks greener on the other side;
until you jump the fence and see for yourself."
– Anonymous.

19 ▊

The Miller Returns

The last convict ship, the *Hougoumont* arrived in Fremantle in mid-1868 with 75 convicts on board. By the time John Arnold arrived back in Perth in 1878 – ten years since that last convict ship – almost all the convicts from that vessel were now on Tickets of Leave or conditional pardons. So, time was fast fading people's memories of convicts. Perth was also growing, and labour was still in short supply. In 1877, a telegraph line from Adelaide to Perth was completed. The colony was becoming less isolated with the improving communication.

Government buildings were going up in the centre of the city. John now saw large and impressive government offices housing the cabinet, treasury, titles office and post office. The central business area – a city block to the north and west of Government House – had a mix of shops and cottages. Some residential developments had started in the west of the main area and minor industrial development was concentrating in the east of the central area. Work had also commenced on the construction of the railway from Fremantle to Guildford.

Labour was valued and work was available for those willing to work hard. John started looking for work in a flour mill. He heard that Shenton's Mill across the river on Mill Point Road was now closed, and after talking with people who understood the milling business, John quickly realised that if he wanted to live in Perth he would not be able to find work in a mill because they were now further up the Swan River in Guildford and beyond, or down around Fremantle.

After listening to the chatter about town John understood that Frederick Sherwood had in 1857 established a brewery on Sherwood Court just one town block from Barrack Street and Government House. It was called the Black Swans brewery after the black swans that lived in and around Perth on the river and lakes. The brewery was now owned by John Ferguson and William Mumme. This was in walking distance from where John and the family lived. John also heard that Ferguson and Mumme were planning that year in 1878 to move the brewery to a new site on the west of the town on the shore of the Swan River at the foot of a small hill called Mt Elisa. Mt Elisa overlooked the town and the Swan River and formed a part of the 400-acre Kings Park to the west of the town.

In the Noongar language people referred to this area as Ga-ra-katta. The name is a concentration of two Noongar words, katta meaning hill and ga-ra meaning either a bird, an edible root, or an orchid. The site had been used over the years as a resting place for travellers moving to and from Fremantle, as a tannery and was the site of the first steam powered flour mill and timber mill. It was also the site one of Perth's convict guard quarters and a convict hiring depot. There were natural springs there, man-made bores and some water wells which provided a ready supply of clean water for the brewery and depot.

As John had worked in construction and in milling, he found work on the new brewery site. It was walking distance from where he lived and only one and a half miles from the centre of the town.

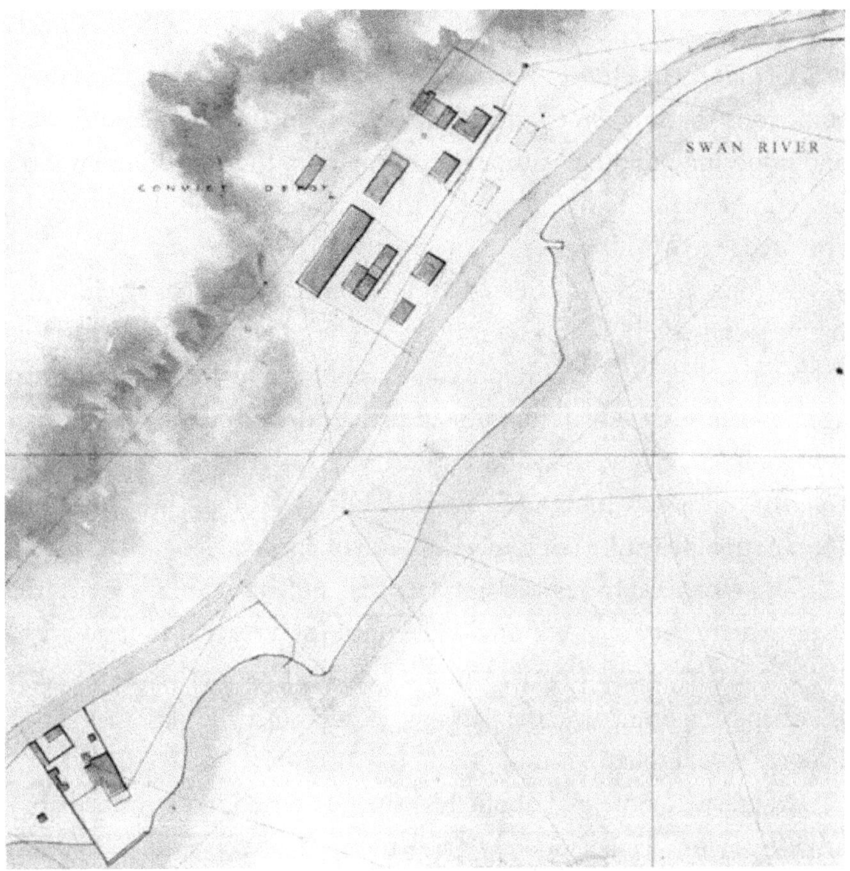

Convict depot at base of Mt Eliza
source public domain – Drawn by W. Phelps surveyor, 1864
Bottom left is the old mill. Top right is the road to Perth, SRO
Original Plans of Townsites.'

One morning John rose early, as was his habit, and set out to walk across town – up and down Barrack Street to the river and westwards to the brewery construction site at the foot of Mt Eliza. As he walked down Barrack Street past the Town Hall, he saw an army guardhouse with a forbidding little turret structure and assumed the street got it name originally from an army barracks that must have existed on that site many years earlier. As he continued down the street some nice government gardens appeared on his left and just a little further east was Government House. He knew some of the convicts who had done some construction work there a few decades ago. It was a nice, elaborate and imposing building he thought. Further on, the courthouse was on his left. At the river, he turned right to the west and headed along the river's edge to Mt Eliza.

As John passed the convict depot, which was located before the brewery construction site on his right, he saw an old familiar face. It was John Cosgrave. When John looked at his old friend, he noticed he had aged enormously – as John guessed he had done too. Cosgrave's hair was completely grey, long and very thin. His beard was long and grey too. In some ways John Cosgrave looked very frail and weak whereas John Arnold felt still strong, alive and full of energy.

John Cosgrave recognised John as well and waved him over to the depot where they chatted for a while until John needed to head off to the construction site to start work. They filled each other in on what they had been doing over the past few decades since they last met. Their lives were a complete contrast.

Cosgrave commented about his past, "I started work immediately after I got my Ticket of Leave and travelled out to York as I heard that there was some labouring work there. I worked in farming and construction or wherever I could find labouring work. Sadly, I never had the opportunity to own a property, run a business or take on any supervisor roles. I never remarried. People just saw me as an ex-convict who they trusted but only for labouring type roles. My two daughters Ann and Catherine both travelled out to Western Australia by sailing ship and re-joined me in 1859. It was amazing to see them in Fremantle. When I left, they were two little girls and arrived as young women. Ann settled immediately in York, met and married James Pitts a year later in 1860 when she was 19 years old. James was a farmer. Between then and now in 1878 they had ten children ranging from 17 years old to a newborn. They seemed to move regularly around the Northam farming areas, from Northam to Greenhills, Malabine, Wilberforce, Woodside and back to Northam. Unfortunately, with ten children to house and feed there was no room for me to stay with them".

"I got my conditional pardon in January 1863, but it didn't mean much to me just that I had some fewer restrictions. Catherine married John Coyne a year later in 1864 in Northam. Catherine, like in Ann's marriage, moved around the farming areas like Northam, Greenhills, Yarralong and back to Northam. Now they have four children ranging in ages from 13 years to four years of age. Sadly, once again with a family of six there was no room for an aging father like me to stay with them".

"I moved from York to Toodyay. As they had some construction work there and there also were a few ex-convicts who had settled down by the Toodyay River. I was friends with a couple of them from the days in Fremantle." John Arnold knew Toodyay was not far from York and a bit closer to Perth as he had also travelled through there before. It was still near to Northam so John Arnold assumed his old friend could occasionally travel to Northam to see his daughters.

Cosgrave continued "Toodyay was good for me and from time to time I would walk down along the Toodyay River on a Sunday and visit the ex-convicts who lived there and my friends. They seemed happy and content to grow their vegetables by the river and sleep in the small huts they built. The locals in Toodyay seemed to not bother them. So, when the work dried up in Toodyay, I decided to move back to Perth so I could get some permanent shelter, meals and support in this convicts' depot."

John Arnold knew that as his friend had never remarried, like many ex-convicts, he never had the stability that he enjoyed with Mary. He could see his old friend was destitute and living in the old convict depot to survive as food and shelter were provided. John was saddened to see an old friend end up this way.

After a short while they separated, and John continued to the brewery construction site. After that, they would occasionally see each other early in the morning and catch up for a chat. Sometimes John felt Cosgrave waited for him so he could have some company. Probably he did. A few years later John heard his old friend died in 1881, a destitute old man at the Perth Invalid Depot on the 12th of August. Later he heard that John's daughter, Ann, passed away in 1886 at 45 years of age leaving behind ten children. It was tough in the newly developed areas and many people were isolated. John knew from his experience in York, Greenough, Geraldton and Dongara that life in those areas could be incredibly challenging and he was one of the lucky ones to have a companion like Mary to work together. He also heard that Catherine had four more children but that was the last John heard of John Cosgrave's family.

A few years later gold was discovered in Western Australia, and it changed Perth, the capital city, and Western Australia permanently. Charles Hall and Jack Slattery found gold in Halls Creek in 1885 and it triggered the Kimberley gold rush. Harry Francis Anstey found gold near Southern Cross in 1887 and it started the Yilgarn gold rush. In 1891 Michael Fitzgerald, Edward Heffernan and Tom Cue found gold in Cue starting the Murchison gold rush. Arthur Bailey and William Ford found gold in Coolgardie in 1892 and Patrick "Paddy" Hannan, Tom Flanagan and Dan Shea famously discovered gold in Kalgoorlie in 1893. Perth and Western Australia attracted vast numbers of people in this period and beyond with each seeking their fortune. With the injection of thousands and thousands of new people and the promise of great wealth, the memory of the past convict era faded even more quickly into history. The Fremantle prison was no longer a convict prison, but a state-run prison for local convicted criminals.

For John, age had caught up with him by the time gold was discovered although the thought of prospecting for gold certainly appealed to his adventurous spirit. When gold was discovered in Coolgardie, he was already 77 years old, so he decided to stay in Perth, but it certainly did have a significant effect on his family in very many and diverse ways.

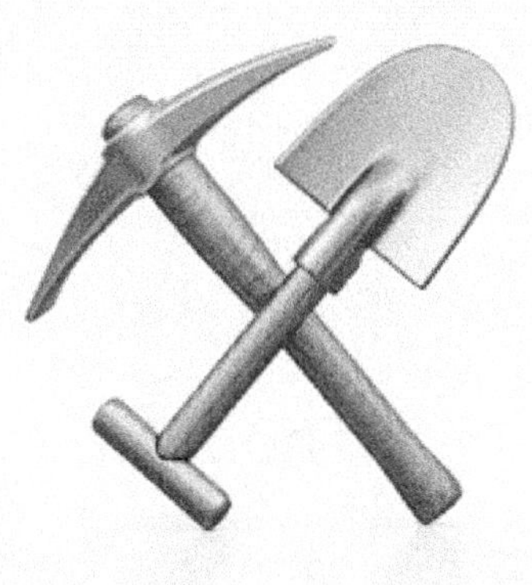

(Image – public domain)

"The night too quickly passes,
And we are growing old,
So let us fill our glasses,
And toast the Days of Gold.
When finds of wonderous treasure,
Set all the West ablaze,
And you and faithful mates,
All through the roaring days."

Henry Lawson – "The Roaring Days" 1889

20

Thomas Francis Elliott

Thomas Elliott walked down dusty Beaufort Street in the northern area of Perth. It was a clear sunny August day. Winter was almost over, and the weather was already warming up, but Elliott felt comfortable in his suit and tie. He liked to dress well, and given that he owned four drapery shops, he could afford to as well. It was late on a Sunday morning and he was due to arrive at midday for a meal at Elizabeth Arnold's house to meet her parents for the first time. At Brisbane Street he turned left and momentarily glanced across the road to the east corner of Beauford Street and Brisbane Street. There was a vacant area of land there and Elliott knew his friend was planning to build a hotel on that corner and call it the Brisbane Hotel. His friend had asked Elliott if he wanted to invest in the hotel but Elliott liked his drapery businesses, and the hotel was not planned to be completed for another three years so it was too soon to start investing in that project. He also liked to keep his cash close to him and manage it himself.

As he walked down the road, he glanced across Brisbane Street and looked at the large park that was being developed there. It was going to be called Birdwood Square. Elliott thought that was an odd name for a park. He liked regal names like Queens Park or Kings Park like the one overlooking Perth and the beautiful Swan River. King Arthur Park would be a much better name he said to himself. Maybe someone in the government was called Birdwood he thought. Elliott was not a tall man but of average height. He was strong across the shoulders from a lot of manual work prospecting over in the Victorian Goldfields and out in the Western Australian Goldfields around Coolgardie and Kalgoorlie. Now in his mid-30s – middle-age – his waist was thickening and his once thick head of fair hair was thinning and receding at the front, but he had persisted with a large thick moustache. It was his trademark look, he thought, as were the nice clothes and the gold ring on the little finger on his right hand.

Elliott owned large drapery shops in Perth, Coolgardie, Kalgoorlie and Kanowna, and profited nicely from workers' need everywhere for clothes, work-ware, hats, curtains for home windows and canvas for tents. Many people considered him to be wealthy, which he was, but they knew little of where his wealth came from as he kept that a secret. Later that day he would tell John Arnold his story and about that secret.

He first met Elizabeth Arnold when he advertised for a dressmaker to work in his Perth business. He manufactured clothes from imported fabrics, so a qualified dressmaker was an important part of his business. He imported the latest patterns from London, and his tailors and dress-makers made beautiful dresses and suits plus a good range of work clothes for the people of Perth, the farms and Goldfields. In answer to his advertisement, he had received a beautifully written letter stating that Elizabeth had six years' experience as a dressmaker, was trained by her mother who also was a very experienced dressmaker and seamstress and worked at another draper in West Perth.

When Elizabeth walked into his shop he was taken aback – petite and slim with long fair hair – she was beautiful. She was well dressed too in a dress that she said she had made only last week. He was expect-ing a working-class girl who would be simply dressed but diligent and hard working. Here was something else. She spoke with a slight English accent which he assumed came from her parents, and she spoke well, clearly and politely. Elliott had lost his wife recently from a prolonged illness, so suddenly found himself thinking of this 20-year-old woman in ways other than as just an employee. Not surprisingly, Elizabeth found herself employed at T F Elliott – The Popular Draper, shortly after.

This led to Elliott walking along Brisbane Street on that late morning in August. Elizabeth turned out to be everything she promised. She arrived a bit early, left a bit late, worked tirelessly producing beautiful garments and continuously worked to get better. Her work was precise and her stiches perfect. She communicated well, made few mistakes and got along well with the other dressmakers and tailors. Elliott found himself coming by the area to excessively check on her work but mainly to just be around this attractive woman. Over time he asked questions and found out that she was not being courted by anyone, and one day he asked Elizabeth to give her father a letter from him.

When Elizabeth arrived home, she showed the letter to her father who opened the envelope, read it through and said to Elizabeth, "Thomas Elliott was asking if he could escort you out on a Sunday afternoon. It seems to be a very polite letter and he just seems to be trying to do the right thing and ask my permission. What would you like to do?" Elizabeth was shocked. She paused and thought about it as she had only ever seen him as the big boss who owned the businesses. She had never thought of him any other way. She said, "Oh, I do not mind. He seems like a nice man and is firm but fair to everyone who works in his business. I heard that his wife passed away a while ago but other than that I do not know too much about him."

John asked Mary, who looked at him and Elizabeth, and replied, "Why don't we invite him over for tea on Sunday afternoon. I would like to meet him too." John wrote a polite reply inviting Elliott to a meal on Sunday midday. John Arnold also wanted to meet anyone who was going to court his daughter.

The houses were relatively new in this area and the house at the address he was given was a single-storey weatherboard cottage. It was modest but new with timber cladding and a hipped iron roof. As Elliott stood outside, he could see it had a double room frontage, most probably with the lounge room on one side and a hallway down the middle.

Bedrooms would fill the other side at the front and the two middle areas on either side of the house. The full width of the front of the house was a front veranda which had a bull-nose roof supported by turned timber posts. Timber valances decorated the joints between the timber posts and the beams running across under the roof. It was a lovely home. In the middle of the house was a wooden entrance door with paned glass windows either side of the door and a fan light above. A low white timber picket fence separated the property from the verge. There were a few small plants within the front setback and Elliott could see clearly that Elizabeth's parents cared for the house and garden.

Thomas Elliott knocked on the entrance door and Elizabeth answered promptly. She ushered him in. She was beautifully dressed as usual. She introduced him to her father John, mother Mary and a little boy. The boy was very well behaved, and Elliott guessed he looked around four years of age. Elizabeth called him OJ. Elliott thought Elizabeth's father looked old, maybe 80, but he spoke nicely with a faded Irish accent. He could see where Elizabeth got her stunning looks from as he looked at Mary Arnold. She looked only to be in her fifty's, but he reasoned she could easily be ten years older with her pale English skin and dark hair that had yet to turn grey. Mary placed everyone at the table and went into the kitchen to bring out the meal. Elizabeth helped and the young boy joined the two men at the table. After saying grace, they all ate a midday meal of roast beef, potatoes, peas and carrots. Mary had even made a Yorkshire pudding and gravy to go with the roast and boasted that the vegetables came from their own garden which was at the back of the house.

After the meal John stood and excused himself from the table and politely asked if Thomas would like to join him to smoke a pipe outside on the front veranda as it was a beautiful afternoon. John wanted time to talk with Elliott alone. Once seated, Thomas Elliott knew to be quiet and not speak first. He had learned in business to let the other person talk first and, in business, not make the first offer when he was trading. It had been successful for him. John took his time to light his pipe and waited until Elliott did the same. John started the conversation by talking a bit about his life. Elliott kept quiet. John preferred to share some background information about himself and family which he knew would built up more trust with Elliott.

John explained that he left Ireland during the potato famine after his parents died and travelled on his own to Liverpool and Bradford. Here he took up work in a woollen mill as he could not use his farming experience or his trades in milling and linen weaving. It was there he met Mary and they got married. After they were married and had their first two children James and Mary Catherine, John sailed to Western Australia to look for a new life away from the big, crowded industrial cities in England. He continued explaining that he first went to York to work in a wheat mill until Mary and the two children arrived at Fremantle. From there they travelled up to Greenough to first work in a wheat mill there and then take up farming wheat, hay and other crops on their own farm. After successfully doing this for years they moved to Champion Bay in the north where he ran a successful building company with three employees for several years. John said he then missed the farming, so they moved back down past Greenough to Dongara where he bought two hundred acres and started farming again for wheat, hay and other crops while still doing some building contracting and milling in Dongara. After working for many years, they decided to move down to Perth so the family could have more opportunity. At this point John paused and smoked on his pipe while waiting for Elliott to talk. Elliott listened to John's story and asked "so Mr Arnold why did you leave the farm in Ireland"? John replied "those were exceedingly tough times with the potato famine. People were dying by the thousands, and I read in a newspaper many years later that one third of the whole Irish population died or left the country during those years". Elliott shook his head. He had no idea about that hardship.

John realised that he had left out a lot of details like his conviction, imprisonment, torture, whippings, shipment to Fremantle and Ticket of Leave. He felt he had done his time many years ago and it should be left in the past. He also knew Elizabeth knew nothing of that past as the family never discussed it. In addition, with the significant increase in people from the east and overseas coming for the gold rush, he believed these details should be forgotten. Peoples' memories on convicts were fading fast, and the new residents simply did not care to know because many were coming from difficult circumstances themselves and were looking for work, prosperity and a better future.

At first Elliott started to talk slowly. He respected the old man and appreciated his frankness and how hard it must have been to lose his parents and be forced to leave his country. He said he was born in Collingwood, Melbourne, in 1860. His father was a skilled coach builder, so he joined his father initially in the coach building business to learn the trade. However, the lure of gold in country Victoria was too much for him so he left Melbourne to find his fortune in the gold mining areas. He worked for several years in gold mining including digging, crushing and refining, and then learned the skills of prospecting from some of the older prospectors. He spent several years unsuccessfully prospecting and in 1890 he heard about gold being discovered in the west.

Elliott said he started to read more and found out that Charles Hall and Jack Slattery discovered gold in Halls Creek. Then Harry Francis Anstey found gold near Southern Cross in 1887 and Michael Fitzgerald, Edward Heffernan and Tom Cue found gold inland of Greenough at a place they called Cue in 1891. The far-reaching excitement of the gold discoveries drew people from all over the world. People emigrated from Africa, America, Great Britain, Europe, China, India, New Zealand and the South Sea Islands as well as coming from the mining centres in the eastern areas of Australia like Queensland, New South Wales, Victoria, Tasmania and South Australia.

"So why did you decide to move over to the west?" John asked. Elliott looked over and said, "Well there was so much excitement around that everyone including me thought that gold was just lying around to be picked up. On reflection I know that was stupid, but the rumours were rife, and the west is such a vast area so I thought there must be an opportunity for me. So, I packed up my possessions and moved over. In 1892 when Arthur Bailey and William Ford discovered gold at Fly Flat near the present site of Coolgardie, I moved to the area to start prospecting as it was a new area with plenty of unexplored land so plenty of opportunity. However, it was hard, barren and uncivilised. In 1893 Hannan, Flannagan and Shea then discovered gold in Kalgoorlie and even more people flocked to the area." Elliott stopped and was silent as if he was thinking back remembering the tough times he had.

When he started talking again, Elliott became excited, intense and more fluent. "Then in 1893 the land values in Coolgardie were dropping and there was a severe drought. I thought I was done. As a final effort I met with five other men to have one last go at the prospecting. It was 1894 and I was 33 years old turning thirty-four that year when the six of us went south of Coolgardie early in the year. I put all the money I had into the prospecting venture and together we purchased a horse and dray and enough provisions including water to last a few months. We also bought some picks, shovels and some basic crushing equipment. I thought at the time that I was getting too old for this work and the hardship, so it really was my last opportunity.

"Initially, we looked south of Coolgardie but without success and after a few months we decided to work our way back to Coolgardie and to look for work with another team where they could be paid wages. I even thought of leaving Coolgardie and going back to Melbourne and re-joining my father in the coach making business. During the days, the six of us would scatter over a wide area looking for signs of a gold bearing rock source. One day, John Mills, a young Irishman from Londonderry in Northern Ireland, was prospecting alone and he sat down in the late afternoon to have a smoke. He rubbed his boot along the ground and across some rocks, and he caught a glint of a shiny substance. He looked more closely and washed it with some of his drinking water to see what the bright spot was. He was startled to see it was gold. He got out his pick and chipped away at the rock and took a piece off, washed it and it was full of gold. In his excitement he started picking away at the outcrop and all the stone was literally held together with gold.

"Mills gathered a hessian bag full of rock samples, slung it over his shoulder and walked back to camp to meet the rest of us. He tried to look glum as if his day was wasted. All of us had unsuccessful days and our mood was sombre. Mills put his bag of samples down and after the evening meal said he had found some interesting rocks. He stood up, walked over, picked up his bag of rocks and poured out the samples carefully on the ground at their feet.

"Each of us picked up a rock and looked at it. We were staggered as we all found quartz rock which was literally held together with gold. Suddenly the mood of the camp changed, and dozens of questions poured out of our mouths. How big was the outcrop? Were all the other rocks like these? How far away was it? Mills responded that it was not far away, and the amount seemed unlimited. At dawn we packed up the camp, hitched the horse and dray and set off for the site where Mills found the outcrop. After some difficulty we found the spot and we all started using our picks to chip off samples of quartz from the outcrop. We all found similar samples and the deeper we dug the more quartz we found with gold. It was exciting as it certainly seemed to us that we indeed had found a large lode of gold. After working for a few hours, we stopped and discussed what to do. We decided to set up camp and get ourselves organised to dig up the rock, break it down, hand pick up the pieces of gold and melt it down into buttons of gold. We all settled down to the demanding physical work of hand digging and crushing the rock with our rudimentary tools."

Elliott paused from his dialogue, looked at John Arnold and relit his pipe. It was mid-afternoon and the sunshine was still bright, but a slight breeze was building up from the south. Arnold kept quiet and Elliott continued his story.

"Initially, the thrill of the gold discovery kept everyone excited and at the end of the first day we all fell asleep exhausted. After the first week of toiling in the sparse countryside and hot weather the work became progressively more difficult. Hand digging hard quartz rock was hard enough but the crushing of the rock into finer particles was exhausting. The picking up of the gold through the digging and crushing process was the easiest part and this job was rotated among us to ease the exhaustion. All of us were resilient men used to this demanding physical work and hardships, but the continuous process was wearing us all down. The use of the furnace was also hot and exhausting work plus it required a continuous supply of wood which needed to be cut or collected from the nearby bushland, carted into the camp, and burned to keep the calcining furnace in operation to produce the buttons of gold".

Elliott continued, "After a few weeks because of the richness of the lode we had collected about eight thousand ounces of gold, valued at thirty-two thousand pounds at four pounds per ounce. This was a vast fortune to us and despite the demanding work we were all excited with an expected five thousand three hundred pounds each for the initial few weeks work".

Gold prospecting Coolgardie – 1890s

(Source – public domain)

After a brief pause as if Elliott was reimagining the scenes out there in the remote bushland he said, "One evening we sat around the campfire and discussed the next steps. Given we had been working out in the bush for several months and working this area for a few weeks we were concerned that we had not applied for a mining lease over our discovery. If we did nothing someone else could see what we were doing and get a mining lease over that area. Alternatively, we could apply for a lease and run the risk that word would get out and there would be a rush of people turning up to prospect around our lease. We knew that by law any new mining leases would need to be publicised once we had a lease. So, we could not keep it a secret as all applications would be posted up outside the Warden's Court in Coolgardie. After much discussion we all decided that two of us should go into Coolgardie and get a mining agent to apply for a lease of twenty-four acres over the area where we were mining. Mills and Huxley were selected to go while the rest of us kept on mining".

"So, Mills and Huxley then went into Coolgardie. After arriving in town, they made sure they looked tired and beaten and told the agent, Walter Henry Lindsay, how they had been prospecting for a few months but had not found anything so far. However, they thought one area looked promising for small yields and they wanted a lease over twenty-four acres to cover it just in case they found something. Besides, they were tired of moving around and this was a suitable place to camp for a while. They concluded that they had little money and hoped for as small a fee as possible".

"I later met WH Lindsay. He was about 25 years old and a few years older than Mills, but he had been in and around the area for over eight years since he was 17 and he told me he was always on the look-out for an opportunity. While he processed the lease application for 'Londonderry' he decided to follow Mills and Huxley to see what was there for himself. A day later he set out to look for the lease area. He was not an experienced prospector nor bushman, so he found the travel difficult and slept rough in the bush each night. He had seen many small prospecting and rough mining operations, so he knew what to look for. On the third day he saw smoke from what must have been a large fire in the distance, so he started walking towards the smoke. As he approached the area, he noticed a significant clearing and saw some of us working in a small pit, others breaking rocks by hand and a large open-air furnace. He had seen this before, so he knew what it meant".

"We were surprised to see him as it is isolated out there, and you rarely see anyone. Initially we told him little but bit by bit our excitement spilled out and given we had the mining lease we told him everything after pledging him to secrecy. We told him about the eight thousand ounces of gold we had. Unfortunately, the news of the extraordinary find could not be kept secret for long and eventually the people in Coolgardie found out, got wildly excited and rushed to see the Londonderry gold find. With the news, many prospectors applied for leases all around the area. Soon the areas surrounding where we were working were wild with activity".

"We kept a close watch on our mine and lodged the eight thousand ounces of gold in the Union Bank of Coolgardie. Mills even took to the bank some impressive nuggets displaying the thick strands of gold. These impressive specimens were under guard at the bank but were inspected by many of the wealthy syndicates who were looking for prospective investments. Gold fever affected not just the individual prospectors but attracted many wealthy groups and individuals aiming to cash in on the gold discoveries as a successful mine could produce significant cash for years if not decades".

"After a while we all decided to sell the mine to one of the interested parties as it needed significant investment in mining, crushing and refining equipment and we decided that we could not continue the back-breaking manual work, nor did we want to spend the hard-earned money setting up a bigger mining operation. As such we started negotiations."

Once again Elliott paused and reflected in silence. John Arnold looked over at him, stood up, stretched and went into the house where he asked Mary if she could make some tea with something to eat. Elizabeth was nervous and asked her father, "So what do you think about Mr Elliott?" John thought for a minute, looked at his daughter and replied, "Well he is certainly telling me a fascinating story so far, and seriously, he seems a nice man who would be good for you to spend more time with."

After tea was served, Thomas Elliott continued. "For some reason, the opportunity to purchase this extraordinarily rich deposit became a high-profile sale and it attracted the attention of people around Australia and even back in England." John reflected even he had heard about the discovery. "As such there was a great deal of competition," Elliott went on. "Representatives inspected the specimens and visited the mine under our close watch. The successful bidder was a Lord Fingal from England. During May in 1894 he travelled to Australia and when he heard about the Londonderry find he diverted his trip to arrive in Albany and then on to Perth where colony Premier John Forrest met him and introduced him to the Coolgardie Mining Warden John Finnerty. Finnerty explained the Londonderry find to Lord Fingal and both met with us and visited the mine site. We then had some negotiations and we accepted Lord Fingal's offer of £296,000. With the £32,000 from the gold, we had recovered, this yielded £328,000, or approximately £55,000 less some costs to each of us."

Thomas Elliott paused at this point and John Arnold thought about the £55,000. When he was working in Dongara for Leverman he was earning four pounds and ten shillings or four and a half pounds per month, so £55,000 represented 1018 years of work for John. Before John could say anything, Elliott added, "I am not a proud man. The time working in the bush was hard and I learned a lot about mateship and humility there so while the money seems a lot, I am not here to impress you. It is simply a true story that I wanted to share with you. I can see too that you have worked hard to become a successful landholder, so we have something in common."

Elliott continued his story. "When Lord Fingal was in Coolgardie, he and the others met him. He said he had big plans for the mine and after the mine was sold, I followed its progress. After the negotiations, the mine was covered over with a strong steel plate, sealed and remained that way for months. In November 1894 two boxes of the impressive samples from the Londonderry lode arrived in London and were displayed at Lord Fingal's business. They created something of a gold fever. The mine was put into a company as an asset and the business was subsequently floated on the stock exchanges in London and Paris for £750,000".

"The mine was then reopened after the float and mining restarted. However, by April 1895 a horrible truth became apparent that the Londonderry lode was a freak small rich patch. It was found that the gold was only present in the surface outcrop and a few feet underground. What was left after a brief period of mining was a barren reef." At this point Elliott paused again and John asked if it ever yielded any more gold to which Elliott added, "Many people tried but no more gold was found in that immediate area. So, I took my money and put it in a bank in Perth and bought a home and waited for things to settle down. I then decided to open drapery businesses to supply the settlements in the gold mining areas. Property was cheap at that time, and shortly after gold mining was reinvigorated, especially in Kalgoorlie and Coolgardie."

Elliott stopped talking and thought about the fact that he had left out a few details in his story. One was that he was married and his wife had very recently passed away. The second was that he had not been a particularly good husband and spent a lot of time away from her. And finally, he did like a drink. The rumours were that he was the person who went into Coolgardie, got very drunk and told everyone of the riches of the Londonderry mine. He could not remember the last part as yes; he did get drunk but could not remember showing off gold nuggets and discussing the gold discovery.

At this point John Arnold stood up and went inside the house to talk with Mary and Elizabeth. He looked at them and said, "I think he is fundamentally a good man and I think he will look after Elizabeth. What do you think Mary?" Mary added, "Well I agree, and he is about the same age as you when I met you, so his age was appropriate". He then asked Elizabeth if she wanted to see him next weekend to which she replied she did.

John went back out to the front veranda and sat down. He thanked Elliott for his story as it was both very impressive but sad too for the new owners of the mine. He added that it was nice to meet and get to know each other. He also approved that he could spend some time with Elizabeth. John then said that the little boy inside was Overend John Arnold who was born in September 1891. He was Elizabeth's son. He added if he wished to ask Elizabeth to marry him, he would need to formally adopt Overend in the process. John said, "Elizabeth became pregnant a few years ago and the man ran off from his responsibilities. In many families this would have created a dilemma and, in some cases, it would have been a disgrace on a family, but for Mary and me we have a different view. That little boy is Elizabeth's precious son and our wonderful grandson, and we feel very privileged to have him in our family. We have been through a lot hardships in life. There were tough times and good times and having OJ in the family is one of the exceptionally good times."

John Arnold and Thomas Elliott parted company that afternoon. Thomas told John that he appreciated his time and honestly. He would very much like to see Elizabeth and felt much better sharing each other's backgrounds and advising him about Overend.

Elliott walked back down Brisbane Street and passed that park again. Once again, he thought it would be better named after a King, like King Arthur. "Arthur, I like that name," he said aloud.

Early the next year Thomas Elliott and Elizabeth Arnold were married in Melbourne. He was thirty-six and she was twenty-one. Overend was formally adopted by Elliott and his name became Arthur John Elliott. OJ became AJ. Elliott liked regal names.

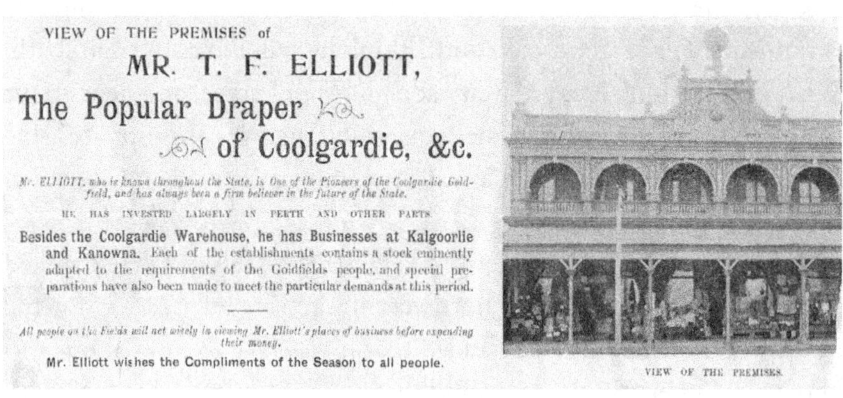

Thomas Frances Elliott's advertisement for his drapery business
(Source – public domain)

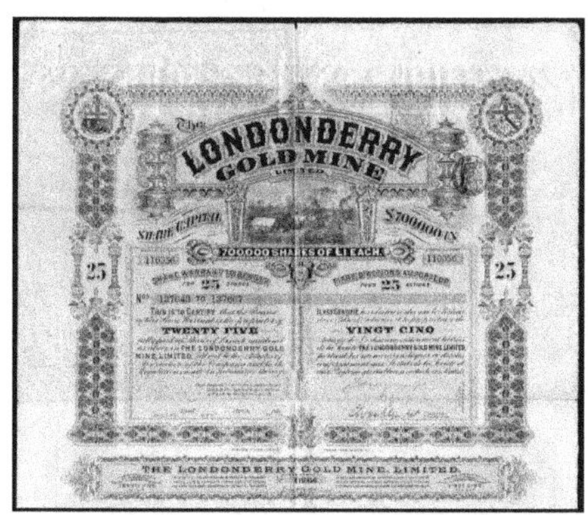

Share certificate of the Londonderry Gold Mine
(Source – Public Domain)

Six Londonderry gold discoverers, the Coolgardie Mayor and one
other reported to be Lord Fingal
(Source – public domain)

"Don't dig for gold, sell shovels. The secret to getting rich in a gold rush is selling picks."
Mark Twain

21

Henry William Beamish Talbot

Henry William Beamish Talbot, HWB to his family and friends, walked along the dusty road in Kalgoorlie. He had an old tattered wide-brimmed hat on his head to protect his pale Irish skin. The hat was ringed with sweat as it was hot, dry and dusty. Henry was a tall thin man, who while used to challenging work on the farm, was still lean and sinewy. He had never filled out regardless of how much he ate. His father always said Henry was too curious, too intelligent and too active to put on weight.

Henry moved to Kalgoorlie with his family when he was 19 years old. Originally, from Cork County, Ireland, the family migrated to New Zealand in 1882 when he was eight. They were looking for a better environment and a place with more opportunities than what Ireland offered at the time. When his father heard of the gold discoveries, firstly in Victoria and then in the west of Australia, they moved to Kalgoorlie in search of gold. His father had visions of becoming a successful farmer in New Zealand and then a successful gold prospector in Kalgoorlie. He knew a lot about farming but little about prospecting or mining, but he felt he had to try.

The gold prospecting around Kalgoorlie was fruitless for both Henry and his father. They had few skills in that area, so his father decided to move the family down to the southwest of the colony to start farming again as he decided that he was much better at farming than gold prospecting. After spending a brief time helping the family settle and start farming, Henry missed the challenges of prospecting and moved back to Kalgoorlie. This time he decided to find employment and learn the skills of prospecting properly. The first job he took was as a junior field assistant in Coolgardie in the government's Geological Survey of Western Australia department. It suited Henry very well as he felt he could learn a lot about geology, geological mapping and exploration techniques. These were all areas that fascinated him. While he did not have any formal qualifications in these areas, he felt that by being around these professionals he could learn a lot and receive valuable experience. Plus, it was a government job, and it paid much better than farming or fruitless prospecting.

Shortly after getting his first job Henry went into TF Elliott's drapery store in Coolgardie to buy himself a new hat to keep the sun off his head and face. He received his first pay so could afford a new purchase. It had been many years since he bought himself anything. As he wandered into the store he was surprised by the range of lovely clothes and goods that were displayed, not only inside the store but on the walkway outside as well. Once inside he was approached by a lovely well-dressed young woman. "May I help you?" she asked politely. Henry looked at the lovely young woman. He was shy with women as his experience with ladies was minimal, especially with well-dressed lovely ladies like the one who was speaking to him now. He had spent all his life so far in remote farms or out in the dry arid parts around Kalgoorlie and Coolgardie prospecting. However, he responded that he would like to buy a new hat.

She was patient and kind as he tried on a range of hats. There was a lot to choose from including stiff bowler and derby hats, felt slouch hats, and billed stocking soft caps. Most were small and narrow-brimmed, but Henry wanted a broad brimmed hat regardless of the fashion. He particularly liked the rabbit felt slouch style hats as the brims were wide and would give him protection from the sun. Besides, a hat would last him for years so he selected carefully. The young lady would look at him with each hat and offer suggestions like the hat was too formal or too old fashioned. Once she even laughed when he tried on a bowler hat. It was funny she said. Once he made his selection, the young woman introduced Henry to the owner of the property, Mr TF Elliott who collected the money and wrote out a receipt. Mr Elliott introduced the young lady as Miss Teresa Arnold, his sister-in-law from Perth.

As Henry took his purchase outside the young lady escorted him to the door as TF Elliott had instructed her to do for all customers. Henry stepped onto the shop's sidewalk and into the sunshine. He put on his new hat, and he did something he never had the courage to do before. He asked with a stammer if she would see him on Sunday afternoon to which she kidded him and said, "Well Mr Talbot, you are a bit forward today but yes that would be nice." Over the next year Henry and Teresa spent more and more time together. Teresa told Henry the story of the family's background in farming and construction in the mid-west coastal areas of Western Australia and how her parents moved to Perth when she was nine years old. They were now settled in Perth. Her younger sister Elizabeth was married to Mr Elliott, and Teresa and her other sister Annie moved out here to the gold mine areas for work for TF Elliott. They also did dress making in their spare time for TF Elliott to make some extra money. Her older brother James was also here working in mining and construction.

Henry promised that with the railway line now between Perth and Kalgoorlie, they would travel to Perth and he would like to meet her parents. She was concerned as her father was old and frail and she wanted to see him – and for him and her mother to meet Henry. Late in the year, Teresa and Henry travelled by train to Perth in time for Christmas, which was a priceless time for both the Arnold and Talbot families. All the Arnold family were together for the first time that year, so it was a great celebration. John was now 82 years old, and Elizabeth was expecting her and Thomas's first child. Arthur John was six.

The month after Christmas Elizabeth had a baby girl and she was named Alice Eve. It was a joy for Mary and John to have another granddaughter. The next month was February and one afternoon Mary heard someone drop off a letter at the house. This was odd as they rarely received letters. She went outside and it was a letter in an official government envelope. Even though Mary could not read she knew it was important and observed from the writing on the outside that it had John's name on it. That much she could recognise. Hurriedly she took the letter inside and called for John. He did not reply.

John had, over the past few years, built a timber structure at the back of the house which he called the fern house. He nailed wooden slats on top and down the sides of the wooden structure 30 feet by 12 feet . He then added garden beds and shelves to hold the various ferns and other plants he bought, collected or was given. It had become his quiet, cool, green place where he would sit, read, rest and smoke his pipe. At the back of the fern house he built a small arched walkway which went to the back area where the vegetable garden was located. Sometimes he would bring out his old fiddle and play a few of the old soft tunes he remembered. He would look at and touch the well-worn inscription on the back, 'To my loving son John – Dadai' and think of the times long long ago on the farm in Ireland with his family. He still had his mother's rosary beads too. Often, he would drift off to sleep sitting in his chair in the afternoon.

This time when Mary saw him sitting on his chair in the fern house, she quietly called his name and again received no answer, so she figured he was asleep. She touched his shoulder and shook him gently. He did not respond. Then his head fell forward, and Mary gasped. She grabbed his hand, and it was cold like Mary Catherine's so many years ago in Greenough. Mary dropped to her knees and let out a loud sob. Tears rolled down her cheeks as she held his cold hand in hers. Elizabeth found her there later sobbing with her hand in his. They had been married for nearly 48 years.

With that John was gone. The doctor who signed off on the death certificate said he had a mild heart attack, and as he was old and frail, he passed quickly without any pain which is why he did not move from his chair. John was buried in a beautiful suit that Mary and Elizabeth made for him. It was black with a white shirt and green tie to represent his Irish heritage. Mary embroidered a small white dove on the edge of the coat sleeve and on the tie as her trademark, but it was much more than that in her mind. The dove represented to her family, love, freedom, opportunity and adventure. John had given her all these things in life, and not just for her but for her children as well. She knew the road they travelled together was at times very hard and unforgiving but through their hard work and determination they had forged a good life for themselves and opportunities for their family. Mary took John's mother's old rosary beads from the small wooden box that John stored his few precious things in and carefully wrapped the beads in his hands in the coffin. She did that so he could go to his mother and his God in peace.

The government letter that arrived on the day John died was forgotten in the turmoil of his death and funeral. It sat on the top of a box where Mary dropped it in the back room of the house. One day Elizabeth saw it and opened it. It was dated 23rd of February 1898, notifying John Arnold of his discharge papers. He was now a free man at 82 years old.

Thomas Francis, Alice Eva, and Elizabeth Elliott (nee Arnold)
(Source – family archives)

Henry William Beamish Talbot
(Source – family archives)

Teresa Talbot (nee Arnold)
(Source – family archives)

"Life brings tears, smiles and memories: the tears dry, the smile fades, but the memories live on forever."
Anonymous

22

The man from Guernsey

Mary Arnold looked at the young man in front of her. He had travelled out to Kalgoorlie with HWB Talbot and Elizabeth Elliott who wanted to see Mary about their planned marriage. Both their spouses had passed away a few years ago. HWB's wife was Mary's daughter, Teresa, who died eight years ago after being married to HWB for only two years. The young man was Walter Le Page and he had been seeing a young lady called Alice Eva Elliott, Elizabeth's only daughter. Henry wanted Walter to meet the old lady. Mary had moved to Kalgoorlie from Perth shortly after John Arnold's death as some of her children – James, Teresa, Annie, Elizabeth and Ellen – lived there or in the nearby mining town of Coolgardie at the time. Recently she had been sick with a weak heart and Henry felt, at her age of eighty-nine, it would not be too long before she passed away. Henry was a man of great dignity and felt it was important for Walter to meet her and show respect for Alice's grandmother and Elizabeth's mother.

The old lady smiled and looked at Walter. He was taller than her at around five foot four inches tall, slightly built at around one hundred pounds but had lovely blue eyes, fair hair and an honest face. He seemed a nice young man she thought. Her eyesight was fading, her hair was grey and she stooped when she walked but her mind was as sharp as always. She still sewed nice clothes to bring in some money. Her hands had never failed her. She showed Walter some of the dresses she was making, and he commented how wonderful they were and added that his own mother Clara also made nice clothes for some local families back in Guernsey when she was alive.

After they shared some tea from lovely old English teacups and saucers, which she saved for special occasions like these, she looked at Walter and said in her faded English accent, "So Walter, tell me a story. My husband John always liked listening to people's stories and so do I." Walter thought for a while, looked at his empty teacup, thought back through his life and picked what he felt was a critical milestone and started his story. He started to talk slowly at first, hesitated a bit as he got his thoughts together and then the words came out easily in his polite English speech. He decided for some reason to start the story when he was a young boy.

A long way away, in a small town called Saint Peter's Port on the small British island of Guernsey off the Normandy coast of France, a slight young boy was looking out to sea. His thin hand shielded his pale blue eyes from the bright mid-morning sunlight. It was summertime so the weather was warm and he was dressed in shorts and an old white shirt that was long in the sleeves and hung loosely below his belt. It was a hand-me-down from his older brother John James who everyone called Jack. His hair was blond, and his face freckled from too much time in the sun on his pale skin. He was carefree as boys are at ten years of age. It was 1906.

He was watching the ships carefully sailing in and out of the harbour from his perch high up on the hill overlooking the town. He had walked from his home in The Vale which was along the northeast coast of Guernsey and up to Cambridge Park on the hill. He liked it up there as the view was beautiful and the parkland was peaceful, unlike the continual noise at home from his fourteen siblings. His viewing spot was on the edge of the grounds of the Catholic school run by the nuns. There was also the nuns' farm next to the school grounds which was used to supply them with fresh produce and occasionally Walter would help himself to some of the berries and apples from their garden if no one was looking.

He was watching out for his father to sail home as his mother mentioned that his father's ship was scheduled to arrive soon. Walter knew that the words "arrive soon" could mean anytime in the next two or three weeks but it was a Saturday, and he liked the walk along the coast. He also liked his own company and watching the ships. In the distance over to his right across Belle Greve Bay and Goubean Beacon he could see the 700-year-old Castle Comet that was situated to the right at the entrance to the inner harbour. It was originally built to protect the harbour and the town those many years ago. The daily noon gun firing of a 32-pound cannon would signal his time to leave and head back home to have his midday meal and do some chores.

Walter loved seeing his father come home and listening to all the exciting stories of his adventures overseas. His older brother even told him that his dad once sailed on the Cutty Sark which was a famous British clipper. It was one of the last tea clippers built and one of the fastest he said. His father told him the *Cutty Sark* spent only a few years shipping tea before transporting wool from Australia, where the ship held the record time to Britain for ten years. He also liked the sound of Australia as it seemed so far away, mysterious and exciting. It was a big, exciting place full of sheep, wheat, wool and gold. His father said they also had a unique animal called a kangaroo which was up to six feet tall and hopped on its two hind legs. What Water did not realise was that each time his dad came home his mother became pregnant – hence the fifteen children plus two children that died in infancy in 25 years of marriage.

When the canon boomed the midday blast across the harbour Walter stood up and started the journey down the hill using the track that all the school children used during the week to get to and from school. It was steep and he quickly was at the shore and walking along the water's edge home. As he neared The Vale, he noticed there seemed to be a lot of people near his home. As he got closer, he could see all the neighbour adults and a few police officers. Some of the women were crying and fussing about with his younger brothers and sisters. He could not make any sense of it. There were never lots of people around his house. Suddenly, his older brother John James came running to him, grabbed him by the shirt and hugged him. "Our mother is dead," he said with tears in his eyes. Walter looked at the ground bewildered. John continued, "Mother took a couple of the young ones down to the beach and suffered some pain from being pregnant, collapsed and fainted. The young ones did not know what to do so they just stayed with her."

Clara Le Page died from a miscarriage with her 18th child. She only had the young children with her, and they were alone on Bordcaux beach that morning. No one saw her and the children were too young to raise help. Walter and his fourteen siblings were cared for by some relatives until William returned from his sea voyage. He was overwhelmed as he had not been a full-time father before plus it meant he could not go back to sea as someone needed to stay with all the children, especially the younger ones.

After a short while William went to see his old friends, Herbert Brookes who was the manager of Manuelle's Quarrying Company, and Graham Lock the manager of Mowlem's Quarry to see if there was work for him. He needed the work. All the major quarries in Guernsey were located to the north of the island in the area known as The Vale which was where William's family lived on Vale Avenue. Guernsey was famed for its solid blue granite which was quarried in The Vale. As he had been a qualified mason before he went to sea, William was offered a role as a stonemason. In Guernsey at that time the quarry jobs were split into a range of roles. The quarrymen worked in the quarry splitting sheets of rock down the vein to extract rough chunks of stone. The rocks then went to a sawyer mason who took the chunks of stone and shaped them into the required shape and size using saws. A banker mason then took the stones into the workshop and honed the stones into the shape and size required by the building designs. The carver masons used their artistic ability to create patterns and designs in or from the stone, such as animals, figures or other types of designs. Often a carver mason is also a memorial mason who carves gravestones, statues and memorials. Finally, the fixer mason fixes the stone permanently onto building structures using various forms of cement. William's skills were as a banker mason. He was particularly good at understanding geometric shapes, angles and technical drawings.

In the evenings after their meal and when the house was clean and organised, he still told all his children the stories of his adventures and even mentioned the *Cutty Sark* and her trips to that land down south, a long way away, called Australia. On Sunday afternoons, after church and the midday meal, William would often take his young sons into the work shed out the back of the house and do some woodwork with them. William loved making pieces of beautiful furniture and he wanted these skills to be passed onto his sons as it was an effective way to make nice furniture for the home. Clara had been passing on her sewing skills to her daughters before she passed away. William had a small range of hand tools, like a drill and some drill bits, a wooden folding ruler, a wood square for measuring angles, a scribe compass, a simple protractor, a beautiful sharp saw, a wood plane, a few sharp chisels and a bench with a vice to hold the pieces of timber. He took particular care of his tools to make sure the saw, chisels and drill bits were kept razor sharp, and covered when not in use. He would draw up what he wanted to make on a piece of paper with a pencil and carefully measure all the parts before he started. His motto was, 'Measure twice and cut once.'

John and Walter loved the stories and the time they spent with him making furniture. They even got to do the French polishing of the furniture when they got old enough. They often planned how they too were going off to sail the seas, explore the world and the land down south called Australia. The boys started work when they were twelve, with John finding work in the Guernsey greenhouses in his youth. Greenhouses were all over the island growing tomatoes, mainly for the English market. He was skilful with his hands, and with the woodwork lessons from his father, he quickly fitted into a maintenance role. The weather on the island was ideal for that business.

However, John was young and restless. When he was seventeen, he had a discussion with his father who said, "John there is no future for you here in Guernsey. You can stay working in the greenhouses, but I suggest you go out and explore the world. It is a big, exciting place and with the new steamships you can travel wherever you want, and quickly, compared to the sailing ships of old." After that discussion John and Walter discussed what to do and John decided to take his father's advice and travel. His father promised to give him some money to help him along the way. John pulled out a coin and tossed it in the air. He said, "Heads it is Perth, Australia, and tails it is Rio de Janeiro, Brazil." They watched the coin spin in the air and drop onto the dusty ground. They looked down and the head of King George V looked back up at them. John was seventeen and it was 1910.

Walter missed his big brother after he left. He was fourteen and was working in the greenhouses too as he was also skilful for his age at maintenance and timber work. The work was good and the money he earned helped the family, but his plans were to join John in Perth once he too was seventeen. So, he concentrated on saving some money and building up the practical skills he would need in the future. He figured if he travelled and lived in Australia like John he would need skills to help him.

When Walter turned seventeen, he asked his father for advice on what to do. John had been sending letters back describing life in Perth and all the adventures he was having. So, Walter too said his goodbyes and boarded a steamship for Perth, Australia, and set sail. It was July 1914. He was 17 years old, just a few weeks before his 18th birthday. Little did he know that World War I had started while he was in transit to Australia, and Britain declared war on Germany on the 4th of August, 1914, shortly after Walter arrived in Perth.

Walter was met joyfully by John and together they lived in a boarding house just to the north of the Perth central district. The boarding house in North Perth was run by an older lady whose husband had passed away and she rented out rooms in her home to make an income. Walter found work as a moulder's assistant in a pipe making factory where they made cast-iron water pipes. It was in a suburb called Subiaco. The advertisement read that they were looking for someone who was at least 16 years old, enjoyed working with his hands, had a feeling for forms and structure, had an aptitude for mathematics, was able to read three-dimensional drawings, be patient and practical, be able to work accurately, had good health, strength, stamina, good coordination and good eyesight. With his knowledge of furniture making from his father and the maintenance work at the greenhouses in Guernsey, his skills fitted the job well. John was working in the railways.

However, the First World War was happening. The first Australian Imperial Force (AIF) consisting of 20,000 men departed for Egypt to defend the Suez Canal in November 1914 and initially John James and then Walter joined the AIF. John James had been in the Royal Guernsey Militia for a year before he came to Australia, so he had some good training. He joined the AIF in August 1915, a year after the war started. Walter joined the AIF in March 2016 into the 44th Battalion, which was formed in Claremont, Perth in February 1916. It was an all-volunteer battalion under the command of Lieutenant Colonel William Mansbridge. It formed part of the 11th Brigade of the 3rd Australian Division. After a period of training the 1023 volunteers embarked on the vessel *Suevic* in June 2016 and headed for England. They did further training on Salisbury Plain and by November Walter was in the front trenches in France acting as a French-English interpreter as he could speak French from his upbringing in Guernsey. John was an army driver.

At this point Walter's words faulted and his head dropped onto his chest. Mary thought she could see some tears in his eyes. After a while Walter looked up at Mary, Elizabeth and HWB and wiped away the tears with his handkerchief. He said quietly, "At this point the story ended and turned into a nightmare."

After a short while Walter continued, "I don't talk about this normally, but when I arrived in France into the front trenches it was, apparently, the most severe winter experienced in northern France in 36 years. The ground was massively churned up by the ongoing bombardments. The ground was waterlogged from the freezing rain and became a muddy quagmire and almost impassable. It rained almost continuously throughout October and continued into November. The following month there was almost continuous frost and snow, which made it worse. It was freezing cold. The stench from the dead, foul water and raw sewerage regularly made me choke back the bile in my throat. Rats were a common site and often I could not stop myself from vomiting".

"We went into real combat on the 13th of March, 1917, when we committed to a major raid which ultimately proved unsuccessful. I remember clearly we sent a raiding party into the enemy trenches at 11:40 p.m. under the cover of artillery, smoke barrages and darkness. Over time the fighting continued, and I saw many of my companions die tragically and even more horrifically injured. I saw first-hand, for the first time in my life, what a 303 bullet or a hit from the enemy artillery can do to a person. I was an innocent, young, village boy from Guernsey, so I was completely unprepared for the trenches and the bloodshed. To give you an idea of the carnage, after I was injured in June 2017, the following month the battalion fought around Broodseinde Ridge in France and out of 992 men only 158 were uninjured. By the end of the war the battalion I was in was down to just eighty men out of the 1023 volunteers who started out from Perth".

"In June 1917, I was at the front trenches and a German artillery shell exploded just to my right-hand side and blew me off my feet. I landed in the muddy bottom of the trench under a shower of dirt with a tremendous ringing in my ears, mud splattered over my face, and I remember trying to clear it out of my eyes with my muddy hands. I was stunned and deaf. I tried to stand up but fell repeatedly as my balance was affected so I crawled through the mud and slush to a safer part of the trench. Regularly I would collapse exhausted and disorientated into the mud and slush with my hands flailing to get leverage to keep crawling away from the noise and battle. Some other soldiers helped me up into a sitting position and much later that day the medics came with a stretcher and took me away. The blast effected not only my ears but my brain as well. I was in a permanent fog. For many days my ears were ringing, and I still could not balance to stand up. With the deafness and some other physical disabilities in my legs I was transported to a field hospital and then back to England in July".

"My injuries rendered me unsuitable for active service and I returned to Fremantle on the vessel *Pakeha* in August 2017 for home service. I was in Fremantle Hospital until October that year and formally discharged in November 2017. My Military Star, British War and Victory medals meant little to me as the experience was horrific with all the senseless death and destruction. My brother John saw out the war in Europe, embarked for Australia in May 1919 and was discharged by July that year. In the end Australia lost 60,000 lives and many more were left unable to work or function in life because of the injuries and severe trauma. John and I were two of the lucky ones".

"When we were both back in Perth I restarted my role in the pipe factory and the company started to train me up to be an engineer with the aim to help convert the pipe casting operation into a steel pipe manufacturing factory. My brother John was supported through the military veterans' support scheme to formally train as a carpenter."

When Walter stopped talking, he seemed exhausted and relieved to have been open with Mary about his life and some of his feelings. He felt there was a nice connection with the old lady. She had listened, taking in everything. He also had told things to Henry and Elizabeth that he had not told them before. Mary looked at Walter with her blue eyes then Henry and Elizabeth in turn and said, "Thank you Walter for sharing that with us and I think the future generations are in safe hands with people like you and my family. When you shared your story, I can't help but think back about my life and some things John said to me before he died. You know after all the difficulties in our lives with the Irish potato famine, the poverty, the slums, the industrial revolution, his conviction, the brutality of the British penal system, the separation, loneliness and then the tough times farming in the Outback, I often think about how I feel now at an old age approaching my last days." She paused and then continued, "The best phrase I can summarise it with, is that after everything, I feel grateful and blessed for my life, the experiences I have had, this wonderful country, my family, the people I have shared it with and especially John."

Mary passed away in Kalgoorlie, Western Australia shortly afterwards in 1920.

To my Australian Family
When days are short, and nights are more than lonely
I'll sit there gazing into flames
Thinking of those whose smiles were ever kindly
E'en though I can't recall their names
Friendships are the basis of life's treasure
I'll guard those riches as a miser counts his hoard
Thank you O'lord for giving me full measure
And bless the place where memories are stored

Kath Baldwin – Walter's niece – Darwin, Australia
11th September, 1972

John

Dr Bill Edgar wrote in his book *The Precarious Journey of Her Majesty's Convict Transport Ship 'Nile' to the Swan River Colony, 1857,* "Life was still physically hard, and the new country could be harsh, unforgiving and lonely. But the convicts and ex-convicts were now far from the depressed agricultural landscapes or the vast, burgeoning, industrial cities of their former countries. And, eventually, with a pardon granted, perchance to dream?" For John and Mary Arnold, the changes in their life were enormous but there were rewards. A typical male in the industrial cities of Victorian England had a life expectancy of 39 years. John lived to eighty-two. His life while hard had freed him from the punishing potato famine in Ireland and the poverty and disease of the industrial cities in England to give him a long and interesting life with a loving wife and family.

Mary

Mary played an especially significant role in John's life. It was typical in those times for a wife to forget about her husband who was convicted and subject to transportation to Australia. It is estimated that from a survey of eight convict ships holding 2200 convicts there were eleven reunions between married couples, or 0.5 per cent. Most women simply had to survive in England and needed to move on with their lives. Poverty was common. It is also estimated that of the total number of convicts shipped to the Colony of Western Australia approximately 15 per cent married. For the ones who were not married their lives could often be extremely lonely and desperate. Alcohol was a common problem although reconviction was not. Mary Arnold was the exception who lived through years of desperation in England and then travelled with her two children across the world to be reunited with her husband. However, with the two of them, working together, they made it all work.

Mary continued as a dressmaker and continued to use her signature embroidery of animals on the clothes she made, though she never again embroidered a dove. She lived at 54 Dugan Street, Kalgoorlie in 1910, 276 Piccadilly Street, Kalgoorlie in 1912 and Addis Street, Kalgoorlie in 1920. Mary died of cardiac failure in Kalgoorlie aged 89 in 1920 and is buried there. Her funeral was attended by James, Catherine, Ellen, Anne and Elizabeth. Teresa had already passed away. Mary's father was documented as Christopher Casey and her mother as Bridget Doolan.

James

James Charles Arnold lived a long life and died at 92 with dementia in Leederville in Perth on the 2nd of June, 1943. He is buried at Karrakatta Cemetery, Perth. It is believed John Arnold's father's fiddle was left with James after John died. Its fate after James's death is unknown. The name of the cemetery has a remarkable resemblance to the Noongar word 'Ga-ra-katta' which was the Noongar word for Mt Elisa.

Catherine

Catherine Arnold married James Hoyne, a blacksmith, in Fremantle at St Patrick's church aged 22 on November 26, 1883. She died in Perth age 56 in 1922 just two years after Mary passed.

Ellen

Ellen Arnold married George Dowdy in 1910 in Katanning, West Australia, lived in Wagin and died at 74 in 1944.

Teresa

Teresa Jessie Arnold married HWB Talbot on January 13, 1910 at the office of the district registrar in Fremantle and she died of a heart attack shortly afterwards in Perth aged 48 in 1912. They lived at 30 Lawler Street Subiaco, Perth.

Annie

Annie Arnold married Henry Lynn Barnard, commercial traveller, at 25 years of age in Kalgoorlie on the 31st of May, 1899 at St Mary's Church. She worked as a dressmaker/draper's assistant with TF Elliott in Coolgardie. She died in Perth aged 70 in 1938.

Elizabeth

After Thomas Francis Elliott died in 1917, Elizabeth Elliott married HWB Talbot in Perth in 1921. Her sister Teresa had died in 1912. Elizabeth died June 6, 1939, at 63 in Perth and is buried in Karrakatta Cemetery.

Arthur John

Arthur John Elliott married Florence MacWilliam in Perth on the 14th of February 1920. Arthur was twenty-nine and Flora was twenty-seven. Thomas Elliott was identified as the groom's father. HWB Talbot signed as a witness. Flora's parents were John and Joan (nee Martin). Arthur John Elliott died in Perth on February 23, 1923. He was thirty-one. He died of hematemesis which is vomiting of blood probably from a stomach ulcer. He then had heart failure from the stress of the severe vomiting and was buried in Karrakatta Cemetery. Arthur and Flora had one son called John. The name Arthur John has been passed down through several generations.

Alice Eva

Alice Eva Elliott married Walter Le Page on 4th August 1923 and had five children: Veronica, Arthur John, Arnold, Elizabeth and Doreen. Their wedding was at the Sacred Heart Church, Highgate Hill in Perth. Alice Eva Le Page (Elliott) died aged 57 on the 19th of February 1954 in Sydney.

Thomas Francis Elliott

Thomas Elliott continued as a businessperson throughout his life and in 1907 ran the Goomalling Hotel, Western Australia. Nothing is known of his significant wealth as it never passed down to the next generation. He died in Perth of tuberculosis aged 57, on the 13th of September 1917 and is buried in Karrakatta Cemetery. The name Elliot has been used again in later generations.

Henry William Beamish Talbot (HWB)

HWB's father is documented as John Shrewe Talbot and his mother as Eleanor White. HWB Talbot led a long and successful career as a geologist. In 1908, Talbot joined the Canning Expedition to survey a possible stock route from Wiluna to Halls Creek in the east Kimberley. Talbot returned to Perth 426 days after setting out.

Later that year he led a party of six men and sixteen camels on a reconnaissance excursion from Laverton to the Warburton Range. While on a trip, Talbot, geologist Edward de Courcy Clarke and camp hand JW Johnson were attacked by Aborigines. Talbot was slightly injured in the arm and chest, but Johnson was more seriously wounded, ultimately dying from his injuries. The rumour was that they saw the Indigenous Australians walking towards them but they appeared unarmed. However, they were dragging their spears along the ground by a thin rope which was connected to their toes and the spear.

In 1922 he joined the Freney Kimberley Oil Company exploring for oil in the Canning Basin. In 1933 Talbot joined Western Mining Corporation as its first senior geologist. Talbot moved to Perth in 1953, then to Nannup where he died in 1957. The name Talbot has been used again in later generations.

Henry William Beamish Talbot's grave – Nannup,
Western Australia
Gravestone – kindly donated by the Geological Society of Australia,
BHP Billiton and Readymix Australia

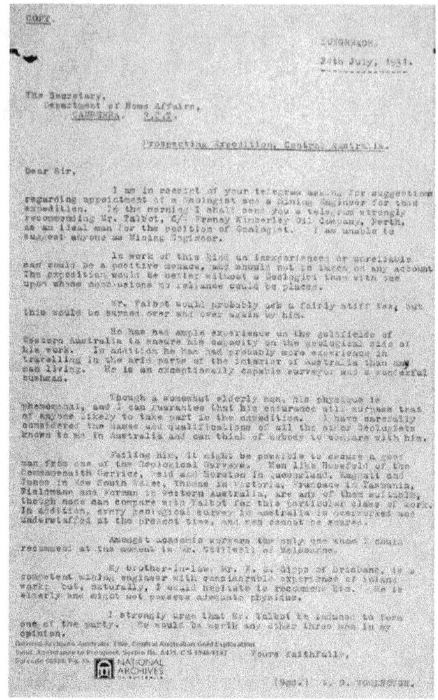

Letter to the Department of Home Affairs regarding HWB Talbot.
(Source – public domain)

Walter Le Page

Walter Le Page (engineer) married at age 27 to Alice Eva Elliott (dressmaker) aged twenty-three at Sacred Heart Church, Highgate Hill, Perth on August 4, 1923. They lived at 67 Bulwer Street, Perth. Alice Eva passed on to Walter her family approach to paid work. It was, "Wherever you work arrive a bit early, leave a bit later than required, work hard, do real quality work and learn to get better at what you do." Walter learned from that and became the Humes' factory manager and ultimately moved to Sydney to oversee the manufacturing of steel pipes for the Snowy River Scheme. All his children moved to Sydney progressively over time. Walter Le Page died aged 77 in 1973 in Sydney.

William Le Page - circ 1895

Clara Rachel Le Page (nee Febrache)

Alice Le Page (nee Elliott – 1918)

Walter Le Page (circ 1925)

John Arnold

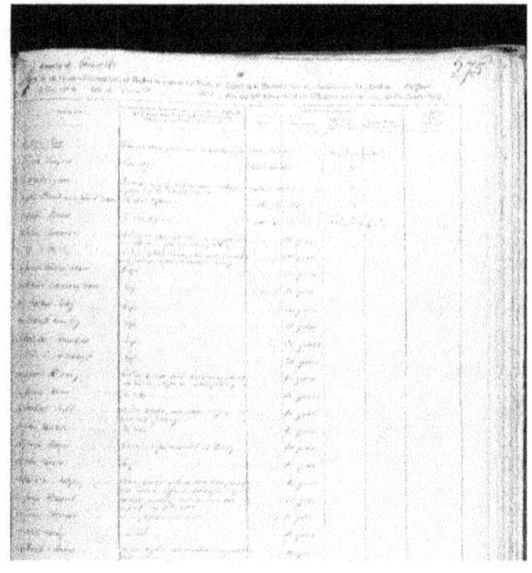

Conviction paper 6th December, 1852 – death sentence

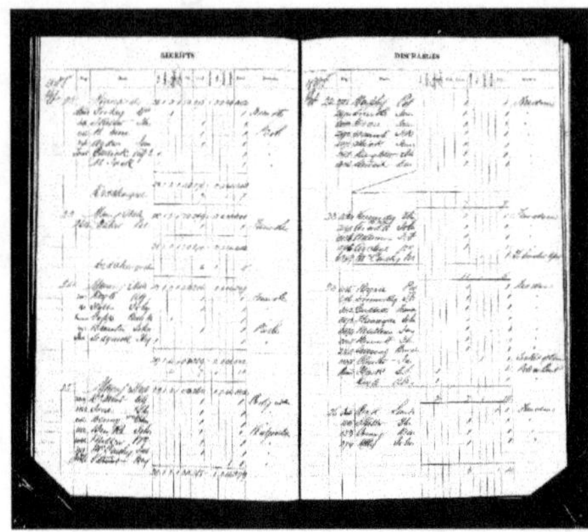

Discharge papers 23rd February, 1898 – 46 years for burglary

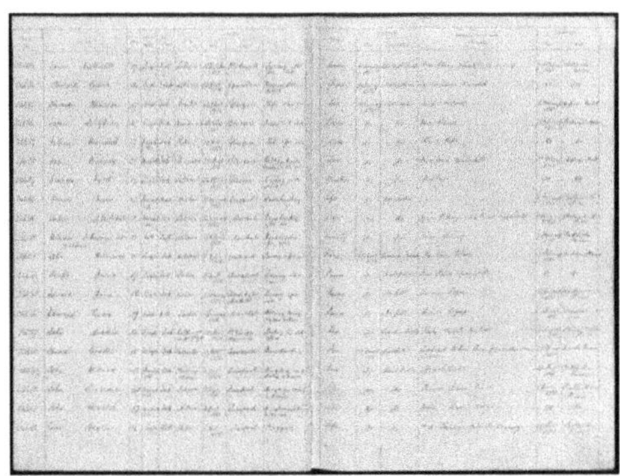

Transfer record Kirkdale House of Correction to Portland Prison. December, 1853

Character record – Fremantle Prison

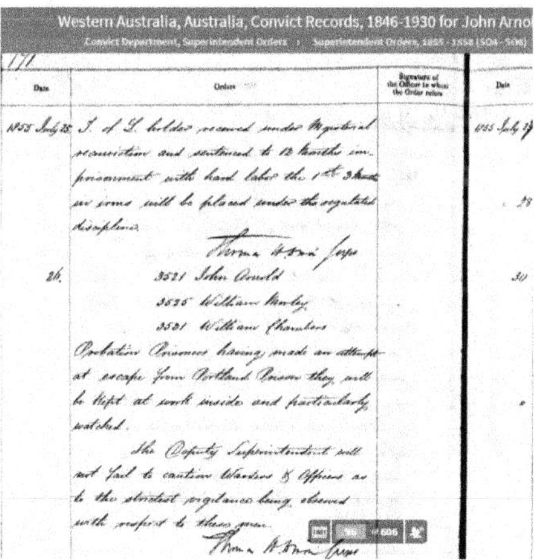

Record – Fremantle Prison

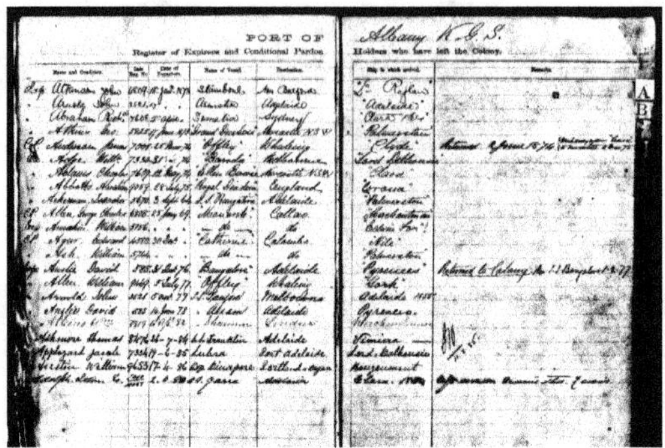

John Arnold – departure records, Port of Albany

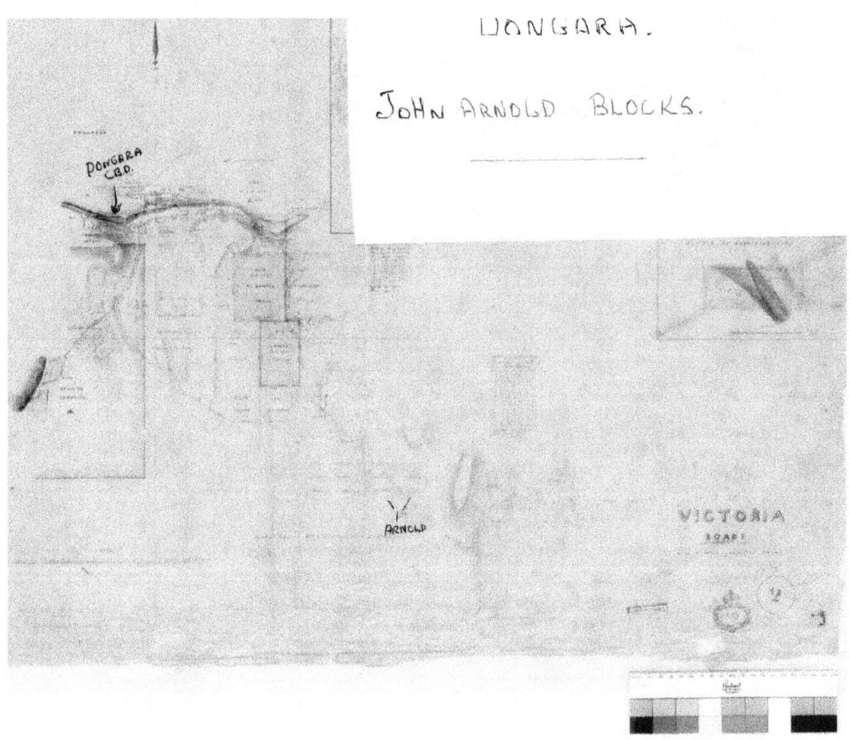

John Arnold – property in Dongara

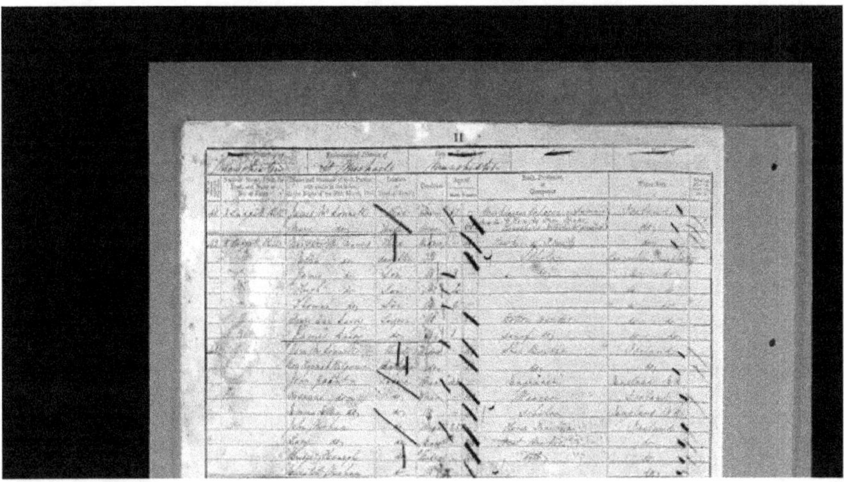

Mary Ann Arnold (nee Casey) England Census 1851

Fremantle Prison

(Images taken by Michael Le Page)

The Fremantle prison was constructed by convicts in the mid-1850s and stayed in continual use for nearly 150 years until 1991. It was a place of hangings, floggings and chain gangs. The gallows and flogging triangle have been preserved to show the reality of life during those times. John Arnold was flogged on the triangle there and housed in the solitary confinement cells in Fremantle. Over time the prisoners included English convicts, local criminals and prisoners of war. It still stands today and is a museum.

Fremantle Prison whipping frame – note the tie-off points at the top, middle and bottom.

Fremantle Prison – ablution bucket

Fremantle Prison – solitary confinement
cell. Note the slot at the bottom where
food was passed.

Fremantle Prison – example of what an Association Room
looked like.

Greenough

(Images taken by Michael Le Page)

The village of Greenough is situated approximately 25km south of Geraldton and 380km north of Perth in Western Australia. The Greenough Flats are the coastal flood plain of the Greenough River which flows from the inland catchment area into the sea. During the 1860s Greenough was a growing agricultural area. The impact of wheat rust on the crops plus seasonal drought, floods and poor prices caused the region's decline. The historic settlement has been kept as a cultural village by the National Trust and can still be visited.

Greenough courthouse, police station
and jail

Greenough Christian school

Greenough school student's desk

Greenough community

Greenough village hall

Greenough Village

Typical Greenough tree

Michael Le Page lives in Perth, Western Australia. This is his second book. He is a writer and has lived and worked in Australia, Indonesia, Singapore, and the United States of America.

He studied the regional history of this era and became captivated by the life and times of John Arnold and his family. While Michael never met them, they left enough footprints on this world for him to follow.

www.ingramcontent.com/pod-product-compliance
Lightning Source LLC
Chambersburg PA
CBHW051559030726
47592CB00001B/359